VEERA HIRANANDANI

How to Find What You're Not Looking For

Kokila

For my parents,
who taught me how to be brave.

KOKILA
An imprint of Penguin Random House LLC, New York

First published in the United States of America by Kokila,
an imprint of Penguin Random House LLC, 2021
First paperback edition published 2022

Copyright © 2021 by Veera Hiranandani

Visit us online at penguinrandomhouse.com.

THE LIBRARY OF CONGRESS HAS CATALOGED THE HARDCOVER EDITION AS FOLLOWS:
Names: Hiranandani, Veera, author.
Title: How to find what you're not looking for / Veera Hiranandani.
Other titles: How to find what you are not looking for
Description: 1st. New York : Kokila, [2022] | Audience: Ages 8-12. | Audience: Grades 4-6.
Summary: Twelve-year-old Ariel Goldberg's life changes when her big sister elopes following
the 1967 Loving v. Virginia decision, and she is forced to grapple with both her family's
prejudice and the antisemitism she experiences, as she defines her own beliefs.
Identifiers: LCCN 2022024154 | ISBN 9780525555056 (paperback)
Subjects: CYAC: Family life—Fiction. | Interracial marriage—Fiction. |
Prejudices—fiction. | Jews—United States—Fiction. | East Indian Americans—Fiction.
Classification: LCC PZ7.H5977325 Ho 2022b | DDC [Fic]—dc23
LC record available at https://lccn.loc.gov/2022024154

Printed in the United States of America

ISBN 9780525555056

2nd Printing

LSCH

Design by Jasmin Rubero
Text set in Adobe Devanagari

How to Be the Lazy One

It's harder than you think.

First, lie on your messy bed wearing your Wonder Woman pajamas that are too small because you've had them since you were nine. Then, watch your older sister, Leah, pin up her hair for dance class. She sits in her black leotard at the small white vanity, her back straight as a board, a magazine cutout of Paul Newman taped to the corner of her mirror. She uses at least fifteen bobby pins for her bun. Count in your head while she sticks the pins in.

One, two, three. She's rushing because she has to be on the #4 bus by 9:00 a.m. for pointe class at Madame Duchon's Dance Academy. She dances there every day except Sunday. You're not even sure how she spends so much time at dance and still does well in school.

Leah seems to do well at everything.

Not you. You're the lazy one. You're just trying to keep

up, but along with all the other things Leah does, she helps you keep up.

Four, five, six.

Ma wishes Leah didn't take dance on Saturdays because of Shabbos, but Leah says it makes no sense for her not to dance if Ma and Daddy work all day at Gertie's, their bakery. Then Ma says Leah's right and that maybe they should be more observant and not work on Saturdays. Daddy says the bakery wouldn't survive if they closed on Saturday in this town and that's more important. They argue about the rules like that sometimes, how Jewish you're all supposed to be.

Seven, eight, nine.

On pin ten, Leah suddenly stops and puts her hands over her face. Her shoulders start to shake. You lean forward in your bed, confused, to get a closer look.

Leah hardly ever cries. You're the crier. It's the only way anyone pays attention to you. You cry when you're sad, or mad, or when you watch *Lassie*. Sometimes you even cry when you're extra happy. You get it from Daddy. He's a crier, too.

Leah manages to keep a smile on her face most of the

time. If she's upset, she gets serious and walks away, her shoulders straight, her head held high.

But today, on a warm Saturday in early June, as the sun tumbles through the window and the birds chirp and the smell of Ma's Sanka floats in through the bottom of the bedroom door, Leah sobs into her hands, and it terrifies you.

"Leah," you say, jumping out of bed and over to her side. "Don't cry. What's the trouble?"

She turns to you. She picks up a tissue off the vanity, presses it to her eyes, then blows her nose. "If I tell you a secret, will you promise to keep it forever?" she says.

"Forever?"

"Yes, forever," she says. "It's the biggest secret I've ever had, and if you don't think you can promise, I won't say it."

Keeping a secret is not your favorite thing to do. Secrets make your stomach hurt. You can count on one hand the secrets you've kept. You once took a report card out of the mailbox and hid it in your schoolbag for a week. But you got caught. Sometimes when you hang out with your friend Jane, you make it seem like you have other friends. But you don't. Occasionally you steal

3

cookies from Gertie's and keep them in a coffee can in your room. You've never had to keep a really big secret before, and certainly not forever.

Leah's cheeks get blotchy, and her eyes start to fill again with tears. "Oh please," she says. "I have to tell someone, and I need it to be you."

Leah saying she needs you—is there anything more special than that? Maybe if you know her secret, some of her specialness will spill over onto you. She bites her lip and grabs your hand.

"Okay," you say, taking a deep breath. "I promise."

She holds up her pinkie and wraps it around yours. "Oh, Ari, something crazy has happened."

"What? What's happened?" A flush of sweat starts collecting on your top lip.

"I've fallen in love," she says, your pinkies still linked together, her eyes still locked on yours. You let go of her pinkie and take your hand away.

"You've fallen in love? How? With who?" you say.

She gets up and starts to pace a little, so you sit down on your bed. You want to give her room.

"I've never felt this way about anyone. It's like I can see my future," she says.

She looks scared when she tells you this, and it makes you feel a little scared. You haven't known anyone in love before. You've watched the soap opera *Days of Our Lives* with Ma, and it doesn't look like much fun. It seems that people start having lots of problems when they fall in love.

If you think about it, you've been noticing some odd things about Leah, like the way she hums a tune everywhere she goes, even when Ma makes her clean the bathroom on Sundays. She wears her best clothes every day. She leaves a trail of Chanel No. 5 behind her, and she never used to wear perfume. She always seems to be thinking of something else.

"Who is he? Do I know him?" you ask her.

As she walks back and forth, she tells you that the boy she's in love with is not a boy at all. He's a young man about to graduate from college. He already enrolled in graduate school this fall because he wants to keep studying and doesn't want to get drafted into the Vietnam War. She met him six months ago at Rocky's Records in town. He's from India, but he lives here now and works at Rocky's after his classes because he loves music.

And he wants to marry Leah.

"Married? Now? You can't be serious," you say as your heart pounds in your ears. You don't know what any of this means, and you don't want anyone to take Leah away from you. How would she have any time to be your sister if she got married? It makes you want to give her secret back.

"I'm eighteen. Ma got married at eighteen," she says, her eyebrows turning angry. "Lots of girls get married at eighteen." She presses her hands to her cheeks as if she's trying to hold herself in.

"I suppose so," you say, still thinking she's lost her mind. But it's true. You think of Betty Campbell and Donna Marino, two girls who got married right after high school. They had their pictures in the local paper, and they looked like the plastic dolls Daddy keeps at the bakery to put on top of wedding cakes.

You remember feeling a little sorry for them, just going straight to the boring grown-up world with no in-between. You thought Leah wanted an in-between.

"When are you going to tell Ma? And Daddy?" you ask her.

Leah shakes her head. "Honestly, I can't even imagine it. I need more time. Remember, you can't utter a word. But this isn't just some silly crush on a boy. This is serious."

"You'll have to tell them eventually," you say. Leah doesn't reply. "Are you really going to get married? To a boy from India? Is he Jewish?"

"He's not a boy," Leah says loudly, and anger washes over her face. She takes a deep breath. "And of course he's not Jewish."

"Well, I don't know."

"He's Hindu," she continues in a smaller voice. "I'm worried about what people will think if we get married."

You nod slowly. Leah is the one who's supposed to follow the rules. It's no secret Ma and Daddy want her to go to college and marry someone Jewish. She already enrolled at Southern Connecticut State for the fall, though if it's anything like your town, there won't be many Jewish boys there.

Leah sits back down at the vanity.

"But I'm also worried about what will happen if we don't. I really love him," she says and starts to dab her face with her pink powder puff, erasing the streaks her tears left on her cheeks. "Sorry, I don't mean to be a drag."

"It's okay," you say and go over to her. You put a hand on her shoulder. "You'll figure it out." But what you really mean is that she'll figure out that she's not in love or thinking about marrying anyone.

How to Keep a Secret

About a week later, neither of you is worried anymore, because it's almost summer vacation and it feels like you're in a movie—Leah's movie—and your beautiful, smart, talented older sister trusts you with her secret love story.

You've never been close to being in love, and that's just fine. Yes, you're only eleven, and all the boys you know are kind of mean or smelly or both. You can't imagine ever feeling that way about any one of them. Who would ever love you like that? You aren't that pretty. You aren't that smart. You certainly don't feel smart at school, especially when you write.

Writing is to you what dancing is to the clumsiest person in the world. Daddy says your hands need to get stronger, not your brain. But you think he's wrong. You think it's your brain. You heard your tutor last year telling

Ma that she thought you had something called a learning disability. Ma sent that tutor away.

Still, Ma makes you knead bread dough to make your hands stronger. You like helping at Gertie's. There, your hands work the way they're supposed to. It hasn't made your writing any better, though. Ma calls it chicken scratch. It's not just hard to write, it's hard to think of what to write. Sometimes you can't even read your own writing. It's like a secret code.

As you walk into the bakery, you feel the afternoon heat surround you like a heavy cloud. It's hot outside and even hotter in the bakery. You don't know how your parents do it.

In the afternoons, you usually help Ma with cookie dough, and then Ma walks home with you at five to get dinner going, but Daddy's in the bakery from four in the morning until seven at night, except on Mondays, when the bakery is closed. Daddy has the strongest hands of anyone you've ever known, and his handwriting is beautiful. He writes the daily special on the chalkboard every day in perfect curly cursive.

Daddy stands across the room, forming bread dough

into loaves. You can tell from the brown caraway seeds that look like ants in the mass of sticky white that it's rye. Daddy's hair is plastered on his forehead, and he moves slowly in the heat. He looks up.

"Have any homework, Muffin?" he says.

"Already did it," you reply, which is almost true, except for the questions you had to answer about your reading. You did your math, though.

Ma and Daddy always let you have a little break before they put you to work, so you grab a cold cola from the fridge and collapse on the stool near the pastry table. Just touching the cold glass of the cola bottle makes you feel better.

After a few minutes, Ma comes over. "Why are you always reading those ridiculous comic books?" she says to you as you flip through the latest *Wonder Woman* while sipping your soda.

You want to say to her that you don't read ridiculous comics. You read *Wonder Woman*. You've tried *Superman*, *The Flash*, even *Aquaman*, but nothing is as good. Something about the pictures helping the words go together in small chunks feels like the puzzle piece your mind is missing. If only all schoolbooks could be like comic books.

Before you figure out your answer, Leah comes bounding through the swinging doors. She often stops by after dance on her way home. Ma doesn't make her help as much as you. She says it's because Leah's older and busier, but you think it's because Ma doesn't want Leah to get used to working at the bakery. She wants her to do other things.

Usually, Leah's still in her dance clothes, but today she's in a red-and-white miniskirt, and her hair is down. She must have gone home first and changed.

"Ma, how can you stand it in here? Let's turn on the fan. We'll all melt," she says, waving her hand in front of her face. She goes over and turns on the big fan in the back and opens the door a few inches.

"Well, look at you," Ma says and runs her eyes carefully over Leah. "A secret date?"

Leah doesn't miss a beat. "A secret date, I wish," she laughs, then changes the subject. "Ari, want to walk with me to the Sweet Scoop?"

You nod and quickly close your comic book. The last

place you want to be on this sweltering afternoon is the bakery.

"Can I?" you say, turning to Ma.

She eyes you carefully and then looks at Leah again. Does Ma know what Leah's up to? She's always telling you she has eyes in the back of her head. When you were little, you used to move her hair aside, looking for those eyes. Also, your sister is a great liar, which makes you wonder if she's ever lied to you.

"But I need you to help me with an order of oatmeal raisin," she finally says.

"Ma, give Ari a break," says Leah. "It's so hot."

You don't like making oatmeal raisin cookies. The batter is lumpy. You also hate raisins. You prefer making chocolate chip or black and whites.

"Let her go, Sylvia," Daddy calls. "She's here almost every day." He's the softy.

"Fine, go," she says, waving her hand without looking up. You and Leah don't wait for her to change her mind, and rush out the door.

Leah has been bringing you with her to meet Raj at Rocky's and go on his break with him. That way it will look less suspicious. This is the third time you've gone with her.

The three of you have a routine. You get Raj at Rocky's and then go to the Sweet Scoop. After you order your ice creams, you all walk through Stallings Park, the smaller park on the edge of town that is loud and filled with young people sitting on blankets, playing music on their transistor radios, and sometimes smoking cigarettes. Ma told you and Leah if she ever catches you smoking, she'll never let you go anywhere without her again, even though Ma sometimes smokes a cigarette after dinner.

At first you were nervous and decided that you wouldn't like him at all. But Raj was so nice to you, you couldn't help liking him. He kind of looks like Elvis, but with darker skin, and always buys you a double fudge ripple cone. It doesn't feel like anyone is taking Leah away from you. In fact, you get to be more a part of her life than ever.

Today, as the three of you walk through the park, Leah says, "Can you believe Ma used to bring me here when I was little? Now the families go to East Meadow." East Meadow Park on the other side of town is bigger and quieter, with more flowers and no teenagers. Occasionally, a grown-up, usually a man in a suit carrying a briefcase, cuts through Stallings to get to the train station and squints his disapproval at a blaring radio.

"I always went to East Meadow when I was a kid," you say.

Leah looks at you and laughs. She rumples your curls. "You're still a kid."

You frown at her and duck away from her hand. You want to stick your tongue out at her, but then she'd be right.

"I'm almost twelve, which is practically thirteen. I'm basically a teenager, just like you."

"First of all, you've got a while before twelve," Leah says. "And second, I'm seven years older than you. Don't be in a rush, Ari. Nothing's wrong with being a kid." Her eyes travel away from you and back to the park. Her mouth falls out of its smile, and she suddenly looks sad. *Then why are you rushing,* you want to ask her.

"I like it here," Raj says, slicing through whatever Leah is feeling. "It reminds me of a park near my flat in Bombay. My cousins and I would play cricket there."

Leah takes Raj's arm, her eyes sparkling. "Tell me more about your family. I want to know everything about you."

You roll your eyes, walk a little bit ahead of them, and plop down on a bench. You lick your melting cone and wonder what kind of game cricket is. Does it involve actual crickets? You want to ask, but it seems like a question a little kid would ask.

"We're going to take a walk, okay?" Leah calls out. This is also part of the routine. They usually leave you on a bench for a little while to eat your fudge ripple while they wander behind a cluster of oak trees. A few days ago, you saw them feed ice cream to each other and kiss. You turned away, your cheeks on fire. Now you know why they go behind the oak trees. A part of you wants to spy on them, and a part of you wants to run far, far away.

After a little while, the three of you stroll back to the store, but they don't hold hands in case they run into anyone they know. You like listening to their conversations. They discuss all sorts of things. They talk about music a lot: the Beatles, the Doors, Jimi Hendrix, the Rolling Stones, Aretha Franklin. They argue about which band is their favorite. Raj likes the Doors the most. Leah thinks the Beatles are groovier.

They talk about serious things, too, like the war in Vietnam, Dr. Martin Luther King Jr.'s speech in New York City that spring against the war, and the protest marches for civil rights and peace that they want to be part of. Today they talk about the uprisings happening around the country, and you wonder what they mean. Leah says she understands why Black people are so upset. Raj says riots aren't the way to change things, that nonviolent protests are more powerful, like what Gandhi did in India, like what Dr. King is doing now.

"But don't you think that the Black community has no choice but to fight back and defend themselves against hundreds of years of racism and violence? What if peaceful protests aren't enough to change things? Have you read Malcolm X's autobiography? And look at what the Black Panthers are trying to do," Leah says. "It must take so much courage." Leah crosses her arms. You've never seen her speak this way to anyone. Other than Dr. King, you don't know who she's talking about.

"But how can we really understand, Leah?" Raj says.

"We have to do more. We're both not part of the majority. How can we not understand?" she replies.

You watch Leah's face, then Raj's. Are they mad at each other? You can't tell.

"I think I have a different perspective rather than a better understanding," Raj says. "When I came here, I felt like the best thing to do as an immigrant was try as hard as I could to blend in so no one would notice the color of my skin. Does that make me a coward?"

Leah gets quiet. She shakes her head and reaches out to squeeze Raj's hand quickly before letting go. You feel more confused than ever. You think about protests and riots and what they are for. You wonder what Raj means by blending in. You didn't know Leah paid so much attention to the news.

You also learn more about Raj. You find out that he grew up in Bombay, a big city in India. That he has two much-older brothers, one still in India and one who lives here. You find out that his favorite flavor of ice cream is pistachio and that he loves pizza.

Another thing you find out is that Leah and Raj go out every Tuesday night to a pizza parlor two towns over so no one sees them. Ma thinks Leah is in her pointe class. You know lots of secrets now, which started off feeling special, but the feeling is getting heavier and heavier as each secret stacks upon the other. What Leah and Raj don't talk about in front of you is their future.

After this trip to the park, back at Rocky's, Raj gives Leah a present, the new Beatles' album. She jumps up and down and throws her arms around him. Everyone in the store looks at them. You don't like the way people stop and stare. You want to pull Leah away, but she doesn't seem to notice.

Then Raj goes back to work, and Leah and you walk home.

"I know I promised to keep your secret," you say after you get far enough away from the store. She faces you, clutching the Beatles' album against her chest.

"Yes, you did," she says, waggling her finger at you, a panicked expression on her face.

"I still promise," you say. "But when are you going to tell Ma and Daddy?"

You read the title on the album: *Sgt. Pepper's Lonely Hearts Club Band*. You wonder what it means. Were the

Beatles changing their name? Your hands feel sticky with ice cream. You press your thumb and forefinger together, and they stay stuck that way.

"I'm just so happy. I don't want anything to ruin it. I feel guilty about being so happy."

"Why would you feel guilty about being happy?" you ask.

"Because there's so much wrong with the world," she says and starts walking again.

There is, according to the newspapers. But you look around your town. You see someone driving by in a blue Chevy convertible. You see people walking down the block in sunglasses, sipping soda pop, riding their bikes, happy to be out on such a nice Saturday. This world seems okay.

"Do you know what happened at Rocky's last week? A guy came in and heard Raj talking. Then he asked John, the manager, why he had foreigners working there and not Americans. He asked Raj if he was here legally. Raj said he was a US citizen, and the fellow demanded to see proof and wouldn't leave! John had to threaten to call the cops until he finally left."

"Gosh, that's terrible," you say. Now she's walking so quickly, you can barely keep up.

"But our love is stronger than the racist establishment."

"'The racist establishment,'" you say, trying out her words. Lately, Leah says things that feel so grown-up and strange, like they belong in someone else's mouth. Leah stops walking, so you stop. You can see her cheeks becoming red, her chest going up and down like she's out of breath. The air is sticky and still.

"I'm not naïve, Ari. I see the looks people give us when we walk down the street. It's not going to be easy for me and Raj."

"So maybe you shouldn't get married?" You're starting to feel like you're walking into a pool that's getting too deep for your feet to touch the bottom. A worry for Raj and Leah, in a new way, a way you hadn't even thought about before, is nagging at you. Other people won't like them together, not just your parents. You shake your head. You're ready for Leah's secret love-story movie to end and to go back to just Ariel and Leah—the way it used to be.

"But then they would win," she says.

"Who would win?" you ask, but Leah doesn't seem to hear you.

"It's not just what Raj faces. We know about prejudice," Leah says.

"We do?" you ask, and again that feeling of the pool getting deeper takes hold of you. Now Leah is a few feet ahead. "Hey, slow down," you call, because it's too hot to walk this fast.

She stops and faces you again. "Of course. I once heard Ma and Daddy tell their friends how the bank wouldn't give them a loan because they didn't think a Jewish bakery would do well here. Daddy had to convince them that his baked goods were for everyone. He even brought them a box of cookies to prove it."

"I didn't know that," you say, and it makes you wonder what else Leah knows that you don't.

"And Ma and Daddy's friends from synagogue, you know the Feldmans? They tried to sign up for that golf club in Milton, and they were told that membership was full, but then the Cunninghams joined a week after."

"But that's not fair," you say, and it feels like Leah has

ripped the cover off something ugly and confusing, something you don't want to see.

"And remember what that awful boy did to you last year?"

"I don't like to think about that," you say and bite your lip. But you do think about it, a lot. You and Chris Heaton had both wanted the last empty swing. You got there first by a second, but Chris insisted he was first and told you to get up. You refused. Then he leaned in and touched your head.

"Where are your horns?" he asked.

"What?" you said, brushing his hand away.

"My dad told me Jews have horns," he said and touched your head again. "Like the devil."

"Get away," you said and then touched your own head, wondering if there was something you had never noticed before.

He kept asking where your horns were, getting louder and louder. He wouldn't stop. So you picked up a small rock and threw it at him, but it hit him in the face.

You had just wanted to stop him, not hit his face. He stared at you, frozen, holding his cheek. Then he ran off and told the playground monitor, acting like you had shot a cannonball at him. You got in more trouble than he did, detention for a week, and all he had to do was talk to the principal.

At home, Ma and Daddy had explained what the horn statement meant—how it had to do with a wrong translation in the Bible saying that Moses had horns instead of light around his head when he came down from Mount Sinai. Ma said it was still used as a slur today and that some people actually believed it was true. It felt like someone had slapped you when she told you this. How could anyone believe such a ridiculous thing, as if you were a different kind of person or maybe not even a person at all?

Ma had been furious and wanted to talk to the principal. "That boy should be suspended! We can't let this go," she had said. But you begged her not to; you were afraid it would only make Chris worse. Daddy agreed. "Let's not make a fuss, Sylvia," he had said. "We don't need that kind of attention. Think of the bakery."

Back then, you had wondered what kind of attention Daddy meant. Now you wonder what really changes people. You had tried stopping Chris with the rock, and it did stop him, but you don't think it changed him. Should you just have let him take the swing? Should you have sat there silently, refusing to leave? You don't know if that would have changed him, either. When you play it over in your mind, you never come up with a good answer.

Suddenly you hear someone calling you. You look up to see your friend Jane coming down the street with her mother. The two of them live on the floor below you. You ride the bus together to school.

"Why, hello, girls," Jane's mother, Peggy, says, taking off her big round sunglasses. "Where are you coming from?"

You and Leah glance at each other.

"The Sweet Scoop," Leah says.

"That's where we're off to. If June is starting off like this, we're probably in for a long, hot summer," she says, fanning herself.

You both nod.

"Oh, oh, oh!" Jane shrieks, jumping up and down. Everyone looks startled.

"What on earth?" Peggy says, putting her hand to her chest.

Jane points at the Beatles' album. "How did you get

that? I thought Rocky's was sold out. They said they weren't getting more until next week."

Leah looks down at her hands like she forgot what she was holding.

"Oh, this, well, I—"

"She put it on hold the day it came out," you say. "But you can come over and listen if you want."

You see Leah's shoulders drop in relief.

"That would be far-out! Thanks! See you in school tomorrow, Ari," Jane calls as she and Peggy head to the Sweet Scoop.

"That was clever of you," Leah says after they walk off. "Imagine if we saw them with Raj . . ."

"Yeah, Peggy would have definitely said something to Ma." Peggy and Ma are sort of friends; at least they like to chat in the laundry room on Sundays, but Ma doesn't seem to have time for many friends.

Leah's face changes, and she gets that hard look with her eyebrows knitted together. "Eventually, someone is going to see us and tell Ma and Daddy. I want them hearing the truth from me first," she says. "I'm just going to do it. I'm going to invite Raj over."

"Oh good," you say and give Leah a little hug. You aren't sure how Ma and Daddy are going to react to Raj, but at least you won't be the only one to know anymore. You both walk home, and your whole body feels lighter, like Leah just took something out of your hands and decided to hold it herself.

How to Eat Dinner

When you get back home, Ma's whirling around the apartment with a rag and a bottle of Mr. Clean. Sunday is Do-everything-else-instead-of-working-at-the-bakery day for Ma. Daddy opens the bakery from noon to five and always comes home for an early dinner. You and Leah are supposed to clean the hall bathroom, your room, and bring the laundry downstairs to the basement washers. Leah makes you do it all with her right after breakfast so she can have the afternoon to relax. Sunday's the only day she doesn't dance, so you understand.

Sunday is also the best time to ask Ma for something since she's usually distracted and impatient to get her work done. Leah doesn't waste any time.

"Ma, do you need any more help?" she asks.

Ma doesn't look up as she wipes down a cabinet. "Too late for that. Almost done."

Leah walks over to the stove, which is empty. No pot of boiling soup on a hot day like this. She goes over to the fridge, opens it, and closes it. "What are we having for dinner?" she asks.

You perk up from the couch, where you'd collapsed as you looked for the comics in the Sunday paper.

"Just making some egg salad. Too hot for anything else," Ma says and stops cleaning. She wipes her forehead with the back of her hand.

You slump back down. *Ugh, egg salad.*

"Could I have a guest over next Sunday evening?" Leah asks, not looking at Ma. She busies herself with rearranging the fruit bowl.

"A guest?" Ma says, pushing back a bit of hair that's fallen out of her bun. "Who?"

"A boy I like."

As you flip through the newspaper, pretending not to watch them, you notice that Leah calls Raj a boy, not a man.

Ma waves the green towel she's holding. "Ah, so there *is* a boyfriend. I thought so, the way you've been going around lately, all gussied up," she says. Then she grabs the orange fly swatter hanging on the doorknob and starts going after a fly buzzing around the fruit.

"There's nothing wrong with trying to look nice," Leah says. "So, can I?"

Ma's eyes narrow on the fly that has now landed on top of the refrigerator. She takes a big swipe at it. "These flies. They're all over as soon as the weather gets humid. So can you what?"

"Have him over to meet you." Leah's voice shakes a little. She's had a few boyfriends come over—one Jewish boy she met at Temple Beth Torah, and one boy from school who was not Jewish. That was last year. Ma and Daddy didn't like the boy who wasn't Jewish, and told her that.

Ma said they didn't like him because he didn't thank them after the meal. But you don't remember the Jewish boy thanking your parents, either. Honestly, your parents didn't like either of them that much.

"Who is this boy? Another gentile?" Ma was now suddenly wiping down the kitchen counter furiously.

"Ma, nobody uses that word," Leah says and looks at

you with a big question in her eyes. You shrug. What can you do? Now the fly lands on the bowl of fruit.

"Oh, you're a goner now." Ma lines up the swatter.

"He's not a gentile," Leah tells her.

Ma brings the swatter down hard on an apple. "Got-cha!" Then she turns her attention back to Leah.

"Oh? Well, I guess so."

"That's swell. Thanks, Ma!" Leah says and hurries out of earshot before Ma can ask any more questions.

Later, back in your room, you sit on your bed while Leah brushes her hair at the vanity over and over. If you brushed your curly hair after it dried, you'd look like you'd stuck your fingers in an electric socket. That's why you keep it short. But Leah has smooth waves, not tight curls like you.

"If they just meet him . . ." Leah starts to say. She begins brushing faster and faster. "Maybe they'll let go of their ingrained prejudice. And who uses the word *gentile* anymore? I guess it's better than *goy*. Maybe Hindus are gentiles? Does it mean anyone who isn't Jewish?"

"I have no idea," you say and place *Sgt. Pepper's Lonely*

Hearts Club Band on the turntable. You lower the needle carefully. You hear a scratchy sound, and then it sounds like a band warming up. You and Leah look at each other, puzzled, but then the song bursts from the little speaker, and you both smile. The new sounds carry you away as you listen to song after song. It's like every track opens a door and shows you a whole new world.

As the music plays, you think about what Leah just said. *Gentile. Goy.* You know those words. Sometimes your parents use them to describe someone who's Christian, but only to each other or you and Leah, never in front of anyone else.

When the first side of the record ends, you get up to flip it over. "What's 'ingrained prejudice'?" you ask.

"You'll see," Leah says. "I want to hear the other side."

You sigh and put the needle down but lower the volume. You plop down on your bed again and stare at the bumpy white ceiling. "So if you won't answer that, then tell me why you think we moved here."

She stops brushing. "What do you mean?"

"We don't go to synagogue that much, just on holidays and sometimes on Friday nights. Ma and Daddy didn't send us to Hebrew school. We only see Aunt Esther and Uncle Isaac's families in Brooklyn every few months, and they hardly ever come here. But Ma and Daddy want you to meet Jewish boys. And I guess the same goes for me if I ever date anyone."

"Oh, stop, you will," Leah says.

"I don't even want to think about it," you say and roll onto your back, hugging your knees to your chest. Then you roll back up into a sitting position. "But if they care so much, wouldn't it have been easier to stay in Brooklyn, where there are more Jewish people and we didn't feel so, I don't know—"

"Separate," Leah says and goes back to brushing.

"Yeah. Do you feel that way?" You haven't thought about it much before, how you feel about religion or about being Jewish. It was something you just were.

"I guess, sometimes. It depends. I don't feel that way with Raj. In my opinion, religion shouldn't matter so much. I mean, if Raj and I get married . . ." she says and gets quiet. You wait. You wait some more. She sits back in her chair, thinking.

"What were you going to say?" you finally ask.

"Nothing. You ask too many questions, Ari. Can we just listen to the music?" she says.

"Tell me," you say. You won't ever stop asking Leah questions. Who else can help you figure out the world in the same way?

But Leah just goes over to the record player and turns up the volume. The music fills the room, and it's too loud to talk anymore.

The following Sunday, after you've all straightened up, put in the laundry, and Ma has Mr. Cleaned the whole place down, the smell of roasting chicken takes over the apartment. Leah asked Ma specifically to make chicken. She told her it was because she makes the best roast chicken in the world, but she told you privately that Raj doesn't eat beef. She said lots of Hindus are vegetarians, like his parents, but he eats chicken and fish.

You wondered if being vegetarian for Hindus was like keeping kosher, the way some Jewish people do, like Aunt Esther in Brooklyn, and the way Ma and Daddy don't. You're just relieved Leah made sure chicken is served, because you wouldn't want to be in the room if Ma spent all day making brisket and Raj wouldn't eat it.

You're watching Ma take a steaming tray of roasted potatoes out of the oven when the doorbell rings.

"I'll get it," Leah says, bursting out of the bedroom in an orange minidress you've never seen.

"A little short, don't you think?" Ma says, wiping her hands with the dish towel, but Leah doesn't respond and opens the door.

Raj is standing there with a bouquet of roses, looking as handsome as a movie star. You walk over and inch behind Leah. They lock eyes, and it makes you feel embarrassed.

"Thank you, they're just lovely," she says, taking the flowers. Ma is still in the kitchen. Daddy is reading the paper on the couch, not facing the door. "Daddy, Ma, come," Leah calls. Ma takes off her apron. Daddy gets up. Then they see Raj, and both of your parents stop in their tracks. Daddy, probably realizing he's being rude, starts to move again, clears his throat, and shakes Raj's hand.

"Hello," he says. "I'm Mr. Goldberg. Nice to meet you."

Ma comes over, finally. "Mrs. Goldberg. I'm sorry, what was your name again?" she asks, not holding her hand out.

"I didn't say. It's Raj," he says. "Raj Jagwani."

"Let me go put these in water," Leah calls in an odd

singsongy way and walks the flowers over to the kitchen, leaving Ma, Daddy, and Raj all staring at each other.

"Hi," you say, giving him a little wave. Ma and Daddy turn to you abruptly, as if they'd forgotten you were there.

"You must be Ariel," Raj says and smiles. He holds out his hand. "Leah has told me a lot about you."

You smile back shyly, acting as if you've never met, just the way Leah told you to. You shake his hand.

"Okay," Leah says, coming over. "Why don't we all sit down here before dinner and have a chat." She gestures to the couch. Everyone walks over and sits down in an awkward silence. Then Leah asks if Raj would like something to drink.

"I'm fine," he says. But Daddy asks for a seltzer. Leah rushes off to get him one. When she comes back, she mentions Raj is a business major at the University of Bridgeport.

"Well, young man," Daddy says. "The best way to learn about business is to run one of your own. College can't teach you that."

"That's true," Raj replies.

Leah squirms in her seat. Ma looks at her nails. The silence falls like wet snow again.

"I'm going to check on the chicken." Ma stands up and heads toward the kitchen. She calls you to help her.

"Did you know about this boy?" Ma whispers when you're standing next to her over the stove.

"No," you say.

Ma studies your face. "Never mind," she says. "I truly don't know what Leah is thinking."

"He seems nice."

All she does is hand you the salad bowl, pick up the platter of chicken, and bring it to the table.

You all sit down at the table, and the food gets passed around while Raj compliments the apartment. There's some talk about how hot it is for this early in the summer. Then Leah says Raj will be entering the graduate business program at New York University this fall.

"Your parents must be proud," Daddy says.

Raj laughs. "I hope so. They wanted me to be an electrical engineer. That's what my father does. But I'd like to run my own business one day."

"So where exactly are you from, Raj?" Daddy asks.

Leah sits up straighter and looks tense.

"We live in Danbury," Raj says.

"No, no," Daddy says. "Before that."

Raj refolds his napkin before placing it on his lap again. "I was born in Bombay. We came to the US a few years ago for my father's job."

"You speak English very well," Ma says and passes him the potatoes.

"I learned growing up," Raj replies, taking the platter.

"Oh." Ma wipes her mouth. "I didn't realize they taught English in India."

"Yes" is all Raj says.

"And I assume you speak Indian as well?" Ma asks.

"Not Indian, Sylvia. Hindu," Daddy says.

You don't think that's the right answer, either. Leah and Raj eye each other for a second.

"Actually, Hindu is my religion. I also speak Hindi, Sindhi, and a little Urdu. But mostly English now."

"My, so many languages," Ma says. "Very impressive. I do think that if people are going to live here, they should learn our language."

You think of how Ma and Daddy speak Yiddish all the time to each other.

Raj gets a hard look in his eye. You feel bad for him, having to answer so many questions. You notice that Leah touches his arm.

Then no one talks for a bit, and all you can hear is chewing. It makes you want to plug your ears.

Ma swallows and dabs her mouth. "Will you go home after your program?"

"Home?" Raj asks.

"Back to India," Ma says.

"We just became US citizens, so I suppose Connecticut is home now. We visit my grandparents in Bombay as often as we can, but it's a long trip."

"I can imagine," Ma says. "One of my friends traveled in India a couple of years ago. She brought back the loveliest jewelry, but the food made her very sick."

"How do you know it was the food?" Leah asks.

"That's what she said," Ma says.

Raj takes a long sip of water.

"So your plans are to stay here permanently?" Daddy asks.

Raj squints. "Yes, that is the plan. It would have been a lot of trouble to go through if it weren't."

"Trouble?" Daddy asks. "Isn't it an honor?"

"Daddy," Leah says in an extra-calm way. "I'm sure Raj just means that they wouldn't have naturalized if they weren't planning to stay. Isn't that right?" Leah glances nervously at Raj. She's starting to look as if she might faint.

"Can someone please pass the salad?" you call out loudly. All eyes suddenly shift to you as if they'd forgotten again you're even there.

Raj grabs the bowl near him, hands it to you, and smiles. "I think we can all agree it is an honor to live in this great country."

After that, Leah tries to steer the conversation to the bakery and gets Daddy to talk about bread making, something he can talk about for hours. It turns out Raj is interested in baking and explains to Daddy how naan is made in a clay oven. Daddy tells him how to make pumpernickel, and they both seem to enjoy the conversation, though you, Ma, and Leah start to glaze over because you've heard Daddy talk about bread too many times.

Raj makes Daddy laugh, though. Even Ma smiles when he tells a story about the first time his family tried Wonder Bread and how it stuck to the roof of everyone's mouth. You like the way Raj's forehead crinkles up when he laughs. *It's going well*, you think. *Of course they like Raj.*

After more smiles, dessert, and the shaking of hands, Raj leaves. As soon as the door closes, Ma turns to Leah.

"What were you thinking, surprising us like this?" she says. Then she tells Leah she doesn't want her seeing Raj anymore.

"I knew it!" Leah yells and points at Ma. Leah never yells. "You're prejudiced."

"Prejudiced? It's the world, not us," Ma says. "I'm thinking of your future."

"Ma, the world is changing. Did you see what happened this week? The Supreme Court ruling, *Loving versus Virginia*?" She goes over to the stand in the living room where Daddy stuffs the newspapers and comes back with a copy of Tuesday's *New York Times*. She puts it on the kitchen counter and taps the page.

"Look," she says. You walk over and look. Ma and Daddy do the same.

Justices Upset All Bans on Interracial Marriage, the headline says. Then Leah reads the first sentence of the article. "'The Supreme Court ruled unanimously today that states cannot outlaw marriages between whites and non-whites.'" She stops reading and faces Ma again.

"I see," Ma says.

"What does it mean?" you ask Leah.

"It means that it's legal everywhere now for different races to marry," says Daddy.

"But it wasn't illegal in Connecticut," Ma says. "And that's not what this is about."

"Oh no?" Leah says. "You should have seen the way you both stared at Raj when he walked in the door. I had to pick your jaws off the floor. And you should know what prejudice feels like, living in this narrow-minded town."

"This narrow-minded town has given you opportunities I only dreamed of. I don't have anything against the color of his skin," Ma says.

"Leah, you know we're not like that," Daddy says.

"So the first thing you noticed about Raj was his religion? I know that strangers look at us funny in the street. You don't want me to be with him because of his religion *and* his skin color."

Ma takes a deep sigh. "Leah, listen to me," she says. You're all still standing around the kitchen counter, the newspaper open in front of you. "This is not about him. It's about what it means to be Jewish, about having a Jewish family someday. Isn't that important to you?"

"It's okay that you have a little crush. He's very charming. But that's all it is," Daddy adds.

"Yes." Ma smiles at Daddy. "I'm actually glad you had him over for dinner. You saw for yourself that it wouldn't work. It'll be easier to let it go now rather than later."

"This isn't a little crush. I love him."

Ma rolls her eyes. Daddy looks away.

"I think he's nicer than Leah's other boyfriends," you offer, but no one even glances in your direction. They go back to staring each other down. "He brought flowers," you try again.

"Leah, you have no idea what love is," Daddy says.

"See," Leah says, looking at you with her hands on her hips. "This is why I didn't want to tell them."

You open your mouth, but you don't know what to say. She walks over to the roses.

"Well, if you don't want me to see him anymore, then you don't get to enjoy the flowers." She grabs them out of the vase by the tops of the stems so she doesn't prick herself and shoves them in the garbage. Then she hurries off to the bedroom you share and slams the door.

Ma and Daddy stand there for a moment. Ma starts speaking in Yiddish to Daddy. She speaks it better than Daddy, but he knows enough to keep up. They learned from their parents, but they never taught you and Leah. You think it's because they wanted to keep it for themselves, a secret language. You only understand some words. You hear Ma say farblondjet, then meshuggener. Those words you know. It means they think Leah and Raj are all mixed-up and crazy.

Ma marches to her bedroom, still muttering to herself, and Daddy follows, leaving you alone in the living room.

You walk over to the flowers in the garbage and pluck out the largest rose. You put your nose in the center of the flower and breathe. The smell is sweet and comforting, the petals silky smooth to the touch.

It seems a shame that the rose will die in the garbage. You once did flower pressing in school, so you know to break off the top part of it. Then you put it between the pages of one of the big art books Ma and Daddy keep below the coffee table. After you press it closed tightly, you open the book again and see the print of the red petals staining the pages like watercolor paint. You decide to close it again and hide it on a shelf in the coat closet. Maybe you'll tell Leah about it later, or maybe you'll just keep it for yourself.

How to Spy on Your Sister

Leah doesn't ask you to go to the Sweet Scoop with her anymore. She barely speaks to anyone at all. Ma and Daddy only let her go to her dance classes and make sure she's either home right after or helping at Gertie's. You wonder if she actually goes to class, and Ma must have wondered the same thing, because a few Mondays after the dinner, you hear her on the kitchen phone.

"Hello, Miss Duchon, this is Sylvia Goldberg, Leah Goldberg's mother. I wanted to call you and see how Leah was doing? Oh no, everything is fine. I just wanted to make sure she was getting to class on time and doing well? Yes? Oh, that's wonderful. Thank you."

After she hangs up, you head into the kitchen, pretending you haven't heard a word, and pour yourself a glass of milk.

"She doesn't talk to you anymore about that Indian boy?" Ma says.

"He's a man," you say.

Ma squints at you. "Ari, I don't think you understand."

You grip the glass tighter. You hadn't meant to do this, to be in the middle. You've been in the middle of Leah and Ma before. Leah tells you something, and then Ma tells you something. You know they both want you to deliver their messages, but the messages have never been this confusing.

Ma puts on her yellow apron and ties it tight around her waist. She lowers her voice like she doesn't want anyone to hear her.

"It was hard enough when your father and I got married," she says. "My Orthodox parents didn't think Daddy was Jewish enough for me. My sister feels the same way. It has always been a problem. It's part of why it's easier for us to be here."

You take a sip of milk and nod. It's like you've somehow always known this even though she never talks about it, that moving to Connecticut wasn't just for the bakery.

"But this. I've never seen Leah look that way at anyone. It's better that I break her heart before . . ." Ma trails off and rubs her forehead.

You put your glass of milk down on the counter. "Before what?"

"Before it's too late," she says.

"But what if they really love each other? What's the harm?" you ask.

"She's turning her back on her heritage. She doesn't know what it will cost her down the line."

"You and Daddy stayed together for love, right?"

"This is an entirely different situation. We didn't turn our backs on anything. Daddy and I are both Jewish; that's the important thing. Even though my parents had questions, they still approved of our marriage. They knew we would bring up Jewish children together and keep our traditions. I don't want Leah to make a worse mistake."

"So you and Daddy made a mistake?"

Her face changes, and she opens and closes her mouth. "Of course not. Honestly, I don't know where you get your ideas sometimes."

"But you said—"

"Set the table for dinner, please." Ma cuts you off and hands you four plates.

"But—"

"Don't hok a chainik," she tells you, which means to stop bothering her immediately. Then she starts peeling potatoes so fast, you're afraid she'll nick herself with the peeler.

Later that evening, after Leah gets home, you all sit in the living room, watching the news. Daddy lounges in his big armchair, and you and Leah curl up on the couch. Ma sits in the small wooden rocking chair. You watch Leah watching the television, the light of the screen dancing in her eyes. A commercial for Ivory detergent comes on, and the woman in the commercial talks about how smooth her hands are from using Ivory, so young-looking that people still think she's a teenager.

"Lies," Ma says and laughs.

You look at Ma's hands as she mends a loose hem on her green-and-white dress. They look fine to you, still youthful even after all the mixing, slicing, and kneading she does at the bakery. But her shoulders are slouched. She looks tired. She never stops. Even when you're all lazing around in front of the TV, she's still fixing something, taking care of something.

"Leah, put your hand up to Ma's," you say.

Leah looks at you, surprised. "Why?"

"Because. Show her that her hands still look like a teenager's."

You want to make Ma and Leah look at each other. It's like you're four boats tied to a dock, but Leah's rope has come untied and she's starting to float out into the ocean.

"I don't want to get up," she says.

"It will only take a second. Just show Ma that her hands still look like yours."

Ma waves you away. "Oh, stop."

Daddy looks up from the paper, his glasses slipping down his nose. "You look the same as the day I married you," he says and winks at Ma. Ma waves him off, just like she did to you.

Leah just sits there, staring straight at the television. You get up and take her hand and tug a little on her arm.

"What is wrong with you?" she says and pulls her arm back.

"Leah," Daddy says. "Be nice."

"Nice," she says. "You want me to be nice?"

You, Ma, and Daddy all stare at her. Her voice gets louder.

"Because I don't think it's very *nice* to tell me I can't be with someone I love."

"Not now," Ma says.

Leah stands up, puts her hands on her hips. "Then when? When are we going to talk about this?"

"I didn't mean to make you upset," you say to Leah, but maybe you did. You wanted her to say something, anything. She turns and glares at you.

"Don't be mad at me," you say.

"I'm not mad at you," she says and takes a deep breath. "I'm mad at them." Her shoulders fall a little. The broadcast goes back on. "Mostly at her," she says, pointing to Ma.

"Little girl," Daddy says. "Don't talk to your mother that way. As long as you live in our house, our rules."

No, you think. *Don't put it like that, Daddy.*

Leah crosses her arms and sits back down. You all continue watching in silence, but you don't think anyone is paying attention to Mr. Cronkite.

After a few minutes, Leah speaks again. Her voice is calm. "You're right, Daddy. I'm sorry." Then she gets up and puts her hand on top of Ma's. "See, Ma. Ari was right. Your hands look just like mine. Youthful as ever."

Ma beams at Leah, pats her hand. You're not sure why everything is suddenly okay. You sink back into the couch, feeling like maybe you've fixed something.

The truth is Ma does look younger than a lot of mothers you see. She puts on a cold cream mask and uses globs of hand lotion every evening before she goes to bed. She always wears a smart dress with nice shoes, does her hair up in a neat bun, and finishes off her look with a coat of fresh lipstick every day, even at the bakery.

In the middle of the night, you hear Leah get up. She drops a hard object, maybe a book, and you open your eyes a tiny bit as she moves toward the door. Moonlight shines through the window, making Leah look like a ghost in her white nightgown. She opens the door and slowly closes it behind her. After a minute, you get up and look at the clock. It's one thirty in the morning. You rub your eyes and press your ear to the door to see if you can hear anything else. Standing there, your eyes fall on the surface of the desk that is empty now for the summer but is usually filled with schoolbooks and papers.

You think of how Leah is always willing to help you with your homework. She does it during the evenings with the door shut so Ma won't get involved. She knows you don't like the way Ma helps you with your writing, tapping her fingers on your paper impatiently, constantly telling you to slow down and focus.

Sometimes Leah will even write down things for you, a little messy so it still looks like your handwriting, but better. She said it isn't cheating if it's still your words. It's so much easier for you to only have to think of what to say without also having to write it, and Leah knows that. She has a way of helping you better than anyone.

As you press your ear harder against the door, Leah's voice from the kitchen travels in muffled bursts through the cracks. Is she talking on the phone? You open the door carefully and make your way down the little hallway that separates your bedroom from the living room and kitchen area. You stand with your back against the wall and peer around the corner, like a spy. Leah's back is facing you.

She holds the yellow receiver to her ear, the cord dangling down. You lean in and try to hear what she's saying.

"I can't live like this anymore. I miss you," she says. Then more muffled talk. You catch the words "Raj, you don't understand. That's just the way they are." A minute goes by, and she's quiet, listening. She starts to talk again. "Don't be like that. Your parents haven't understood, either," she says in an angry whisper. "Are you saying you don't love me the way I love you?" she continues, panic creeping into her voice. More silence. Then she says, "I know. I'm sorry. But aren't we supposed to be the strong ones?"

There's another long silence as she holds the phone to her ear. "I have to go" is the last thing she says before putting the phone gently back in its cradle. Her shoulders start to shake. After a minute, she turns. You run back into your bedroom and jump on your bed, but as you pull the covers up, you realize you forgot to close the door. You wonder if you should get out of bed again, but it's too late. Leah stands in the doorway.

"Were you spying on me?" she asks, wiping her eyes and sniffling.

"No," you say.

"I didn't leave the door open."

You don't answer. She plops down on her bed.

"What's going on? Were you and Raj fighting?" you ask.

"Shhhh," she says, looks at you for a few seconds, then lies down. "It's all fine."

"It doesn't sound fine," you say.

"Raj thinks we should wait. But we had a plan. I trusted him."

"Wait for what? A plan?" you ask. You thought Leah had told you everything. You wonder how many secrets she has.

"You can't tell them," she says.

"Ma and Daddy? Tell them what?" You really wish Leah would make more sense.

"About the phone call."

"I won't," you say. "But what plan? Please tell me, Leah. You know I'm good at keeping secrets."

"There's no plan, not anymore," Leah says and lays the back of her hand over her forehead. Sometimes she falls asleep like that. "Don't worry, Ari. It's late. I'll tell you more in the morning."

Leah doesn't say anything else. She just lies there, her hand on her forehead. You think about what she said, how she couldn't live like this anymore. You wonder what makes her feel that way. Is it Ma and Daddy being mad at her? Is it having to be apart from Raj? Is it having to share a bedroom with you? Leah wondered if Raj loved her the same way she loved him, but you wonder that about Leah, whether she loves you as much as you love her. You watch her body rise and fall with her breathing. You drift off, too, and when you wake up, her bed is empty.

You rush out of the room, barely awake, and to your relief, Leah and Ma are sitting there, just like any old morning, while Ma has her Sanka and Leah sticks her spoon in half a grapefruit. She's in her dance clothes, her hair wrapped tight in a bun. How did you not hear her getting ready?

"There you are," you say, a little out of breath.

They both look at you.

"Where else would I be?" Leah says.

You squint at her.

"We need to get you a new pair of pajamas," Ma says, and you look down at your tight Wonder Woman pj's.

"I hope they make these in a larger size, because I plan to wear them forever," you reply, puffing out your chest. You cross your wrists like Wonder Woman.

Ma shakes her head and takes another sip of coffee. "Leah, tell her she needs more ladylike pajamas."

Leah takes another scoop of her grapefruit. "Wonder Woman *is* a lady, Ma," she says. Your heart lifts, and you smile. You feel like the old Leah is back. Maybe she and Raj broke up last night on the phone. You like Raj, but you don't like what's happening to your family. You don't want Leah to be sad, but maybe it'll be easier for everyone this way.

"Gotta go," Leah says. "The bus." She grabs her bag and gives both of you a kiss on the cheek and a hug, which surprises you because she never does that. Then she walks out the door.

How to Write a Poem

Nearly two months later, the first day of school starts like any other. You sit at a desk with a stack of textbooks and notebooks stored neatly inside it and wait for the teacher to tell you to read, write, add, subtract, and divide. Gripping your pencil as tightly as you can, you hope it all feels easier this year. Your teacher is new to the school. Her name is Miss Field. She has the longest hair of anyone you know. She also wears a long skirt and very long earrings, which look nice dangling against her long neck.

First, Miss Field asks everyone to share their names and their favorite fruit. You say apples to keep it simple even though the real answer is the strawberries you once picked with Leah at a farm four years ago. They were still warm, as sweet as candy, and stained your lips red. Leah said it was nature's makeup and rubbed some juice into her cheeks like blush. Ma didn't let Leah wear makeup yet. Then she put some on your cheeks, too, while you laughed and laughed. You get a pain right in the center of your stomach thinking about it. It feels like a memory from another person, another life.

After the names and the fruit, you expect to be asked to take out your math textbook or told when the first spelling quiz will be. But something different happens.

Miss Field says the class is going to write a poem. You hear the sighs leak out as everyone finds their composition notebooks. Then she asks the class to write about what their summer sounded like. You don't want to think about your summer. Your mind goes right to the last time you saw Leah, that day she hugged you and left for dance class, except that's not where she went.

You push away your thoughts and stare quietly, waiting for Miss Field to explain. Her earrings swing back and forth, back and forth as she moves her head. You watch the fan standing in the corner blowing the hot air around. No one starts writing. Lisa Turner raises her hand because she always has something to say. "Miss Field, how can a whole summer sound like one thing?" she asks.

Miss Field says it doesn't have to sound like one thing.

She says it can sound like as many things as we want it to sound like.

"Should it rhyme?" Lisa asks.

"It can be any kind of poem. It can rhyme or not rhyme," she explains.

"But—" Lisa starts to say.

"Lisa," Miss Field says. "There's no way to get it wrong."

There must be a way to get it wrong, you think, and you'll probably be the one to do it. You've only written one poem in your life. It was in third grade, about the color green. Your teacher said every poem had to have eight lines, but you could only think of two. She said your poem didn't count.

"I won't be grading it, and please don't worry about spelling and grammar," Miss Field says.

You look up and blink. You've never heard a teacher talk like this. You take a deep, deep breath and pick up your pencil. It takes you a while to think of things to write. When your hand touches a pencil, your brain feels as if it's filled with molasses.

Lisa raises her hand and asks, "How long does it have to be?"

"Any length you'd like. It could be one line," Miss Field says. Your shoulders suddenly feel lighter. One line. You can do that. You hear more murmuring and then the scratching of pencils moving on paper.

After a few minutes, you write four words, one short line. You try to keep it straight, but your writing has a life of its own. It grows bigger and wavier the more you write. Usually your teachers give you the little-kid paper with the wider spaces, but that makes you feel stupid.

You think a little more and write another short line. You stretch your fingers out, and after a minute, you write one more. You press the pencil down hard to make the letters clear. When you finish, you have three lines and a title. It feels a little something like baking—take black and white cookies. People think they're hard to make, but each step isn't hard. First, you mix the dry ingredients with the wet ones, the same ingredients in any cookie—flour, sugar, butter, eggs—then bake. The cookies need to cool before you add the vanilla glaze, then the chocolate. Step by step, line by line, it's easy. You can even read most of the letters.

September 5, 1967

Poetry assignment

Miss Field

The Sound of Summer

My summer sounded like

the moment after

the last guest leaves the party.

Miss Field walks around and looks at everyone's poems, every single person. When she comes to you, she picks up your paper and puts on her glasses. She squints at the letters. You expect her to say that she can't read it, that it doesn't count.

"This is very good, Ariel," she says instead.

"Really?" you say. Maybe she's a liar. Teachers never tell you anything you've written is good. They tell you it's too short, or that it needs work, or that they can't read it, or they just correct all the spelling mistakes with red pen.

"Yes," she says.

"No, it's not," you say. "It's just a few words. It doesn't really mean anything." But you know it does. You know you're trying to tell the story of what it felt like after that day in July, when Leah left and didn't come back.

"It is. Tell me more," she says and hands it back to you.

Other kids are looking at you, and your hands start to sweat. You nod and stare at your paper; ideas of what to write float around in your mind. But after a few minutes, Miss Field asks the class to take out their history books, and there's no more time.

When you arrive at Gertie's after school, Ma is taking pumpernickel loaves out of the oven. You go over to the day-old, grab a slice, toast it, and slather it with butter. Then you pull a cola out of the refrigerator, pop it open, and feel the little bubbles tingle on your lips.

"When you finish your snack, we need your help with a big order," Ma says, wiping her flour-covered hands on her apron.

"Okay, okay," you say. Ma is always rushing, but lately she seems more rushed, and you wonder if it's just going to keep getting worse. Daddy comes out of the kitchen, looking hot and tired.

"How's my muffin?" he asks.

"I'm all right," you say and stuff the rest of the bread in your mouth. "Same as always."

Daddy nods. "Me too, Muffin," he says. "Same old, same old."

This is what you and Daddy always say to each other after school. And every day, you know that you are not the same and neither is he. When you and Ma get back to the apartment, you go into your bedroom and take a sniff of the Chanel No. 5 perfume on the dresser, a sixteenth birthday gift that Ma gave Leah. The apartment used to smell of it when Leah was still here, along with her Breck shampoo, but you didn't notice until she was gone and the smell faded away.

A little part of you still hopes you'll find her sitting on her yellow-and-white bedspread, playing the Beatles or the Rolling Stones. Or maybe even the Doors real quiet because Ma hates the Doors.

She would be unpinning her hair from dance class and look up at you. "Hey, Ari," she'd say. "Why do you look so low?" "I'm not low," you'd insist. "Then don't look so serious," she'd reply. She'd ask if you needed any help with your homework, and you'd always say yes, even if you didn't need help that day. When Leah paid attention to you, it always felt like the light around you got a little brighter and clearer. You think Ma felt like that, too, even if she probably wouldn't admit it.

Instead, the bedspread stays smooth and untouched.

You take a seat at your little wooden desk, pull out your poem, and read the three lines again. A few more come to you quickly, which never happens. But this poem feels like finally writing down a list of things you've been thinking about for a long time.

September 5, 1967
Poetry assignment
Miss Field

The Sound of Summer

My summer sounded like
the moment after
the last guest leaves the party,
when all the laughter

and the slicing of cake

and the unwrapping of gifts

and the smiling

and the dancing

stops.

Those who are left

sit down, tired and quiet,

wondering if they'll ever

feel that happy again.

How to Follow the Rules

Today on the bus, you sit with Jane. She's not always on the bus. Sometimes she fakes sick and her mother lets her stay home to watch TV all day. Jane isn't that good at school, either, but not for the same reason as you. She just doesn't care. She says she's going to be a famous actress and live in Hollywood and sticks celebrity magazines between her notebooks. You don't know where Jane's dad is. It's just her and her mother, Peggy, in the apartment. She never talks about her dad.

Most kids in your town live in big houses, but you like living in the apartment building right outside of town. Sometimes, when you pass the big houses with their big lawns, they seem so lonely and separate from everything else. You already feel lonely. The last thing you need is a lonely house.

"I'm going to try out for *Bye Bye Birdie*," Jane says, flipping through an old copy of *Screen Parade* magazine. She holds up a picture. "Don't I look like Elizabeth Taylor?" she asks and smiles, the metal braces on her crooked teeth gleaming in the sunlight. You wonder how she got braces. Ma says they're for rich people. Sometimes Jane talks about her grandparents and their big house in Maine. Maybe her grandparents are rich and they got her the braces. Luckily, your teeth aren't that crooked.

"When are the auditions?" you ask, not answering her question, because other than the color of her hair, she looks nothing like Elizabeth Taylor. Jane has so many freckles, they cover her face in patches. Her thin dark hair that her mother cuts in a short bob hangs close to her chin. Through the picture, Elizabeth Taylor stares at you with her piercing eyes, straight teeth, and perfect red lips. Ma once told you that Elizabeth Taylor is the most beautiful woman in the world. You wonder how one woman could be the most beautiful. Aren't there different kinds of beautiful?

"Next week. Audition with me. Please, oh please," Jane

says. She puts her magazine on her lap and turns toward you. She grabs your arms and squeezes them, giving you a little shake.

She can squeeze all she wants. That will never happen. You shake your head.

"Not on my life," you say and mean it.

"Scaredy cat," she says and drops her grip on you.

"I'll go with you and watch," you say. This seems to calm her down. She turns back to her magazine, and you take out your notebook and open it carefully, hoping Jane doesn't ask you what you're doing. You look at your poem and count the lines in your head. Thirteen. It's the longest thing you've ever written.

When you see Miss Field in class, you notice she's wearing the same long earrings, but she doesn't start with poetry today. She starts with boring old spelling. She writes words and definitions on the chalkboard for everyone to copy.

After she's finished writing on the board, she walks over to you and watches you write. You stop and look at her. She smiles. You smile back but don't start writing again until she leaves. She doesn't watch anyone else write the way she just watched you. She's figuring it out, like every teacher does, that something is wrong.

Just before lunch she asks you to stay behind for a minute. You take in a deep breath and put your things in your desk. She's probably going to give you those handwriting worksheets as extra homework. All your teachers make you do them.

"Did you write any more of that wonderful poem?" she asks and tilts her head to the side.

"No," you say, and your face gets warm. It always does that.

"Okay, well, maybe another time. I got the sense that you didn't finish."

You nod.

"I wanted to ask you about your handwriting," she says.

"I'm sorry. I know it's very bad," you say and drop your eyes to your feet.

"Ariel," she says, taking her glasses off. "You don't have to apologize. Has it always been hard for you?"

"Yes," you say and look up again.

"Has anything helped?" She looks at you carefully.

All those handwriting worksheets you've done, both print and cursive, over and over and over. It doesn't seem to matter how much you practice, though. Thinking of words, of sentences, of writing them down never gets any easier. "Not really."

"Did you like writing that poem?"

"Yes." You did like writing it, the way it focused your thoughts, the way it got some of your feelings out. You think of all thirteen lines sitting in your notebook, and your back gets a little straighter. You could take it out and show Miss Field, but you don't. Not yet.

"I like writing poems, too. How would you like to write another one? Just like you did before, as short as you want."

You just nod again. Why is she telling you all this?

"I'm going to have everyone write more poetry, not just you. But I think you have something to say."

"I guess so," you reply. Doesn't everyone have something to say?

"I'm glad we talked."

"Okay," you say because you're not sure if you're glad. You feel sort of excited and embarrassed and confused.

When you get to the cafeteria, the noise hits you like a gust of wind. Too much noise makes you feel like a thousand people are screaming at once. Ma says you're too sensitive.

Scanning the room, you find Jane sitting with some of the girls in her class. You start walking toward her table, but she doesn't look up, which makes you angry. You feel like she knows you're there but is pretending not to see you.

Then you see some of the girls in your class, but you aren't really friends with any of them. You sit at the end of their table anyway, a little separate from everyone else, and eat your PB&J. The girls ignore you.

You used to be friends with more of them, but as everyone got older, they treated you differently. Maybe it's because you're the only Jewish girl in the sixth grade. Or maybe it's because people think the way you write is weird. Or maybe it's because you keep your hair short and you don't like to paint your nails or wear dresses or makeup. It makes you wonder if there's just one way of being a girl and if you're doing it wrong.

After you're back home, watching the news because it's

the only thing on just before dinner, you notice you don't see Ma in the kitchen. She's not doing her crosswords at the table, either. The silence feels strange. You check in your parents' room, but she's not there. Then you go in your room, and you see her sitting on Leah's bed. Her back is toward you. She sniffs, and her shoulders shake. It reminds you of Leah the last night she was here, when you spied on her talking to Raj and she was crying.

"Ma?" you say.

She jumps and turns around. She takes the tissue she always carries in her skirt pocket and dabs her eyes. "Oh, you startled me."

"What's wrong?" you ask her. The hair stands up on the back of your neck. Just like Leah, Ma hardly ever cries.

"It's her birthday tomorrow," she says. "It's my daughter's birthday tomorrow, and I don't even know how she is or what her life is like." She's holding Leah's letter, even though you know she's read it many times.

"She's with Raj, Ma. She's okay."

"No, no, don't say his name."

On the day Leah left, she put a note on Ma and Daddy's bed, explaining her plan to marry Raj and live with him in

73

New York City. Then Leah sent another letter a few weeks later in August. It said they got married at City Hall and were living in Manhattan. She said Raj was working at a record store in the city and going to graduate school at New York University.

She said she didn't want to go to college just yet and was teaching a dance class and auditioning for dance companies. She wrote that she was eighteen and in love and had to think about her own life. She also said she would only visit if Ma and Daddy wrote back and accepted Raj as her husband, that even the Supreme Court ruled that interracial marriages were legal everywhere and why should her own parents feel any different?

Ma keeps the letter in her night table drawer, and you don't know where the envelope went. You've snuck into your parents' room to read the letter many times. Each time you read it, you hope you might have missed something, like the part where Leah tells you she's sorry she left you all alone. Or where she remembers how good you were at keeping her secret. Or explains why she didn't include a message just for you, her special sister. The answer isn't something you like to think about, because it hurts like a big bruise. Leah simply doesn't love you the way you love her. What other answer could there be?

Ma turns to you. "Promise you won't leave me," she says, her eyes still red. She never talks to you like this.

"I promise, Ma," you say. You don't think you're going to college, and who would marry you? You'll probably live here with Ma and Daddy and make cookies at Gertie's forever.

After Leah left, Ma told you that because Leah married someone who isn't Jewish, she can't be part of the family anymore; it was their duty as Jewish parents to reject her decision, Ma explained. She said it was very painful, but it wasn't just about her and Daddy or Leah and Raj. It had to do with what her parents and Daddy's parents went through; with the Holocaust and the history of religious persecution that Jews will always have to carry. She said you would understand these things when you were older, but you weren't sure you wanted to.

It made you think of the play *Fiddler on the Roof*. Ma and Daddy took you and Leah into the city to see it on Broadway two years ago. Your parents were so excited. Your mother said she never thought she'd see a story about her own people on Broadway. They even bought the soundtrack. Your father still sings "If I Were a Rich Man" when he's frosting cakes at the bakery.

You remember thinking when you saw the play that the family—a Jewish family in Russia from many years ago—seemed so different from yours. In it, Tevye, the father, says he won't speak to his daughter Chava anymore because she's married a non-Jew. You remember how painful it seemed for Tevye but that he felt like he was doing the right thing. Chava was marrying someone who was not only not Jewish, but part of the Russian community who wanted all the Jewish people out of the village, who hated them, who might kill them if they didn't leave.

It made sense to you that Tevye wouldn't want his daughter to marry someone who was part of a group who hated his family. Yet the couple got married anyway. Chava said that her husband didn't agree with his people, that he was different. But maybe their marriage was a good thing, a small act of love in the middle of all that hate?

Except Raj isn't part of a group who hates you. Your family isn't even that religious. You don't observe the

Sabbath. Sometimes you drive down to Brooklyn for the Jewish holidays, and sometimes you don't. It feels like Ma and Daddy are figuring out the rules as they go, so why is this rule so important to them?

You want to know the right answer, to find it sitting in the palm of your hand as sure as a new penny.

"You're a good girl," Ma says and holds out her hand for you to take it. You get a prickly feeling all over. Ma has never called you a good girl before. You don't know whether you're scared or happy. You take Ma's hand; it's a little cold and damp. You wonder if this means Leah is now a bad girl. It used to be the opposite. You get to be the good girl, but only if Leah isn't here.

If Leah returns, you'll move back into second place. For a moment you imagine what that would be like, being Ma's favorite. The thought makes you feel guilty, as if you're taking something from Leah. Ma stands up, smoothing Leah's bedspread.

"I'm going to put in the chicken," she tells you and leaves for the kitchen.

Maybe you do have something to say. You sit down at your desk and start a new poem.

The Rules

There are so many rules.
But people break them
all the time.
Sometimes they get punished,
and sometimes they don't.
But how do you know
which rules are worth breaking?
And which ones you have to follow
even if they break you?

How to Mind Your Own Business

You sit in the theater with all the other kids auditioning, but you're just there to watch. The theater is dark except for the bright stage lights. It smells like wood and dust. You love sinking back into the shadows.

If you could pick one superpower, you would choose to be invisible. You could spy on any conversation you wanted to. There's just so much more you'd like to know, so many more secrets than you thought. The funny thing is that in real life, feeling invisible isn't the same as being able to turn yourself invisible. It's the opposite of a superpower.

You scrunch down in your seat, resting your head back, and wonder what Leah's doing on her birthday today. Would Raj get her a cake? Would they have a party? In a theater, you can't not think about Leah. You've seen her onstage so many times.

Today, everyone seems a little nervous before they start singing, even the best kids. Leah never looked anxious during her dance performances, but she always got nervous on the way in the car. She'd sit silently with her hair scraped back into a tight bun and tap her foot, her knee bouncing up and down.

Daddy would get talkative and start telling all sorts of random stories because he didn't like quiet in the car, but Leah would tune him out. When he'd ask her a question, she wouldn't answer, and Ma would put a hand on his arm to let it go.

You once asked Leah what she thought about before she performed. "I only think about who I'm supposed to be in the dance, like I'm in a storybook, not the real world. Then it feels easier," she said. You wonder if that's how she felt about marrying Raj.

Finally, it's Jane's turn. She stands on the stage, looking very small, the lights making her eyes squint. She clears her throat, tucks her hair behind her ears, and begins. She sings the song "An English Teacher" from *Bye Bye Birdie*.

She sings loud and strong, not high and wispy like many of the other girls. Her voice fills the theater. Everyone sits up straight and claps hard when she's done. You wish that a good stage voice would matter most, but in the school plays you've seen, the prettiest and most popular girls usually get the best parts.

"What did you think?" Jane asks as you walk the long walk home since the bus has come and gone. "Tell me the truth."

You look at Jane, her nose pink from the sun, her brown freckles reminding you of the topping on the crumb cake at the bakery. "You were the best one," you tell her.

"Really?"

"I wouldn't lie about that," you say.

Jane glows, and you feel light in your shoes, like you've just handed her a shiny gift. Then she frowns. "But I'll probably get a chorus part like I always do."

"It's all about popularity," you say.

Jane touches her hair and smooths it down close to her head. "Will it always be about that? For the rest of our lives?"

You're quiet for a minute. You think of Leah in a way

you've never thought about her before. She's inventing her own life, doing something completely unexpected. In high school, she was one of those pretty, popular girls who got the good parts. Nobody teased her about being Jewish, at least not that she mentioned. It seemed like she barely even noticed how lucky she was, or she didn't care. But then you shake her out of your head because if you think about Leah too long, your throat starts to hurt and you have to stop before you cry.

"Maybe only if you follow the rules," you say.

Jane's smile returns. "Yes, I think you're right. I'm giving up rules!" she says. She links arms with you, and you both skip the rest of the way home, Jane belting "An English Teacher." You join her because nobody but Jane is listening. The wind blows your hair around, and you imagine both of you skipping faster, lifting off the ground, taking flight.

The next day in class, Miss Field says you're going to spend every Wednesday, as part of social studies, discussing the news.

"So for our current events unit, once a week, five people will present a chosen headline. I'll pass out a sign-up sheet," she says.

Your heart sinks. You don't want to stand up in front of the class like Walter Cronkite and present anything because that will mean outlines and showing neatly drawn posters to the whole class—things you're awful at. If only you could just talk about what you think. It makes sense when it's in your head, but when you have to put it down on paper, your ideas get all mixed up.

You do like that Miss Field wants to talk about the news. Last year in social studies, it was always about the past. Your teacher, Mrs. Thomas, would write lots of names and dates on the chalkboard, and you were supposed to memorize them for her weekly quizzes.

It's always been hard for you to remember facts that aren't attached to anything else. They feel like falling leaves. You see them for a little bit, but suddenly a gust of wind takes them away and the new ones that fall look exactly the same.

Current events are easier because they are all around you. They are alive. They are stories you hear on TV and on the radio or read about in the newspaper, stories that Ma and Daddy discuss in the kitchen. They think you don't pay attention, but you listen even more now because of all the things you heard Leah and Raj talk about. It's as if the world is dying and being born at the same time.

Miss Field starts writing a timeline on the chalkboard. She's reviewing major events that happened over the summer. She writes down some topics: *The Vietnam War. The protests and riots happening all over the country. The boxer Muhammad Ali sent to jail for not going to Vietnam. The Beatles' release of the* Sgt. Pepper's Lonely Hearts Club Band *album. The Six-Day Arab-Israeli War. Thurgood Marshall being appointed as the first Black justice of the United States Supreme Court. The Supreme Court* Loving v. Virginia *ruling.*

She keeps going. You can't believe how many things have happened in just one summer, but the *Loving v. Virginia* ruling makes you think of Leah again.

After Leah wrote about the Supreme Court ruling in her letter, you went and looked it up on microfiche in the library and found out all about Richard and Mildred Loving, a white man and a Black woman who lived in

Virginia and got married even though it was against the law. They were even sentenced to prison. Eventually a lawyer helped them fight their case, but it took many years.

You think about how it's funny that it's called the *Loving* ruling, because it is about love, but it's also named after them. They had to move out of Virginia for a long time, away from their families, so they wouldn't be arrested. This past June, the Supreme Court finally ruled that no state could make laws against interracial marriage anywhere in this country. You remember the way Leah showed Ma the newspaper when it was announced in June and the way she cut out the article and stuck it on the edge of her mirror, right next to her picture of Paul Newman.

"First," Miss Field says, "you'll choose a topic here to review for us. Then we'll move on to weekly headlines."

You know you're going to choose the *Loving* ruling but copy the topics from the board like everyone else, just slower. Chris Heaton is in your class again this year. He leans over and looks at your paper. You turn your back to him.

"Why do you write like you're still in kindergarten?" he whispers.

He's always picking on you. "Mind your own business," you say, not whispering. Chris Heaton doesn't scare you. Sometimes you even feel bad for him. You know his older brother is fighting in Vietnam. You also know lots of soldiers who go to Vietnam don't come back alive. That probably makes him sad and angry, but that doesn't mean he can be the way he is to you.

Miss Field turns around. "Ariel? Do you have a question?"

"No," you say.

"Okay, let's write in quiet."

You thought Miss Field was different, but maybe she's just like your other teachers. Out of the corner of your eye, you see Chris making a face at you. If you were Wonder Woman, you'd take him by the arm, flip him over, and teleport right out of the classroom before he knew what happened. But instead, you swallow hard and grip your pencil tight.

Later at Gertie's, you throw yourself into an order of chocolate lace cookies. You have your snack, put on your apron, and start creaming the butter and sugar.

After sifting the flour, you realize Ma isn't there. Daddy is getting stuff out of the fridge. Jerry, Daddy's morning baker who usually leaves when you get there, is already gone for the day.

You check in the front to make sure you're right, but only Gabby is there, busy at the register. You go into the back and see Daddy holding a huge tub of butter.

"Where's Ma?" you ask.

"She wasn't feeling well," Daddy says without looking at you. "Can you walk home yourself?"

"Yes," you say and see something funny in his face, something he doesn't want to explain.

"Got to get a wedding cake started," he says and winks.

If Daddy didn't want to tell you stuff, he didn't. It was easier to get information out of Ma, even though from the way they both acted, it seemed like it would be the opposite.

You go back to your cookies, and they come out so thin and perfect, you eat one yourself, even though you're not supposed to. You're only allowed two cookies a day, and never fresh from an order. You sneak one more cookie and have an extra cola since Ma's not there.

At dinner, Ma serves leftover mushroom barley soup

with baked potatoes. She asks you how your day was but doesn't listen to the answer. Then she scoops you extra ice cream and goes into her room.

"What's wrong with Ma?"

"You know how she gets her headaches," Daddy says. At the close of the door, Daddy looks over the top of his newspaper. Ma does get headaches a lot. She calls them migraines and says she even sees flashes of color before they start. That sounds sort of magical to you rather than painful, but Ma sure does seem like she's in a lot of pain when she gets them. Since Leah left, it's been happening more often.

It's strange, because sometimes Ma seems so solid and strong, and other times she's lying on her bed, the curtains closed, with a bottle of aspirin by her side and a cold washcloth on her head. Daddy says her nerves get the better of her. You aren't sure what *nerves* means exactly, but you guess they cause migraines. You hope the nerves stay away from you.

"She's been getting them a lot," you say.

Daddy folds his newspaper, puts it down, takes off his glasses, and rubs his eyes.

"There was another letter today," he says after a few seconds of eye rubbing.

"Really? What did it say?" you ask, leaning forward, a smile spreading over your face.

"She's going to have a baby," he says.

Your mouth falls open, and you drop your spoon. It bounces a bit on the floor, then becomes still on the yellow linoleum. You and Daddy both look at it for a moment because it's a lot easier to look at the spoon than at each other. You bend over, pick it up, and bring it to the sink. Then you dump the chocolate ice cream in the garbage, feeling nauseous. Leah feels even farther away, spinning out into the atmosphere like a space rocket. You couldn't even hold on to her if you wanted to.

"Can I read the letter?" you ask him.

"It's not for you. It's about adult things," he says. He takes his napkin, reaches out, and dabs it at your mouth.

"Stop," you say and drag the back of your hand across where he put the napkin. You don't want your mouth wiped like a little baby.

"Sorry," he says. "You had a bit of chocolate on your face."

"Maybe you don't want Leah and Raj to be together," you say, tears making your eyes sting. "But she's still my sister, and you can't take her away from me."

"I'm not," Daddy says. "Leah has made her choices."

"Then show me the letter," you demand, crossing your arms tightly over your chest.

Daddy's face turns angry. He crumples up the napkin in his hand. "Please don't speak to me that way," he says.

"Daddy, I was with them. We would go to the park. Raj bought me ice cream. They looked so happy together. The only reason everything is sad and hard is because of you and Ma. It's not just about the choices Leah made. You are choosing, too."

"Ari, you don't know the ways of the world," Daddy says, louder now.

"I know that what you're doing is making everything worse," you say. You shouldn't be saying any of this, but sometimes the words just come out and you can't stop them.

Daddy glares at you. "That's enough," he says through gritted teeth.

You run into your room, slam the door, and climb into Leah's bed. Pulling the covers up to your chin, you cry into them. The phrase "the ways of the world" plays over and over in your mind. You try to piece together how all of this happened.

You think of when Leah brought home a Doors album. She said that she had a new record she wanted to play you. You thought she'd bought it, because you didn't know about Raj yet, but later you found out that he'd bought it for her.

She put it on, and both of you sat quietly, hunched over the little red turntable. You'd never heard anything like it. The lead singer, Jim Morrison, sounded like he was telling you secrets you weren't supposed to hear.

"Isn't it groovy, Ari?" she said as you both lay on the floor and listened to the strange sounds of Morrison's voice twisting and turning, even screaming, like he was actually trying to set the night on fire as he sang those words.

"It's like you can feel the whole world changing through the music," she said.

You didn't know if you heard what she heard, but you agreed with her anyway. Leah was easy to follow, like a tour guide, a light. Now with her gone it was dark and foggy. You have no idea what to do next.

You lie there for a long time in your school clothes. Could it really be true what Daddy said—your sister will soon be a mother? That means your parents are going to be grandparents, and you are going to be an aunt. The world suddenly just got a whole lot older.

You wake with a start and realize you've fallen asleep in Leah's bed. You get up, go into the kitchen. The big white clock on the wall says it's a quarter past eleven. Your parents are in their room, door closed, a slice of light peeking out from underneath. You stand there in the dark, staring at their bedroom door, while their voices rise and fall. They must be discussing the ways of the world. You want so badly to see Leah's new letter. You want to pore over every word and find the part that's written for you in between the lines, because there must be something. She wouldn't just forget you like this, would she?

How to Try Harder

On the way to school, you watch Jane read about the Beatles in her magazine. All the girls you know have a favorite Beatle. Paul's pretty keen, but you don't like him the way Jane does. John's okay. Ringo and George, not so much.

"Look at his eyes," she says, pointing at a picture of Paul. "He's staring right at me. It's like he knows everything I'm thinking."

You nod and stare into Paul's eyes with her. Jane has a huge poster of the Beatles on her bedroom wall, and she practices kissing Paul all the time. She says that she actually loves him. You wonder how Jane can know she loves Paul just from a picture. If you ever fall in love, it will be with an actual real person. You've never had a crush on someone real, though. Most of the boys don't notice you at all, or when they do, it's not for nice reasons.

The only crush you've ever had was on Elvis Presley, but you wouldn't tell anyone about that. You don't even know if it's a real crush or if it's just because you love his music. The truth is, he's getting kind of old, and he just got married. Even your mother listens to his music. Everything that's happening with Leah doesn't make falling in love seem like something you want to deal with anytime soon.

You go home that day, still thinking of love, and your fingers itch to write another poem.

The Ways of the World

The world has many ways
of spinning.
Many I don't understand.
But love
is not that hard
to understand.
Doesn't it just spin one way,
one person toward another,
without stopping?

When you write poems, you feel heavier and lighter at the same time. This poem you write in the last page of your notebook while sitting on your sister's bed. You write it as small as you can, and when you finish, you clap the notebook closed and slip it in your desk drawer.

Later that night at dinner, Daddy doesn't seem angry anymore and Ma's headache is gone.

"Ma, I really want to see Leah's letter. Please? Can I?" you try again.

She doesn't say anything and waves away your question with her hand. Sometimes when Ma gets angry, she gets real quiet.

Daddy says, "Adult talk, Ariel. It was for us, not you."

"I know she's going to have a baby. I know what that means," you say and stick out your chin, but your parents stay silent. You think of something to threaten them with. But not leaving, never that. Where would you go?

"When is she going to write me a letter?" you say, your voice becoming small and cracking a little. You bite your lip hard to stop the tears.

Ma leans over and puts her cold hand on your warm cheek for a few seconds, but she doesn't look you in the eye.

Another day goes by and you still haven't found the letter. You've looked in the kitchen drawers, both night table drawers, your parents' dresser drawers, the glove compartment in the Buick. Nothing.

The next afternoon, Ma is back at the bakery like everything's peachy, but you can tell by the fast and furious movement of her hands over the cookies, the bread, the cakes, and the pies, mixing the dough, so much dough, that nobody should interrupt her.

The bakery phone rings on Thursday afternoon. Ma answers and speaks low. She turns her back to you.

"Okay," she says. "I see. Next Tuesday. Yes, we will be there, thank you."

She puts the phone down, washes the flour off her hands, and wipes them on her apron.

"That was Miss Field," she says, looking in your direction.

"Oh," you say, and shame rushes to your face. "Am I in trouble?" You think of the poems you haven't shown her and the outline for your presentation on the *Loving* ruling.

"No," Ma says. "Should you be?"

You shrug and hope Ma can't actually read your mind, though sometimes it seems like she can. "No. Why did she call?" you ask, searching Ma's face for a clue. She searches yours as well.

"She said she wanted to discuss your handwriting. She wants us all to come in for a meeting."

You roll your eyes.

"Handwriting is important, Ariel, even if you don't think so. You have to try harder."

"I try."

"Do you?"

"I swear I do." If she only knew how hard you tried with every letter. Just thinking about it makes your fingers hurt.

"School was hard for me, too. But I knew I wasn't going to college," Ma says.

"Why was school hard for you?" you ask her. This surprises you. She's never said school was hard for her before.

"Oh, I don't know. Maybe I was just lazy, but I don't want you to think it's okay for you to be lazy. I want you to be better."

"I don't think it's okay to be lazy," you say, and Ma is the least lazy person you know.

"We'll see what Miss Field says," she tells you and sinks her hands into a huge metal bowl of risen pumpernickel dough, pulls off a big blob, and shapes it on the counter. She makes a trayful before sliding them into the oven. You wander out into the front. It's not that crowded. A woman looks through the day-old bread basket, and a man is ordering a box of cookies. Gabby nods at you as she takes cookies out of the display case.

"No, that one," he says as Gabby takes out an oatmeal, then a chocolate chip, a madeleine, and a piece of raspberry rugelach. "No, no. The one on the top," he continues, and she finds another cookie for him, but still he's not satisfied. "I want the big one in the back," he says.

A strand of Gabby's hair falls in her face, and she blows it away in a big huff as she puts back perfectly good cookies and takes out new ones. You see Ma's tan leather purse hanging on the hook by your coats. The letter has to be in there, but if you started looking through it, Gabby might notice. You'll find a good moment. It's like there's a sound pulsing through Ma's purse that only you can hear.

You walk home with Ma, watching her purse hang off her arm and swing back and forth during the half mile to your apartment, the golden September sun falling everywhere like honey. Ma talks to you about the flour order, how it's always late, how this makes her so mad, how nobody understands how important flour is to a bakery. Nobody. You nod and kick leaves aside until you get home.

Ma sets her purse down on the console next to the front door like she always does and takes off her wool jacket with the gray fur collar that Daddy bought her last year for their anniversary. She heads to her bedroom.

"Going to change," she calls to you. "Start the meat loaf?"

"Okay," you say and run into the kitchen. The meat loaf sits in a pan, looking lonely in the center of the refrigerator. It's the second time she's made meat loaf this week. You take it out, set it on the counter, and turn on the oven for preheating. You have ten minutes, or less if she's in a rushed mood, which is often.

You walk softly over to the console and unzip her purse. Her leather change purse, a roll of mints, a package of tissues, two Revlon lipsticks, a silver compact, and a folded piece of paper are all neatly lined up in her bag.

You take out the paper with shaking hands and unfold it. It's a letter, but not from your sister.

AGREEMENT TO PURCHASE
REAL ESTATE

The undersigned ("Purchaser") hereby offers to purchase from the owner ("Seller") the real estate located at 61 Main Street in the city of Eastbrook, State of Connecticut, the legal description of which is a storefront bakery and kitchen.

Upon the following terms and conditions:

1. Purchase Price and Conditions of Payment

The purchase price shall be Dollars ($14,000) to be paid in accordance with subparagraph A below:

You read a little more, but the words are so formal and strange, like another language, and you stop. You fold the letter, put it back in Ma's purse, and think about what you've read. Sixty-one Main Street is the address of the bakery, and *purchase* means to buy something. Is someone buying the bakery?

"You didn't put the meat loaf in!" your mother calls from the kitchen.

You hadn't realized you'd been standing at the console, staring at the floor. You rush back into the kitchen.

"What are you doing?" she asks, but luckily you can tell by the way she's hurrying around, putting plates on the table and unwrapping the iceberg, that she doesn't really want to know.

"Sorry," you say and put the rolls in a basket. You can't ask about something you weren't supposed to see. You look at Ma in her short green-and-white dress, her blond hair that's not really blond, up in an elegant bun, her peach lipstick still fresh, highlighting her green eyes. Did she know that this was going to be her life, here, in this small apartment with its tiny yellow kitchen, working at Gertie's all day, making dinner every night for you and Daddy? Because sometimes she seems dressed for another life, maybe the one she wished she had.

"Will we ever leave?" you ask.

Ma stops tearing the lettuce into little pieces. "What do you mean? This apartment? This town?"

"Yes, both," you say, watching her face carefully.

"Don't you like it here? We're lucky to live in a town like this," she says and goes back to the lettuce.

"I guess," you say.

"You go to one of the best schools in Connecticut. Your father and I didn't go to great schools, and we didn't go to college. But you will."

"I will?" You thought she didn't want you to go anywhere.

"Yes, because you'll have a lot more choices than I did as long as you don't end up like your sister. It's up to you now."

"I'm not smart enough to go to college," you say.

"Well, then you better study more. Your father and I aren't working this hard for nothing."

She goes back to making the salad, slicing up a cucumber. She hands you a piece like she always does, and you take it and bite down. You wish she had corrected you instead, had said that you *are* smart. You swallow the cucumber. She's moved on to the tomatoes.

"What about Gertie's?" you ask.

"What about Gertie's?" Ma says and looks away.

"Aren't you going to need me to stay and help?"

But she doesn't answer. She's moved to the oven and is checking on the meat loaf.

"Ma," you try one more time.

"What are you kvetching about? You spend too much time in the kitchen. Go do your homework," she says. You want to tell her that she was the one who asked you to put in the meat loaf. You walk out quietly and slip into your parents' room, where you quickly take another look in every drawer for the letter.

They must have thrown it out. You see Leah's first letter sitting in a drawer, with no envelope. If only you could find a return address, you could write her yourself.

You hurry out of their bedroom, but Ma is now relaxing on the living room couch, watching the news, having one of her drinks that smells like lime and rubbing alcohol in the tall glass. She usually only has a drink when she's really had *enough*, but she's been having them more often lately, along with her headaches.

You wonder if you should sit with her, ask her more

questions, try to get some answers, but you also want to be alone to think. You go into your room and look through the pile of records. Are your parents selling the bakery? Does it have to do with your sister leaving? The bakery, the four of you living here, it all seemed so permanent just a few months ago, like the rising sun. Now you feel like anything could happen at any moment.

You put on one of your favorite 45s, *Return to Sender*, on the little red turntable, lie down on the floor, and turn it up. You like to feel the vibrations of the music through the rug. It was Leah who introduced you to Elvis years ago, and you've loved him ever since. You listen to the words he sings: *We had a quarrel, a lover's spat. I write I'm sorry, but my letter keeps coming back. So then I dropped it in the mailbox and sent it special D. Bright and early next morning it came right back to me.*

The song gives you an idea. You wonder what would happen if you wrote your sister without the address, just put her name on it and sent it to New York City. Would it somehow make its way to her? How many Leah Goldbergs could there be in Manhattan? Hopefully it won't come back.

How to Have a Learning Disability

Miss Field sits in a student desk chair, not her own desk chair, with her legs crossed. Today she's wearing a paisley dress, so many colors swirling on her, it makes you dizzy. You wait with her for Ma to get there. Ma is late. You imagine her rushing to take off her apron, washing the flour off her hands, swiping on fresh lipstick, and hopping on the #7 bus.

"Do you think your parents forgot about the meeting?" Miss Field asks and gives you a gentle smile.

"My mother mentioned it this morning," you say. You don't want to be the one to tell her that Daddy isn't coming, not when there's bread to be baked and cakes to be decorated. Daddy has become one of the most popular cake decorators in the area. He started teaching you how to do a basket weave design with buttercream and make sugar roses because he needs the extra help. You can't do roses yet, but the basket weave is getting easier.

"Okay, we'll wait another five minutes," she says and crosses her legs the other way. "I liked your outline for your current events project. You had a lot of strong facts in there."

"Oh, um, thank you." You feel shy. Teachers don't usually say such nice things.

"Did you know about the *Loving* case before?" she asks.

"Yes," you say and nod. You know you're not supposed to tell her why. Ma told you never to tell anyone about Leah. Your parents have made up a story that she's gone away to school, and that's what everyone believes, their friends, relatives, even Jane.

"So what do you think?" she says.

"About what?" You squirm in your chair, hoping to hear the click of Ma's shoes in the hallway.

"About the case. I noticed you listed all the facts, but remember, for the assignment, you're also supposed to give your opinion. You said the ruling made laws preventing interracial marriage unconstitutional. You also noted that sixteen states still had these laws at the time of the ruling. What do you think about that?" she says and sits back a little in her chair.

"I . . ." you say and stop. Teachers usually have you memorize the answers they want you to know. You're not sure what the right answer is supposed to be.

"Really, I want to know," she says and leans forward, resting her chin on her hand. You look around and see a shaft of light coming through the classroom window. It shows all the bits of dust that you normally can't see. You turn to Miss Field again. Her eyes are lit up, waiting for you. She seems excited and calm at the same time. You wish you felt the same way.

"I think it's good," you finally say. She nods and stays quiet.

"Why?" she asks after a few seconds.

"I think it's good because any two people who are in love should be able to get married if they want to. Even if they're from different races, religions, or whatever. Even if their families don't agree. Even if it changes everything." Your heart is pounding so hard, you wonder if Miss Field can see it through your shirt. You hadn't even said to yourself what you thought, but then you think of Leah and Raj holding hands in the park, kissing behind the oak tree. It had looked so simple in the beginning of the summer.

"It seems that you believe in equal rights for everyone," Miss Field says, her eyes still lit up. "That's good. I do, too, but many people don't. Still, the more people think like we do, the more things will change."

It seems so simple the way Miss Field puts it, but it doesn't seem simple in your house. It doesn't seem simple in the news. You nod and wish you could tell Miss Field the truth.

You wish you could tell her that you don't understand why Daddy and Ma are treating Leah like she isn't part of your family anymore.

You wish you could tell her that you're not even sure which part Ma and Daddy are more upset about—the fact that Raj isn't Jewish or the fact that he's Indian.

Mostly, you wish you could tell her that you're afraid you might never see your sister again.

Before you can say anything, though, you hear Ma's shoes tapping down the hallway.

You and Miss Field turn and watch her walk in the door.

"I'm so sorry," Ma says, looking flushed. "The bus was slow." Even though you have a car, Ma never learned how to drive. That doesn't stop her from telling Daddy how to drive all the time.

"That's quite all right. I know all about the buses around here. You never know if they'll be on time."

Ma's shoulders drop, and she smiles. "Yes," she says and sits down in the empty desk chair next to you.

"I've been talking to Ariel about her wonderful current events project," Miss Field says.

"Oh," Ma says. "She hasn't mentioned it. What is it about?"

You hadn't thought this through. You should have begged Ma to let you go home after school so she would have come alone.

"Ariel, why don't you tell your mother?" Miss Field says as if this would be fun for you.

"It's about the *Loving* case," you mumble and scratch some hardened bit of food off your shirt.

"The what?" Ma says, looking at Miss Field and not you.

"The *Loving versus Virginia* case. Perhaps you've read about it in the papers, Mrs. Goldberg? Last June, the Supreme Court ruled that state bans on interracial marriage are unconstitutional."

Ma glances at you with a question on her face, then back at Miss Field.

"Oh, I'm quite familiar with it," she says, smoothing her skirt.

You squirm in your seat, losing yourself in the orange-and-brown plaid pattern on your pants. They are suddenly incredibly itchy. Ma picks up her purse, puts it square in her lap, and holds it tight.

"I believe you mentioned something about Ariel's handwriting?" Ma says a little louder now. She's starting to use the same voice she uses when the flour order is late. "Isn't that why you called me in?"

You sit forward in your chair and glance at the big clock on the wall. *Tick-tock, tick-tock* goes the second hand. It feels like you've been here for an hour, but only ten minutes have gone by.

"Yes, yes," says Miss Field. She smiles and blinks her

eyes nervously. She suddenly looks so young, no older than Leah. She gets up, goes to her desk, picks up a folder, and returns to her seat.

You never thought a teacher wanting to talk about your handwriting would make you feel so relieved. You take in a breath, let it out slowly, and watch the dust floating in the sun.

Then Miss Field shows Ma examples of your handwriting. She says she's concerned. She says that it's not only your handwriting she's concerned about, but the writing level. She says you're obviously highly intelligent and believes that this isn't your full potential and that she'd like to provide you with extra support.

This is the part you know. This is the part that happens every year, though usually teachers don't say "highly intelligent."

Ma is nodding. She knows this part, too. In some way, it feels comfortable, and you settle back into your chair. Miss Field will start suggesting more practice at home, writing on large, ruled paper. Ma will nod some more, clutch her purse, and say that she hopes you'll grow out of it, like she does every year. She'll tell the teacher how you can knead bread dough, make cookies, and decorate cakes as well as anyone, which isn't exactly true. She'll ask if maybe you're not trying hard enough. If you would just focus more.

It's as familiar as the patter of rain on a roof. But that's not what happens at all.

"So I have an idea. I'd like to bring in an electric type-writer so she can do much more of her work on that. Do you possibly have one at home, electric or not? I'd also like her to keep writing poetry. There have been some new studies that say that students with Ariel's type of learning disability could benefit from both. Have you ever heard of the term dysgraphia? It's not a common term. More people are familiar with dyslexia. It's focused on writing abilities rather than reading."

Dysgraphia. It sounds like a disease. You start to feel scared.

Ma blinks and sits up even straighter. "I don't mean to be rude, but how long have you been teaching?" she asks in her full flour-order voice.

"Three years," Miss Field says. "But I have a degree in special education as well as general education. I'm not a specialist, however. We should get her formally evaluated to be sure."

"Special education! With all due respect, my daughter doesn't belong in any special class," Ma says and stands up. You start to stand, too. "I need to be getting back home," she continues, putting on her coat.

"Oh, Mrs. Goldberg. I certainly didn't want to upset you," Miss Field says. Blotches start to bloom on her face. "But I do believe she has a learning disability that affects her writing. Please stay. Let's discuss it more."

You sit back down, but Ma doesn't. That invisible feeling creeps over you. You could start doing cartwheels, and they probably wouldn't notice.

"I'd rather not discuss it more until I talk to my husband," Ma says.

"I was hoping he'd be here," Miss Field says.

Oh no, that was the wrong thing to say. Poor Miss Field.

"My husband has a bakery to run, otherwise we don't eat," says Ma. "Ariel, let's go."

You get up again and look at Miss Field apologetically. She's standing now, and she's a lot taller than Ma, though you hadn't noticed before. You follow Ma out the door and take one last glance at Miss Field. She gives you a sad little wave.

Typewriters. *Poetry*. A strange word. No teacher has ever suggested things like this before. There's a classroom on the basement floor where some of the kids who can't be in regular classrooms go. Is that where you are supposed to be?

Still, it's good knowing that maybe your trouble with writing isn't because you don't try hard enough or because you're lazy—that there's a name for it. That night before bed, another poem bursts into your head and out your fingers before you can stop it. Each poem becomes its own thing after you write it, something separate, like a living creature. You don't care how messy it is; you just need to get it out.

The Dust

When people look at the air,
they think there's nothing to see.
But when the right angle of light
shines in just the right way,
they're always surprised
by how much dust
has been there
all along.

How to Keep Your Head Down

"I got my part," Jane says the next day on the bus without looking at you.

"Yeah?" you say, wanting to seem surprised.

"The mayor's wife. Not a chorus part, but only one line."

"Well, at least it's not a chorus part," you say, trying to sound hopeful, but you're not surprised. Life keeps disappointing you in the same boring ways.

"I wanted to be Kim or Rosie so much. Honestly, I'd rather be home listening to the Beatles. Did I tell you I finally got my own copy of *Sgt. Pepper's*? Now I don't have to borrow Leah's anymore."

At the mention of Leah and *Sgt. Pepper's*, a memory of Leah sitting in the living room doing her nails, flipping through the latest issue of *Time* magazine, pops into your head. It was after your parents met Raj.

Sgt. Pepper's Lonely Hearts Club Band had been playing faintly from your bedroom. You can even remember what song it was on: track 6, "She's Leaving Home." You had no idea then that you wouldn't be able to listen to that song after that. Sometimes you even wonder if Leah was inspired by it.

Ma was there, too, watching the five o'clock news. You remember the cover of *Time* that week. People with long hair and wearing sunglasses played guitars over a red, blue, and yellow swirly background. It was a story about the thousands who traveled to San Francisco over the summer, spreading the message of love and flower power. Hippies, they were called. On the television, on the radio, in the papers, it was all war, protests, anger, and riots. In San Francisco, though, it was about peace and love.

You read over Leah's shoulder. The pictures showed lots of people with long hair, in long skirts or bell-bottom jeans, playing music and speaking out against the war.

But the article mentioned drugs, too, that they did a lot of drugs. You weren't even sure what that meant—to do drugs—just that drugs were bad. The whole thing seemed strange and dangerous, but kind of exciting, though you knew you weren't supposed to think that. Ma always told you to stay away from the teenagers with long hair smoking in the park or hanging around Rocky's. They looked kind of like the people on the cover of *Time*. "This used to be a nice town, but all the kids are going crazy," she would say sometimes.

Leah had finished one hand, a frosty pink color, and she flipped the pages of the article with the other and blew on the wet polish.

"Maybe I should run off to San Francisco and become a hippie," she said after a few blows.

"That's not the way problems are solved, by taking all sorts of drugs and dancing naked in the streets," Ma said.

"But don't you believe in love? Aren't you against the war?" Leah asked.

"No one likes war," Ma said. "And just when I think President Johnson has things under control, he makes the war worse. I don't know about that man. These are troubled times, I tell you. The country is going to break in half." She got up and switched off the TV.

"Break in half?" you had asked. "How could that even be possible?"

"Don't worry about it. Just work hard and keep your head down. You'll be all right," Ma said as she headed into the kitchen.

"Leah," you said. "You wouldn't do that, would you? Go off and become a hippie?"

Leah straightened up. "Why not? I believe in love, equality, and civil rights, just like they do. I'm against the war."

"Nice girls don't run off and become hippies," Ma called from the kitchen.

"Who says I'm nice?" Leah said and continued blowing on her fingernails.

"Leah," Ma said in a lower tone.

"You're just kidding, right?" you asked.

She looked hard at you and studied your face. "I was, I guess. But hey, if I left, you'd get the whole room to yourself."

"Yeah, but—" you started to say. You wanted to tell her that you didn't want to be here all alone with Ma and Daddy. Who would help you with your homework, your hair, to deal with Ma? She needed to stay around and help you grow up a little more before she went anywhere.

"Do you like the color?" she had said, not letting you finish. She smiled and wiggled her fingers in your face. You looked at her nails, pink and shiny as candy.

"Sure," you had said.

"When they dry, I'll do yours." Something made you agree even though you didn't like polish on your nails. You remember how she painted them slowly, making sure they were perfect. A few weeks later, Leah was gone, but you still had the chipped polish on. You wish you could have kept it on forever.

The memory is interrupted by Jane, who pokes your shoulder. "Hey, Ari, are you even listening to me?"

"Yeah, sorry," you say as the bus goes over a big bump. Jane drops the magazine she was holding on her lap. You both lean over to pick it up. An actress you don't recognize is smiling on the cover. You look at her powdery skin. Her pink lips. Her blond hair. Did she ever ride on a hot bumpy bus smelling of baloney sandwiches?

"Maybe I shouldn't even do the play," Jane says and sighs.

"It's only your third play. Don't sweat it. You'll get better parts," you tell her. You think of what Ma said that day with Leah about keeping your head down. "Just keep your head up," you say to Jane but also to yourself. "And don't follow the rules. You'll be all right."

Jane looks at you and grins. "What do you mean?"

"Be the mayor's wife your way."

You can tell the wheels are turning in her head.

"I like that. Hmm, what would Elizabeth Taylor do?" she says and taps her finger on her lips. "I heard that she asked to be paid a million dollars for the movie *Cleopatra*, and that's what she got. The most any lady in Hollywood had ever gotten."

"So what would you ask for if you could ask for anything in the world?"

"I'd ask for money to write and star in my own play. And I'd want to do it in New York City. On Broadway."

"Sounds like a million-dollar idea to me."

Jane nods, turns toward the window, and loses herself in her own thoughts. You open your notebook and scratch out a short poem. You keep putting down a line and closing the notebook while you think so Jane won't notice. You write it faster than you've ever written anything before.

What Would Elizabeth Taylor Do?

A girl on the bus,
covered in freckles,
her hair frizzing in the heat,
asks this question,
"What would Elizabeth Taylor do?"
as she gazes down the street,
not minding the bumps
or the smell of baloney sandwiches,
and dreams of New York City.
How long will it take the girl
to raise her head up
and figure out her answer?

You walk into your classroom, and Miss Field is arranging papers on her desk. You and Ma haven't talked about what happened yesterday. Ma just took you home and made dinner. She said Daddy needed to stay late, restocking and doing inventory. Then he left this morning super early like he always did.

But restocking probably wasn't the only thing he was

doing. He was probably getting ready to sell the bakery. Were your parents going to tell you? There were suddenly so many secrets. Maybe they had always been there and you just hadn't noticed.

You study Miss Field, her long hair, her long skirt, concentrating and putting things in piles. Is she a hippie?

Someone pushes you, and you stumble forward a little.

"Hey," you say and see Chris Heaton slide into his desk chair. He doesn't look at you.

"Don't you say 'excuse me'?" you say.

"Why should I?" he says. "You were in my way."

Your face feels hot. Your lips are tingling. He starts unpacking his schoolbag.

"I want you to apologize," you say and put your hands on your hips.

He stops taking out his schoolbooks, leans back his head, and laughs a big belly laugh. If you were a cartoon character, you would have flames shooting out of your eyeballs.

"I would never apologize to someone like you," he says. Then he goes back to his stuff. You look at the stack of notebooks and textbooks on his desk. You see his name written in tiny letters on his black-and-white composition notebook. So small and neat and infuriating. A shaft of light comes through the window, showing all that dust.

"What do you mean, someone like me?" you ask. Other kids are starting to watch. He doesn't reply. "Come on, what do you mean?" you say, louder.

"Oh, you know what I mean, reject!" he yells.

Everyone stops talking. All you can hear is your own breathing, and your body starts to act. You couldn't even stop it if you wanted to, because Chris needs to be stopped before he says anything worse. You square your shoulders and sweep your hands over his desk, wiping the surface clean of stuff as it all tumbles to the floor. For a second, looking at the flat, empty surface of his desk, you are satisfied. It feels like you've squashed a big spider.

Chris's mouth drops open, and your eyes meet. You're as shocked as he is. The noises of the classroom come rushing back. Some boys near you are laughing. You hear Lisa Turner say, "Oh lordy!"

Then Chris yells out. "Miss Field! Miss Field! Ariel just pushed all my stuff onto the floor for no reason."

People start saying all kinds of stuff, and Miss Field hurries over.

"Girls and boys," Miss Field says. "Settle down. Please go over your spelling list. We're having a quiz today."

Voices still bounce off the walls.

"If I have to tell anyone again, you'll find yourself in Mr. Wilson's office and cleaning the blackboard after school for a month."

There are a few groans and then silence. Mr. Wilson is the principal, but he reminds you of a police officer. He's very tall, wears heavy black shoes, heavy black glasses, and walks around slowly, looking for trouble. He rarely smiles. His announcements usually include a threat: *Good morning, Eastbrook Middle School. If I see one more student with a water gun, they will receive a two-day suspension. Good morning, Eastbrook Middle School. If I hear a student cussing in the hallways, they will receive a week of detention.*

"First, I want both of you to put Chris's stuff back on his desk."

Chris points at you. You hate when people point at you.

You control the urge to bat his hand away. "She was the one who did this. Why should I clean up?"

"Now, please," Miss Field says in a deeper voice. You kneel down and start picking up Chris's stuff, but once you start, he also kneels down and gathers most of it up, faster than you, and even grabs a notebook out of your hand. Once everything is back on his desk, you both stand up.

"Now, let's step outside in the hallway and then both of you can explain."

You follow Miss Field out, but Chris hangs back for a second. You don't like him walking behind you, but you just keep following Miss Field. The other kids sneak glances at you as you walk past them. Your cheeks must look all blotchy.

Finally you're out, and Miss Field gently closes the door behind her.

She looks both of you over. "So, what happened?"

Chris starts talking immediately.

"Miss Field, I was just minding my own business, sitting at my desk when, when she came out of nowhere and pushed all my books to the floor. Girls shouldn't be bullies."

Miss Field nodded. "No one should be a bully, Chris."

"But especially not girls, and she's a bully," he said, pointing again.

"That's quite enough, Chris," Miss Field says and turns her face toward you. "Ariel, what's your side of the story?"

You feel like you should choose your words carefully, but usually you find it easier to simply say what you think or stay quiet. You take a deep breath. *Be careful.*

"He pushed me out of the way first—"

"I did not," Chris bellowed. "That's a lie. See, she's a bully."

"Let her talk. I need to hear both sides."

Chris crosses his arms and glares.

You stare at your feet. "He pushed me out of the way. I asked him to apologize, but he said that he would never apologize to someone like me, and it made me very angry. He called me a reject. So I shoved his books on the floor. I know I shouldn't have."

You look up now and see Billy Johnson through the glass window on the classroom door. He has a paper airplane raised above his shoulder and is about to throw it.

"Well, I agree with you, Ariel. You shouldn't have done that," says Miss Field.

"Yeah," Chris says.

"But, Chris, you shouldn't have shoved her or called her any names in the first place. That's not acceptable."

"I didn't shove her at all or call her any names. She's a liar. They all are."

"Who's they?" Miss Field asks.

"You know what I mean," Chris mumbles.

"No, I'm afraid I don't," Miss Field says.

But you know what he means. He means Jewish people are liars, but this isn't something you can say out loud, so you shove the feeling down into your body like you're being made to swallow dirt.

"Just forget it," Chris says. "So is she going to get detention?"

You look at your teacher and plead with your eyes: *Don't let him get away with it.*

"You both were a part of this," she says. "Ariel, can you apologize to Chris for pushing his books to the floor."

"I'm sorry," you say quickly. You just want to go back inside. Sometimes when you don't want to be where you are, you start thinking of the bakery. You picture sitting on your favorite wooden stool, a cola in one hand, a cookie in the other, watching Daddy braid a challah, twisting the fat yellow dough into a thing of golden beauty.

"Okay," Miss Field says. "Ariel, there are other ways to handle your feelings, even if someone provokes you first. Talking things out peacefully is best."

You nod slowly and again wonder if this is true. You think about what Leah said in the beginning of the summer, when she and Raj were talking about the protests and race riots. What if people don't change? What are you supposed to do if they keep putting you down, shoving you aside when you've done nothing to them? You look at the satisfied look on Chris's face, his greasy brown hair falling into his small blue eyes. This is all wrong. Chris was the one who was supposed to apologize to you. But maybe if you had stayed calm while you asked for an apology, he would have given it to you.

"And, Chris, I don't know if you shoved her or called her names, because I didn't see that part, but if you did, that's no way to treat your fellow student. Please apologize."

"Why should I apologize if I didn't do anything," he says, crossing his arms again.

"But that's a lie!" you say.

"See, now she's calling me a stinking liar," he says. "She's bullying me again."

"I'm waiting," Miss Field says.

You all stand there, staring at one another. Chris holds you both hostage for a minute.

"I'm not apologizing for nothing."

A spitball hits the window. More people are away from their desks, and the noise level is rising. Miss Field looks at the door and back at you. She turns to Chris.

"This isn't over," she says to him. "You still owe Ariel an apology." Then she opens the door, and you see several people jump back into their seats and pretend to be working hard. You wanted her to force him to apologize right then and there. Why didn't she just believe you? If she doesn't trust you, how can you trust her? It's like she's letting Chris bully her, too.

You sit down at your desk and take out your spelling

list, but you feel a dull pain in your chest again, like something is chipping away at pieces of your heart. You put a piece of notebook paper underneath the spelling list and start writing an answer to Miss Field's question. You keep adding to it all day, and when the dismissal bell rings, the poem is done.

This Is What Chris Meant

When he said
"She's a liar. They all are,"
he meant
that Jewish people are liars,
even though he lies all the time.
But are we?
Is my mother lying to me?
Is my father?
Is my sister?
I feel like
I'm the only one who tells the truth.
So what does that make me?

At the end of the day, as you leave the classroom and head for the bus, Miss Field is near the door, watching people leave and helping them gather their stuff. You take the poem out of your bag and stand there for a moment. Then you drop the paper folded in half right in the middle of her desk. You look back to see if she's watching you. Are you really just going to leave the poem there on her desk? You think about the way Chris accused you of lying, the way he didn't have to apologize. Miss Field told you she thought you had something to say. Well, you do.

How to Try Even Harder

You go to the bakery after school, almost wondering if this is the day you'll find it dark and closed, a red FOR SALE sign hanging on the door. But as you approach, there it is, lights on and bustling, as open and alive as any person.

As you walk inside, the smell of sugar, baking bread, and melting chocolate hits your nose. That's what bakeries do: give people this moment even when nothing's right at all. They should make a perfume out of that smell. That, you would wear.

People are walking around, choosing bread for their dinners and cakes and cookies for their desserts. Cake orders stand in white boxes waiting on the counter. Fresh challah loaves sit in a basket, waiting to be bought for Shabbat dinners, though most people who come into the bakery aren't Jewish and the challah doesn't always sell well. Daddy makes them every Friday anyway. It still makes you wonder why your parents didn't open the bakery in a place where there were more people who are Jewish and would want the challah.

You sort of know the answer, though maybe not the whole answer. Every year on the anniversary of the day your parents bought the bakery, your father tells you the story. He took Ma on a surprise trip to tour the old mansions in Newport, Rhode Island, for their first anniversary. On the way back, they stopped off the Eastport exit because Ma said she was starving and might faint.

They drove into town to get some lunch, and there, across the street from the luncheonette, was a FOR SALE sign. Above it on the awning was your father's name, Max, and that's when he knew his life was about to change.

It had been a butcher shop called Max's Meats. When he called the number on the sign, the real estate agent told him the shop had been taken by the bank and that he could get it "for peanuts." When you were little, you thought he really bought the bakery with a can of peanuts.

"When your dream knocks on the door, you have to answer," he says every time he tells the story.

Gabby calls to you across the counter. "Hi, Ari."

"Hi, is my mother here?" you ask.

"Where else would she be?" Gabby says, and her bright eyes question you. You wonder what Gabby knows. She's been with the bakery for years. Gabby used to babysit you; that's how Ma and Daddy found her. She would make you the most perfect chocolate-chip cookies as snacks. Ma tasted one and offered her a job on the spot. If the bakery was sold, what would happen to Gabby?

You go into the back, take off your jacket, put down your book bag, and get a cola out of the fridge. Ma is rolling out some pie dough. Daddy is way in the back, loading things into the freezer. As you watch your parents, you think of the poem you left Miss Field and wonder if she'll call your parents again. Your stomach turns. You put the cool soda against your forehead.

"How was school?" Ma asks.

"Okay," you say, opening the bottle and taking a long bubbly sip. You watch Ma bent over her work, her eyebrows knitted together. She has a brown-and-white dress on with her kitten heels. Her lipstick is bright, but her skin looks pale. There's no color in her cheeks.

"Ma, do you like baking?"

Ma stops rolling. She wipes her hands on her apron and pats at her hair.

"Why are you asking?" she says.

"I don't know." You take another sip of soda.

She looks at you and then goes back to rolling. You watch her quietly and sip the soda.

"Haven't I told you this?" she says after a minute.

You shrug. "What? Tell me again."

She sighs. She stops rolling and holds the rolling pin by her side. "When we began dating, Daddy started teaching me how to bake. He said he wanted his own bakery one day. I wasn't so sure if I liked that idea. My mother worked so hard in the kitchen for us. I didn't want to be like her, putting meat and fish through grinders, always smelling like garlic and onions. But your father taught me another way. Baking is precise. It's about lightness and beauty. And I fell in love with him and baking. But I still chop onions." She smiled and went back to her pie dough. "And I spend more time in kitchens than my mother did. Go figure."

You get up and butter a slice of sourdough. You think about Daddy teaching Ma how to bake. You think about them being young and in love, just like Leah and Raj. Did they ever share ice cream in a park? Then you shake your head. You don't really want to think of your parents this way.

To distract yourself, you watch Ma place a circle of dough over the pie pan, push it in, and gently pull off the extra dough around the rim. You've done the same thing and can feel the metal rim on your own fingers as you watch her. After, she fills the crust with lemon custard and starts whipping the meringue. The meringue grows bigger and fluffier. It's one of your favorite things to watch, how slimy-looking egg whites become a heavenly cloud before your very eyes. The meringue starts to form stiff peaks. Finally, she spoons it over the filling.

Could they really be selling the bakery? Wouldn't that be selling Daddy's dream? Maybe you didn't understand those legal papers. Perhaps it's not just your writing that's the problem. Other things are hard for you, too. Keeping things organized is hard. Following lots of steps is hard. Paying attention for a long time is hard.

"Ma, do you think something is really wrong with me?"

She turns off the mixer. She looks serious but not mad.

"Are you asking because of the meeting?" she says.

"Yes, Ma. Because of all the meetings. Every year."

"Listen," she says and points at you with the wooden spoon she's holding. A little meringue goes flying onto the floor. "Nothing is wrong with you. I've seen you work very hard, and you will overcome your writing problem. This trouble you have is not because of a disorder like your teacher says. Just don't give in to laziness. School wasn't easy for me, either, but maybe if I'd worked a little harder, I could have gone to college. Instead I'll probably work in a kitchen until the day I die."

You notice she doesn't say she'll work at Gertie's until the day she dies. "But I thought you fell in love with baking," you say. Had Ma wanted to go to college?

"Ari, the point is you're a smart girl even if Miss Field doesn't think so."

"But Miss Field didn't say I wasn't smart." She actually said the opposite.

Ma keeps pointing her spoon at you as she talks. "These young people like your teacher, thinking they can change the world. But it makes things more complicated. Sometimes it's not so complicated. Work hard, be honest, don't dwell. That's all we can do."

You open your mouth to say something more. Whenever you try to talk to Ma, the conversation starts to zigzag, and then it ends before you feel like you understand her or she understands you. You want to ask her what she means when she said she was lazy but never gave in to laziness. Ma doesn't have a lazy bone in her body. In fact, you wish she'd act a little lazier sometimes.

"Now off you go. Gabby needs help in the front."

You don't want to get in the way of that spoon she's waving around, so you hop off the stool and head to the front. You push through the swinging door separating the front from the back area, but you turn and take a last glance at Ma before the door swings closed.

You expect to see her hard at work again, spooning her meringue on the pie. But instead, she leans against the stool, a little hunched over, one hand on her hip, the other hand rubbing her forehead. She looks worried and sad. It scares you to see her suddenly so wilted.

You wonder if the reason they're selling the bakery is because Ma needs a break. The thought of Leah somewhere out there, married and pregnant, must be really tough on her. That's probably why she's getting more headaches. If you just listen to Ma and work harder, you'll get better at writing, at school. It's the least you can do for her.

The next morning, you get up extra early, wash carefully, clean your nails, and smooth a little Breck cream rinse through your dry hair, a trick Leah taught you to make your curls less frizzy. The school dress code changed last year, and girls can now wear pants just like the boys, though you're one of the only girls who does. But today you put on your blue plaid jumper, clean socks, and your Mary Janes. You even swipe on some of the frosty lip gloss Leah left behind: a new beginning.

You try to organize your schoolbag, which is stuffed with loose-leaf papers, folders, and textbooks. You dump everything out and then try to put it back neatly, piece by piece. Then you cram your lunch bag and thermos on top.

"Is it picture day?" Jane asks with a panicked look in her eye when you arrive at the bus stop.

"Can't I just look nice?" you say, annoyed.

The bus comes rolling down the street, and you hurry on, Jane trailing behind you.

"Sure," she says slowly as you both head to the back. "But you're up to something, aren't you? Trying to impress a fella?" A sparkle dances in her eyes.

"This has nothing to do with any silly boy," you say loudly. Some older girls in front of you turn around and giggle, and you shrink down in your seat. "I've got to finish my math homework."

Jane gives you a puzzled look in return. You're not sure why she's making you feel angry. Maybe it has something to do with the fact that she noticed how you looked, that trying to be better is actually different than what the world normally sees. You ignore her for the rest of the ride and do the last problems on your math homework, which you usually try to rush through during the morning announcements.

Carefully, you place your book bag and coat in your locker instead of tossing them in. Most people are in class already, standing in groups around desks. Chris isn't at his desk, but when you sit down, you feel his eyes on you. He must be somewhere watching you. *It doesn't matter,* you tell yourself and take out your books and papers and place them neatly in your desk. Then you clasp your hands in your lap and wait, ready for anything.

"Ariel." Miss Field calls you over to her desk. She's not smiling. *It's okay, it's okay, it's okay,* you tell yourself as you walk over. You will handle it like a very grown-up girl who has never known a lazy day in her life. You will handle it the way Leah would.

"Yes, Miss Field," you say, standing tall before her.

"I'd like to speak to you at the beginning of lunch today."

You nod. Your shoulders slump a bit. *It's okay,* you say again in your head, and you hope that whatever happens, Ma never knows about it.

"Yes, Miss Field," you say politely and return to your seat.

As you stand for the Pledge of Allegiance, your stomach isn't just turning, it's hurting. It starts to hurt more with each hour. As you work your way through several long division problems, your hand starts to hurt along with your stomach. You write slowly, pressing the pencil hard into the paper, and it goes right through. You pause to shake out your fingers. Suddenly a tiny ball of paper lands on your desk.

You look to your left, and Chris is busy with his workbook. You glance up at Miss Field, who has her head down, correcting papers. You open the note, and in tiny dark letters you find the words *you're going to get it* staring back at you.

Chris seems absorbed in his work, too absorbed. You take the ball of paper. You want to write *you don't scare me* in small, neat letters on the back and toss it on his desk. But you can't. You'd never be able to write that on a little piece of paper. You smooth out the paper, stick it in your notebook, and promise yourself not to look at him.

At lunch, you hang back, pretending to rummage in your desk until everyone leaves. Then you walk up to Miss Field. She gets up and pulls over a chair for you.

"Have a seat. I read your poem."

"I'm sorry. I shouldn't have left it for you like that," you say and keep your eyes on your shoes, which are killing your feet.

"Ariel," she says in a gentle tone. "I was alarmed by it. But it's a powerful poem."

You're so confused now. "Oh, so am I in trouble?"

"I'm sorry Chris treated you that way. Has he ever treated you like that before?"

You think of what Chris did to you last year, when he asked about the horns. "Yes," you say.

"I know there aren't many people in this school who practice Judaism."

"No," you say, and now your stomach growls. You put your hand over it.

"There must be some other kids in the grade," Miss Field says.

"I guess. A few," you say and can think of two people who go to your synagogue. Sarah Pearlman and Michael someone, but they aren't your friends. It sounds so formal, the way she puts it, and you think about what it means, to practice Judaism. Ma goes to synagogue more than Daddy. So is Daddy less Jewish than Ma? Where do you fit in? You don't go to Hebrew school. You don't see your cousins very often. You only have one friend, and she's not Jewish. What would it be like if lots of kids were Jew-

144

ish at school and you didn't have to explain that part to anyone? A feeling starts to float up your body, a lightness. Is that what other people feel like every day?

Miss Field sits back and clears her throat. "Chris should not have said what he said. I know he was lying to me."

"So you're glad I wrote the poem?"

She thinks for a second. "I'm glad you're writing poetry about your real feelings, but please come to me if something happens with Chris again. Pushing people's stuff off desks won't solve anything."

"I understand." You still want her to make Chris apologize to you. Was she really on your side? You think of the little ball of paper you got this morning, most certainly from Chris. Something tells you not to show her. You start to get up.

"One more thing before you leave. Have you and your parents discussed what I said at our meeting?"

"A little," you say and smooth your dress over your legs. You're not even sure Ma told Daddy. "I think if I just try harder . . ."

"Ariel, you try very hard. If you have a learning disability, there's more we can do to help you reach your full potential. The goal would be to make things easier for you, not harder."

It doesn't sound easier. "Ma says nothing is wrong with me."

Miss Field opens her mouth to say something else, but then she closes it. Her lips become straight and serious.

"I don't think something's wrong with you. I'm just trying to help."

"Thank you." You both look at each other for a second. "I don't want to miss all of lunch."

"No, you shouldn't. I'm looking forward to hearing your report next week. And keep writing poems. Show me anything you'd like, but just in a different way."

You get up, give Miss Field a weak smile, tug your dress down, and head to your locker. You grab your lunch bag and walk down the hallway, slipping into the bathroom before a teacher asks you for a hall pass. You go inside a stall, but you forgot the toilets at school don't have lids, and you don't want to sit on the open seat, so you come back out and sit on the ledge of the heater near the window.

Ma packed you a tuna sandwich and an apple. You sniff

it, but it just makes you feel nauseous. After a minute, you take a bite and force yourself to swallow. It goes down like a piece of wet wool. You throw the rest of the sandwich out, take a few bites of your apple, and toss that.

There's nothing left to do but wait for the bell to ring. You spend the rest of the day just trying to concentrate on your work, and now you have a dull throb in the middle of your head. Maybe you also have a headache problem like Ma.

You really want to be good and not cause any more trouble for Ma. You want to try hard and do better at school. You don't want to push things off anyone's desk. But you wonder, if you were who everyone wants you to be, would it even make a difference?

How to Miss Her

Dinner is so quiet you can hear your parents chewing the turkey and gravy, and it's disgusting. You press your fork on some peas and mash them down. Daddy raises an eyebrow, and you stop. You taste the mashed potatoes. They're creamy and salty, just the way you like them.

"How was school?" Ma asks, breaking the silence.

"Fine," you say and take another heaping forkful of mashed potatoes.

"Did Miss Field talk to you more about her disability ideas? Tell me if she doesn't leave you alone about it."

"No, she hasn't," you say to keep things simple, and you think of Miss Field today, her bright smile, the extra-calm way she speaks. She seems like she wants to help you. Maybe she's right about some things and wrong about others. Can teachers be that way?

Daddy perks up. "Disability ideas?"

Ma stiffens. "Ariel's teacher called me in for an appointment. She wanted to discuss her writing. She has an idea that Ariel is learning disabled. But I said that Ari doesn't need a special class or evaluations like she's not as smart as the other kids."

Ma gets up and starts cleaning some of the things off the table. You're not completely done. Daddy isn't, either.

"Sylvia, please sit down," Daddy says. Ma puts her dish in the sink and starts wiping the counter with quick motions. You take an even bigger forkful of mashed potatoes.

"Sit down so we can talk? This sounds important," Daddy says.

Ma has an exasperated expression on her face that reminds you so much of Leah it hurts. She sits down slowly on the edge of her seat, still holding a dish towel. Ma doesn't like to sit still for very long.

"I want to know what's going on with Ari's teacher."

Ma sighs. "She wanted to talk about Ari's handwriting. You know these young hippie types, thinking they know everything now."

"But what exactly did your teacher say?" Daddy asks slowly, turning to you.

You think of what Miss Field said about poetry and typewriters. That's not the part that Ma seemed to hear.

Ma takes a deep breath. "It's mind over matter. I never liked school much, either. Ari's just a late bloomer like me." She smiles.

"Ma," you say and roll your eyes. You don't want to think about blooming. It's too embarrassing. "It's not because I don't like school. I mean, I don't like school, but . . ."

"But what?" Daddy asks.

Suddenly you feel so tired from the day, the week, the months, these hard and strange months. You could just put your head down on the table and go to sleep. "Nothing. Really. Can I be excused?"

Daddy looks disappointed.

"*May* you be excused," Ma says.

"Fine. So *may* I?"

"I suppose so. Maybe we should talk alone," Daddy says, looking at Ma. You're out of your seat before he finishes his last word. They switch to mostly Yiddish, so you can't really understand them anymore.

In your room, you put on your Elvis record and open

your notebook to a fresh page. You want to tell Leah everything: how things are so hard at school and that you're not sure if Miss Field is trying to help you or if Ma is right and what's happening to the bakery and why it seems like everywhere you turn is filled with lies. You want to ask her how she feels, if Raj is a good husband, if she's excited about having a baby. You want to ask her if she's thinking about you.

But it would be so hard to write all this. Once your mind comes up with a sentence and you start working on each letter, the idea starts overlapping with another idea, or you forget what you wanted to say in the first place, and you have to start all over.

If only Leah were here so you could say your thoughts out loud, and she would write them down for you, but then you wouldn't need to write her a letter. Writing poems feels different. The lines are short. The idea stays clear. You don't have to think of the introduction, the supporting paragraphs, the conclusion. You just have to think of a few words, write them down, and then you're ready to think of the next few.

As Elvis tells people to step off of his blue suede shoes,

you lie down on your bed, head on the pillow, legs raised, and feet resting on the wall. You look at Leah's empty bed. You hate looking at it. You'd rather look at your own empty bed, so you switch and lie on her bed. It's starting to lose her smell.

Your parents' voices drift out from the kitchen, getting louder and softer and then louder again, but you're too tired to spy on them. You and Leah used to spy on them all the time together, especially when they had company. After a little while you get an idea for a poem. You get your notebook and sit down on Leah's bed to write. Each word appears in your mind one at a time, like it's on a billboard, bright and clear.

Leah, Do You Remember?

Do you remember
when Ma and Daddy
had friends over
to play cards
on Saturday nights?
Do you remember

how we would

spy on them

from the hall bathroom,

trying not to make a sound?

I didn't know

the last time we did that

would be the last time

we ever did that.

You write the poem in your notebook as small as you can with a black ballpoint pen. You don't want to mess up, so you go really slow and bite your lip until it hurts. You do each letter, hoping you don't forget the next word you're thinking of by the time you finish the last. Then, after a long time, you're done.

You hold the notebook up and look at it. It's the neatest thing you've ever written. You almost want to frame it. Ma was right. Look what you can do when you try.

Your hand feels stiff, and the headache you had before returns, but you don't care, because now at least you have something to send Leah even if you can't find her address. If you can't figure out how to find her address, you'll try sending it to her without one. If she gets it, she'll have to write you back. She'll have to remember how much she misses you. Then you'll ask her to help you find out what's going on with the bakery, because you don't want to ask Ma and Daddy yet. You don't want to deal with the answer all by yourself.

In a way it feels like she's dead. You know she's not, but she's so not here. You look at the closet with most of her clothes still hanging in it. You want to wear something of hers. You start rummaging through it all, the closet stuff and then the clothes in the dresser. She's taller and skinnier than you, so you can't wear a lot of her clothes.

Ma always says Leah has a dancer's body. You wonder what kind of body Ma thinks you have. You pull out a pair of white flannel pajamas with little roses on them. The sleeves and bottoms are too long, but you put them on anyway and detect a faint smell of Breck shampoo around the collar. You get back into her bed and let Elvis's velvety voice sing you to sleep.

How to Mail a Letter

That morning you wake up early, but not too early. Daddy leaves a little before 4:00 a.m. and Ma doesn't get up until 6:30. So you pad into the kitchen at 6:00, find an envelope and a stamp in the drawer by the refrigerator, and hurry back to your room like a squirrel with a nut.

Writing Leah's name in the center of an envelope isn't easy, but you do it as neatly as you can and wonder if you should put a return address on it. You hesitate and then write it anyway, even though it's hard to keep your writing in the top left corner. After you put the stamp on, you look at the envelope and remember: Leah's last name is different now. What is Raj's last name? You think and think and think. It starts with a *J*. That you know.

An image comes to you of Leah lying on her bed, sitting up against the pillows, green curlers in her hair, doodling on the back of that *Time* magazine. She left it lying on her bed, and you saw the doodle after, her name and Raj's together like they were married, with a heart around them.

There's no *Time* magazine in the desk drawer. It's not in the night table, either. You stuff the envelope in your schoolbag and go into the living room. Ma seems busy in the kitchen, so you flip through the magazine rack. Ma and Daddy keep old magazines around for years. You find it, and when you turn it over, you see what she wrote— *Leah and Raj Jagwani*—inside the blue inked heart. You memorize Raj's last name, Jagwani, as you stare at the heart. Jane makes the same kind of hearts with Paul McCartney's name. Raj suddenly seems like just any crush doodled in a heart on the edge of a magazine. Was he worth losing you, Ma, and Daddy for?

"Come have your breakfast, Ari," Ma calls.

You stick the magazine in your bag and hurry to the table. Breakfast is a piece of toast and butter. Normally Ma makes scrambled eggs, mamaliga, or at least pours you a bowl of corn flakes and slices a banana in it.

"I'll take my toast with me. I'm meeting Jane early today," you say.

"How come?" says Ma. She peers at you with her lie-detector eyes.

"To practice my presentation. Jane said she'd help me." Ma studies you but doesn't say anything. "I'm giving mine tomorrow."

"I remember. *Loving versus Virginia*," she says and takes a deep breath. Before she can ask you anything else, because you don't want to talk about *Loving v. Virginia* with Ma right now, you grab your toast and head toward the door. "Don't want to be late," you call.

You really do have your presentation tomorrow; at least that part you didn't lie about. You've done a lot of research but still only have a few of the main facts down on the poster board. You learned that five weeks after Richard Loving, a white man, married Mildred Jeter, a Black woman, they were woken up at their home in Virginia in the middle of the night and arrested by policemen. But when you read further, it said Mildred was not only Black but also Indian.

Somehow it felt like you were connected to her, because Leah is married to Raj and Raj is Indian, and Richard and Mildred ultimately won their case. Then you kept reading and found out that Mildred was part Native American, not Indian from India. But still, maybe it could be the same for Leah and Raj. Except what exactly would they win? It wasn't illegal for them to be together. They weren't going to be woken up and arrested in the middle of the night like Richard and Mildred were. Would they win over your parents? Did Raj's parents feel the same as yours? Then you had to stop because your thoughts started to pile on top of one another and became a big alphabet soup.

That was why it was so hard to write and think at the same time. You want to understand your problem more. You want to know if there's a name for what makes writing difficult. Is that what Miss Field is trying to do?

You walk toward the bus stop in case your mother is watching you, then pass it. You decide to write Leah Goldberg Jagwani, New York, NY, on the envelope and walk another block to the mailbox. All the writing is big and messy but still readable. You slide the envelope in the slot and stand there, looking at the dark insides of the mailbox as it falls in.

At once, you wish you could grab it back.

How could your own sister not have written you by

now? She must really not miss you at all. Is this the terrible truth you've never known before? Suddenly, sobs shake your body, and you let it happen, like a wave crashing over you. After a minute, they stop.

"Ariel," you hear someone call. You quickly wipe your tears and straighten up. When you turn toward the voice, you see Jane hurrying down the sidewalk.

"Oh no, what's wrong? Have you been crying?" Jane asks in her usual direct way, her big brown eyes searching for the answer.

"I had to mail something," you say and start walking toward the bus stop.

Jane puts her hands on her hips and shakes her bob back and forth. "But why would that make you cry?"

"I wasn't crying," you say in a small voice. Your throat feels thick. Your face burns with embarrassment.

"Yes, you were."

"I wasn't. We have to get to the bus," you say and start walking faster. She moves in front of you. You try to go around her, but she blocks you. Imagine if you told her what was really happening—that your sister wasn't in college, but had run off and married an Indian man and now they were going to have a baby. Also, your parents have disowned her, she hasn't even bothered to write you a letter, and your parents are selling the bakery for some mysterious reason. Oh, and your teacher thinks you have a learning disability. That's all.

"You're lying to me," Jane says, pointing at you. "And that's not what friends do."

You both face each other like cowboys in a Western movie. Is she going to let it go, or are you going to tell her something? You both stay still until you hear the gears of the bus already leaving your stop two blocks ahead.

"Uh-oh," she says, and now you're both running. Jane yells and you wave your hand, but the bus driver doesn't see either of you or doesn't care and makes a left on the street ahead. You both stop, breathing hard.

"Great," you say. "That's perfect."

"It's not my fault," Jane responds.

"If you'd just ignored me, at least you wouldn't have missed the bus."

"Oh, so you're mad at me because I actually wanted to see what was wrong?"

She stands in front of you, but you walk around her

and keep your head down. Out of the corner of your eye when you pass her, you notice her face crumpling. Maybe she cares about you more than you thought?

"We have to hurry," you say, your loafers slapping the ground hard as you pick up your pace. You wish you had your bike, but if you went home and got it, Ma would get too suspicious.

The walk to school is long and silent. The wind swirls around you, and you wonder when it got so chilly. You and Jane finally get to school and go to the office for a late pass. It's the first time you're late this year. Two more times will land you in detention. When you each receive your pass, Jane heads to her class and you go to yours without a word.

All the kids look at you as you walk into your class. Miss Field is at the blackboard, working out more long division, so you put the pass on her desk, and to your great relief, she just nods and continues with her lesson.

You sit down and start copying what's on the board. You hear Chris whisper "loser" under his breath. You let the word hit you, but instead of looking at him or whispering something back, you grip your pen tighter. It's still so new, writing poetry, but it's become a way to feel better, a way to feel free. It's like finding something buried in the ground, thinking it's a rock, then realizing it's gold. You flip your notebook page over to a blank one.

Loser

Call me a loser
if that's what
you need to call me,
but I'd like
to be the one
who gets to choose
what exactly it is
I'm losing.

Once it's out, you can breathe again. You turn back the page and get to work, pretending your hands aren't shaky and your heart isn't broken.

How to Tell a Story

The next day, you and Jane don't speak on the bus, so you hold the small white poster board that you brought for your presentation on your lap and stare at it. It's not very good. You knew filling it up with your handwriting would only make the other kids laugh at you, so you tried to put the least amount of writing possible on it. But deciding what to write took so long, you didn't have time to decorate it. This is not what Miss Field wants. You think of how the other boards have been: brightly colored, filled with big block letter outlines, drawings, and magazine collages.

When you get to class, Miss Field has your name and Lisa's on the board. Lisa is going first. This makes you both nervous and relieved. After the bell rings, you say the Pledge and Miss Field takes attendance and makes the morning announcements. Then Lisa gets up from her desk, wearing a crisp blue skirt and a yellow sweater, her blond hair perfectly curled around her face. She props up her huge poster and stands in front of the class, holding some note cards.

It's beautiful. She traced and colored in the *Sgt. Pepper's Lonely Hearts Club Band* album cover. There are lots of facts about it listed all over in thick black bubble letters and magazine cutouts of all the Beatles. Flowers and swirly designs in pink, orange, and green decorate the edges.

You gaze at Lisa in her bright sweater and at her perfect lettering on her poster board and start to feel heat rising in your body because after she's finished, you're going to have to get up there with your boring board with its terrible lettering and a lump in your throat.

Lisa keeps standing there, looking out at everyone. Seconds go by, and you see her hands shaking. You can hear people shift in their seats. Lisa is completely frozen. Normally nothing stops Lisa from raising her hand and asking tons of questions. But you haven't ever seen her give a report in front of the class. A few more seconds go by, but Lisa isn't making a peep.

"Why don't you start with the title of your report, Lisa," Miss Field says in her smoothest, kindest tone. She sits in the back of the class. A few snickers leak out. Then Lisa starts.

"Um. This is my current events presentation," she says and clears her throat. Miss Field nods and smiles.

"Um, it's about the release of the Beatles' album *Sgt. Pepper's Lonely Hearts Club Band*."

More snickers. More of Lisa's hands trembling as she grips her notecards. You sit up taller and face her with your full attention.

So far, nobody has done a report on anything really serious, like the Vietnam War or Dr. Martin Luther King Jr.'s speeches. There's been nothing about the protests and riots, nothing about San Francisco and the hippies, or about Thurgood Marshall's Supreme Court confirmation or the Six-Day War, and nothing about *Loving v. Virginia*, but that's a good thing because Miss Field said you couldn't choose the same topics.

But why did you have to go and pick something that makes people think about difficult things like being part of a country that made it illegal for people of different races to get married and even put them in jail for it? Why did you pick a topic that only reminds you of why Leah left? It feels like there are a thousand butterflies in your stomach.

"The album was released in May in the United Kingdom, but here in the United States of America in June," Lisa says.

Then she pauses. You hear Chris laugh a little on your left. You promise yourself you will snicker at him when he does his presentation.

"You can keep going, Lisa. You're doing great," Miss Field says.

"It has many musical influences," Lisa says. "Rock, jazz, blues, big band, circus, and even Indian classical music. The songs on it are 'Sgt. Pepper's Lonely Hearts Club Band,' 'With a Little Help from My Friends,' 'Lucy in the Sky with Diamonds' . . . " Lisa reads and lists all the songs in a flat voice, but it makes you want to listen to the album again, as if it can bring you closer to Leah, as if it could hold a clue. After the last title, more empty seconds pass. Then Lisa says, "That's it."

"Oh, okay, thank you, Lisa," Miss Field says. "And what do you think of the album?"

Lisa shrugs. Her face is bright red. Seeing her uncomfortable calms you a bit. You wonder if that makes you a bad person.

"Do you like it?" Miss Field presses on.

"It's pretty neat, I guess. I haven't listened to it much."

"Then why did you choose it for your presentation?"

"Well, the Beatles are really famous."

"Yes," Miss Field says, giving her a small smile. "Thank you again, Lisa. Very nice poster board. And remember, everyone, I'm inviting you not only to present the facts but also to discuss your opinions."

Lisa quickly sits down and stares straight ahead. You realize how hard it is to know anyone. You would have thought that Lisa's presentation would have been big and loud, mostly filled with her opinion.

You steal a glance at Chris. He plays with a little hole in the leg of his pants, squinting at it, his face curious. If he noticed you looking at him, he would suddenly change into Chris the bully. Is he only that way with you? You see him with his friends on the playground, laughing and joking around. He doesn't seem as if he's mean to them. You wonder what he's like at home. Do his parents know he's a bully, or is he another Chris entirely?

Miss Field suddenly calls your name, making you jump.

You stand up and walk to the front, prop up your poster board on the easel, and stare out at all the faces. There are only four points on your poster—the date the Lovings got married, the date they got arrested, the date they sued the state of Virginia, and the date the Supreme Court announced its ruling.

You wrote it all in capital letters in pencil and then traced it in marker. There are smudge marks all around your words because you had to erase many times and start over until you finally had four clear lines. When you practiced last night in front of your mirror, just looking at the lines made you remember everything you read about the case. It was easy to talk about it by yourself in your room. But here in front of the class, you suddenly can't remember a thing.

It takes you half a minute to state your topic and read the lines on your board. The kids stare blankly at you, and your heart is about to explode through your chest. No wonder Lisa was so nervous. Not knowing what else to do, you go back to the top of the list and read the first line again, slowly.

You see Chris out of the corner of your eye. He's leaning back in his chair, arms crossed over his chest. He looks like bully Chris now. Your eyes meet, and he sticks out his tongue. You're tempted to return it, but not with Miss Field watching you. You look back at your four lines. Chris might think you're a loser, but if that's true, then you have nothing left to lose.

You look at your board again and take a breath. The fact that the points are so simple reminds you of what you know about the case, and your mind lights up. You'll show Chris. You'll show all of them. Ma and Daddy. Even Leah.

"Okay, so I'm going to tell you what these dates mean like it's a story," you say and wonder where your words are coming from. Your heart is still beating fast, but not in a bad way, in a way that makes you feel stronger.

"Because it is. It's a love story," you continue. "But that's not why this case is called *Loving versus Virginia*."

People start to sit up straighter and pay attention.

You point to the first fact, which says *1958: Richard Loving and Mildred Jeter get married in Washington, DC.*

You explain that they couldn't get married near their home in Virginia.

"The main reason was because Richard was white and Mildred wasn't. She was Black and Indian, but Native American Indian, not India Indian," you say.

You start getting distracted by the questions that won't leave you alone. What if Raj and Leah had fallen in love last year in a state where it was illegal? Were the laws only for Black people and white people or all marriages between people with dark skin and light skin? You shake off your thoughts and keep going.

"But five weeks after their wedding, they were arrested in their home at two in the morning. To stay out of prison, the judge said they would have to leave Virginia for twenty-five years," you say. "Imagine if you fell in love, got married, and were told that your love was illegal just because of the color of your skin. Imagine if you were arrested in your own home, in your own bed, because you married the person you loved."

You gaze out and see all these white faces looking back at you. You see the backs of your own pale white hands. There was only one Black student in your grade, Danielle Walker. What was it like to be Danielle in this school? As hard as it is to be you sometimes, what makes you different from most of the students at your school—your religion, your handwriting—can't be seen on your skin.

You take another breath and continue. "After that, they couldn't even travel to Virginia together to visit their families, so in 1964 the American Civil Liberties Union helped them sue Virginia. The case went all the way to the Supreme Court.

"And after three years, they won," you say. "The Supreme Court announced its ruling this year on June 12, stating that it was unconstitutional to make laws against interracial marriage. At the time of the ruling, sixteen states still had laws against it."

Miss Field looks at you and nods. "And what's your opinion about the Supreme Court ruling?"

"My opinion is that I'm happy about this ruling, and

I think it's wrong to stop people of different races from marrying each other."

Everyone is silent, so you keep going. The words are flowing from some part of you that you didn't know you had. "Because laws like this will never stop people from falling in love. People who are in love will still want to be together even if it means their families or other people don't want them to. Isn't love between people a good thing? Isn't it supposed to make things better for everyone?"

After you finish, the class sits under a deep blanket of quiet. You've never talked this way in front of anyone. You wonder if you've said too much.

Miss Field stands up from her chair and starts clapping. She is beaming. "Wonderful, Ariel. Just wonderful." You've never seen her smile so big. Then suddenly the class joins in and claps. To your complete shock, even Chris is clapping. A wide grin spreads over your face, and for the first time, you feel the opposite of invisible. You feel seen.

How to Burn a Loaf of Bread

After school, you decide to walk to the bakery instead of taking the bus. You avoid Jane because you aren't ready for hard stuff yet. You want to coast a bit longer on this feeling. Talking to your class was so different than writing things down. You've never spoken about a topic you actually cared about. It's filled you with something new and powerful.

Halfway through the walk, your body wants to run, so you do—all the way to Gertie's. The breeze blows through your curls, and your schoolbag seems as light as a cream puff. You burst in through the bakery door.

You've decided that you're going to tell your parents about your presentation. You're also going to ask them about the bakery and why they're selling it. You don't have to be so afraid. Maybe you'll even give them the same presentation at home and change their minds. You've never been so ready for anything.

Gabby, who is working at the counter, calls out your name, but you just smile, wave, and keep on going. You give the swinging door a big push with both hands and swish into the back.

"Ma, Daddy," you say, dumping your bag on the ground. "I have something important to tell you!"

But what you see doesn't add up, and it flattens out your smile. Ma is sitting on a stool, slouched and small. She looks at you, startled. Her eyes are red. Has she been crying? Ma never cries about anything.

The first thing you think about is Leah. Is she all right? Did something happen to her baby, to Raj?

"Ari!" Daddy says. "You're back early."

"I am?" Because you're not. Normally you take the bus.

"Have a seat. We need to tell you something."

But, wait, you want to say, *me first.* The expressions on Ma and Daddy's faces, though, tell you not to move. Daddy points to another stool. Ma isn't wearing her apron, which means she hasn't been baking.

"What?" you say, all that good energy turning into bad

energy, into panic. "Tell me. Is it Leah? Is she okay?"

Daddy and Ma blink for a minute, and you do the same, as if adjusting to new light.

"Oh, yes. I mean, I think so," Daddy says. He seems surprised that you're even bringing her up. Ma takes a tissue out of her pocket and blows her nose.

"We have some difficult news," she says. Daddy puts his hand on her shoulder. She looks up at him and stops talking. You search her face for that part of her that keeps on rolling out the dough no matter what. It's something in her face, a crease in her brow. You don't even know exactly what it looks like, but it's not there.

"We hoped that it wouldn't come to this, but we have to sell the bakery," Daddy says.

At first you're relieved. At least *you* don't have to bring it up.

"I know," you say before thinking about it.

Ma straightens up a bit.

"You know? How?" Daddy asks.

You wish you could take your words back. Now you have to explain that you were snooping in Ma's purse, looking for a letter from Leah, and they'll think that you're just a bad girl sneaking around, not someone grown-up enough to hear the whole truth. But then Miss Field pops into your head again, beaming and clapping. The fearless energy from the day finds you again.

"I saw papers in your purse," you say to Ma, squaring your shoulders. "The contract, about selling the bakery. I was looking for a letter from Leah."

Daddy opens his mouth to say something.

"You little mazik," Ma says.

"I'm sorry," you say. "I should have told you."

"Yes," Ma says. "But it's okay. It's better that you know."

"Why, though? Why do we have to sell it?" The sweet-and-sour scent of yeast from bread baking fills the air. Your stomach grumbles. You barely ate lunch. But the smell becomes too powerful, a burning smell.

"Oh no," Daddy says, and he runs over, pulling open the oven door. They do most of the baking in the morning, but sometimes Daddy does special orders in the afternoon. You and Ma spin around and watch him pull out a tray of eight loaves, dark brown to black, with his bare hands. "They're all burnt. Ow!" he yells as the tray slams on the counter. You jump. A few loaves fall off the tray and break apart on the linoleum floor, leaving a scattering of burnt chunks of bread. He holds his fingers. "Damn it all to hell," he yells and walks out the back door.

"Max," calls Ma.

You start to follow Daddy. Ma sighs. "Leave him for a moment. Come here," she says, motioning to you. You walk over to her slowly and stand before her. She puts a hand on your shoulder and then lets it go.

"We've been trying too long to stay afloat with the bakery, and now we have a lot of debt. If it were just up to me, we would have made this decision a year ago," Ma says, the edge returning to her voice. "But why should anyone in this family listen to me?"

Daddy comes back in, and Ma stops talking. He looks calmer. He runs his fingers under cool water to soothe the burn. You and Ma watch him.

"But, Daddy, I thought the bakery was your dream. I thought—" Your throat catches, and you stop. Daddy looks at you, but his eyes are empty. He clears his throat and manages a small smile.

"Dreams are for the young," he says. "They're fairy

tales. The sooner you learn that, the less of a shock it will be."

"So grown-ups can't have any dreams?" you ask.

"Sure they can." Ma suddenly perks up. "It just depends on if you want to deal with reality or live in a fantasyland."

Daddy continues without looking at Ma, just at you. "I went to Caruso's. They need a bread baker. When we close, I might work there for a while until we figure out the next step."

"Oh, Daddy," you cry. "You can't work at Caruso's!" Caruso's is an Italian bakery in the next town that sells ten different kinds of cannoli—the most delicious cannoli, and rainbow cookies almost as good as Gertie's . . . almost. Caruso's was Gertie's main competition.

"Well, tell Caruso's that. They seem happy for me to work there. And there's one more thing," he says, running his hand through his hair. He looks at Ma. There are a few seconds of silence.

Ma takes a deep breath. "We're going to have to move," she says. "But we'll find a nice place, don't worry."

"Move?" you ask. More secrets.

"They raised the rent again," Daddy says. "I'm so sorry, Muffin. We'll start looking at places soon. It still won't be the house we thought we'd get when we moved to the suburbs, but we'll find something nice. Maybe with a patio."

But if money is the problem, how would your parents find a nicer apartment? The ground starts feeling unsteady, like you're on a ship. You become light-headed. It seems like all of this has to do with Leah leaving, like she was the thing holding your life together.

"Does Leah know?" you ask.

Your parents are silent again. They glance at each other and back at you.

"So she doesn't," you say, your voice getting angrier. "Are you going to tell her?"

"That's between us and Leah," Ma says, hard and serious again.

"But you'll tell her?" you ask, biting the inside of your cheek. "You wouldn't just move and sell the bakery and *not* tell her."

"It'll be okay," Daddy says in a stern voice.

"It doesn't sound okay," you say, shaking your head. "I don't feel good. I want to go home."

"Wait for Ma. She'll walk with you."

"No. I don't want to wait. We can't just move and not tell Leah. What if she comes home and finds us gone?" You imagine Leah coming back to surprise you, maybe with her baby. She goes to the bakery and finds it dark and closed. She goes to the apartment and knocks on the door. A stranger answers. You, Ma, and Daddy are in some other apartment without a clue. You back away from your parents, who are starting to feel like strangers. The smell of burnt bread still hangs in the air. You need to get out of the bakery.

"That's not going to happen," Ma says.

"How do you know?"

Ma and Daddy just stand there, silent.

"How do you know?" you say again, louder, the anger filling your body. How could they take this much away? First your sister, then the bakery, and now the apartment. They've even taken what happened today away, the first good thing that has ever happened in school. But there's no point in telling them now.

"These are adult decisions, and you don't need to worry about them," Ma says through a stiff smile.

"What kind of parents are you?" you yell and go right through the back door. It slams, and you run all the way home. After school you were running toward something, but now you want to run far away.

How to Be Alone

You aren't hungry for dinner, so you lock yourself in your room, something you're not allowed to do. You lie on Leah's bed, which has become your bed, and hope that Ma or Daddy will come knocking. You wish they would come and pull you out of your swirling mess of thoughts. If they don't, it will mean that you're right, that they don't love you as much as you thought, either.

They probably think you're just a silly kid with no real problems, that you're just feeling sorry for yourself. Maybe it's true. They've had harder things happen to them. Did they ever lie on their beds like this, feeling sad and alone?

You think about how Daddy's family left Poland years before the Holocaust; they were lucky. But then your grandparents died within a year of each other when Daddy was only seventeen. Daddy once said something about your grandfather having heart problems, and you're not even sure why your grandmother died. Your grandmother on Ma's side died of cancer when you were only a baby. Her name was Gertrude. They named the bakery after her.

You only have one grandparent left, Grandpa Myron, but he lives in Miami now, and you don't see him very much. He's the one who didn't like Daddy because he wasn't Jewish enough for Ma. But these stories feel more like sad legends from broken and faraway places rather than a part of your life. Now it is only going to get worse. More broken things.

You pick up your notebook and chew on the eraser end a little bit, thinking. Then you write.

Broken

My parents
have handed me
something broken,
with so many pieces
I can't tell anymore
what goes where.
Am I even the one
who's supposed
to put it back
together?

You look at your poem, and the lines are slanting down the page, the letters big and wavy. You stand and tear up the poem into little pieces. Then you sit back down. Before the summer, you thought there was the truth and there were lies—nothing in between. Now the truth seems like something your parents pick and choose, like fruit in a grocery store. What they decide on seems to change all the time.

There is a knock. You freeze.

"Can I come in?" Ma's voice trickles in under the door. She tries the doorknob.

You get up and throw the pieces of the poem in the garbage.

"Ari? Please open the door," she calls.

"Coming," you say and undo the lock.

Ma stands there, looking shorter somehow. You can see the dark roots in her blond hair.

"Ma," you say, and she hugs you. You hug her back, tight. Maybe she does love you as much as you think. She smells like Chanel perfume and fried onions, and you cry a little into her shoulder. She lets you for a minute. Then she straightens up. She takes a tissue out of her pocket and hands it over.

"We'll all be okay, Ari. I promise. We're doing this so we don't lose everything. We'll get a good amount for the bakery, save money on rent, and decide what to do next."

"It's so sad," you say. "I thought Gertie's was forever."

"Nothing is forever," Ma says. "But we'll get through it. We're strong."

You think of both your parents and all the kneading, stirring, lifting, and slicing they do. When Ma wears a sleeveless dress, you can see the muscles in her arms. Daddy's hands could knead through iron. But it's a different kind of strength she's talking about.

"What about Leah?" is all you say.

Ma frowns but takes your hand and holds it. "Someday when you're a mother, you'll understand."

You want to tell her that you've tried hard to understand, but you just can't. You know she wanted Leah to marry a Jewish man and have Jewish children, and you don't know what's supposed to happen when a couple is different religions. But isn't Leah being her daughter the one thing that is forever? You also want to say that if she doesn't tell Leah, you'll find a way to tell her.

She lets your hand go and walks out the door, closing it behind her before you can say anything. You stare at the door as you hear her footsteps get quieter and farther away. It feels like the door separates you from everything and everyone else: your parents, your sister, the bakery; Jane, Miss Field, Chris Heaton; the whole twisting, turning world.

The next day on the bus, you can sense the warmth from Jane's leg an inch away from yours. You and Jane have gone days without talking. After your parents' news, your brain is extra mixed-up, extra farblondjet. Sounds are even louder. Your limbs feel heavy and slow. Your bag is full of crumpled papers on top of papers, and you haven't done any homework in days.

You and Jane still sit together on the bus, because there's nowhere else to sit other than next to Charlie Stewart, who smells sweaty and is always drumming annoyingly on the back of the seat in front of him. The weird thing is, you're not even sure why you're still mad at each other or why you got so mad in the first place.

Jane is reading a book, but not a book from school. You can't see the title, but you can tell it's a Nancy Drew mystery from the yellow spine. Other than magazines, she only reads Nancy Drews. She has at least twenty of them lined up in her room.

This gives you an idea. Jane must have picked something up from all those mysteries. Maybe she can help you find your sister? But even if she can't, you still want to be friends again. The difference between having one friend and having no friends is a lot bigger than you thought. It's the difference between never feeling alone and always feeling alone.

"I didn't mean to get mad," you say. Jane doesn't look up. You wait another minute and try again. "I know you were just trying to help."

Jane turns to you. "Okay," she says and goes back to her book.

"So can we be friends again?"

She stops reading and turns to you, her eyes squinting a little.

"Please?" you say, your voice cracking.

"Okay, fine," she says again and then goes back to reading. That's it. You don't want to rush her, but your heart leaps. You ride the rest of the way in silence with a little smile on your face.

After school, the last thing you want to do is go to the bakery, but that's what you do every day after school. You think of just going home and calling Ma, saying you don't feel well, but then she would worry or tell you to stop feeling sorry for yourself. Strangely, the bakery has never been busier, like it knows something, like it's trying to hold on to Daddy, to Ma, to you.

When you get there, Daddy is spreading raspberry jam on Linzer cookies.

"Where's Ma?" you ask, putting your bag down.

Daddy doesn't answer you for a second. "Daddy," you say again, louder.

"Oh," he says, startled. "Didn't see you there."

You sit down on your stool and watch him for a few minutes. He spreads the jam on each half so fast, the edges perfectly clean, going through ten cookies in a minute. Whenever you do it, your jam always gets on the sides, on the bottom, and all over your fingers. Just as you're thinking about how perfectly his hands work the cookies, one breaks.

"Your lucky day," he says, putting one broken piece over the other, jam in the middle, and holding it out to you.

You hop off the stool and take it. It's still a little warm. Each separate flavor—the raspberries, the vanilla, the butter, the lemon zest, the crushed almonds—stands out but also blends into something even better.

"Thanks," you say, wiping a few sticky crumbs off your lip. "So where's Ma?" you ask again.

"At home. She's having a migraine," he says while he fills more cookies. He doesn't look at you.

"She gets them a lot," you say.

He stops spreading and finally pays attention. "Yes," he says. "This has been hard for her. She's worn out."

He doesn't say which *this* he means, but you know what's probably making her head hurt the most.

"Maybe if she talked to Leah, she'd get less headaches," you say, examining your broken cookie, the raspberry jam taste fading on your tongue.

"We're not discussing that," he says, his face turning cold. Last night, you asked them when the bakery will be sold. They said the closing date was three months from now, the date when they have to turn over the keys and the bakery isn't theirs anymore.

The people who want to buy the bakery aren't bakers. They're butchers. In a few months, Gertie's will be filled with slabs of raw meat in the cases instead of cookies, cakes, and pies, just like before Gertie's. It will be like Gertie's never happened.

"I got an A on my presentation at school," you say, puffing out your chest a little, trying to change the subject. Miss Field handed you her grading sheet today with a big blue smiley face on it under the A. It's the first A you've ever gotten.

"Really? That's wonderful," Daddy says, still spreading the jam, but he doesn't even look up. You shrink down again. He doesn't ask what the presentation was about. He doesn't even seem surprised, which is good in a way.

You wonder what Daddy even knows about you and school. He never remembers your teachers' names. He doesn't ask you about your homework when you get home, like Ma does. He leaves it to her to know those things. If Ma keeps getting her headaches and there is no Leah, who will know this stuff besides you?

"I'm going to help Gabby," you say, deciding to leave Daddy alone. "It looks busy out there."

"That would be great. Can you take these out front?" he says, handing you a finished tray of Linzers and starting on a new batch. The tray is still hot, but it's not burning.

Gabby is ringing up Mrs. Applebaum, a regular customer who comes all the way from Milford once a week to get her challah for as long as you can remember. Ma and Mrs. Applebaum often have long chats. She says the grocery store in the next town started carrying challah on Fridays, but nothing compares to Gertie's. She always gets a box of assorted cookies with the challah. Seeing her makes you sad.

"Is Sylvia back there?" she asks Gabby. "I keep missing her."

"I think you've missed her again. She's under the weather today," Gabby replies swiftly as she puts two of the fresh Linzers into a box.

"Sorry to hear that. Well, hello, Ariel," Mrs. Applebaum says when she sees you. "Look at you, so grown-up now."

You smile. She says that every time she sees you.

"Wasn't it yesterday when you and Leah were just little girls running in circles around the display cases?" she says. "How is Leah?"

"She's good," you say quickly and start folding boxes so your hands have something to do.

"She graduated last spring, right? Off to college now? I hope so, a girl as talented and bright as she is."

Gabby hands Mrs. Applebaum her packages. If you say yes, she'll ask you where. You try to think of college names. Mrs. Applebaum waits in her thick camel overcoat and a bright melon-colored scarf tied over her puffy hair.

"Yes," you say slowly, and Gabby side-eyes you. You still have no idea what Gabby knows.

"That's wonderful. Where?"

"New York University," you say because you remember Raj was going there. Gabby stares at you.

"Well, that's good. Does she get to come home often?"

You say no at the same time Gabby says yes. You stand there as surprised as you've ever been. Gabby laughs at you and waves her hand.

"I guess not that much," Gabby says, still laughing in a nervous way.

Mrs. Applebaum looks a little confused. "Well, so nice to talk to you girls," she says and takes her packages. "Please tell Sylvia I send my regards."

Gabby smiles. "Of course. See you next week."

You both watch Mrs. Applebaum leave, her brown pumps tapping on the linoleum.

Gabby goes back to arranging the cookies.

"So you know?" you ask. Gabby stops and stands up. Then she reaches out and gently tousles your hair.

"So sorry, Ari. I just wasn't sure when your parents were going to tell you the news. I couldn't say anything."

"When did they tell you?" you ask. You've always trusted Gabby almost like another sister. Almost.

"Oh, hon, a few weeks ago, but they had to. I have to make work plans."

"So do you know where Leah's living?"

"No, they just told me about the dance program and how they didn't really want people knowing until she's in a performance, but quick thinking on the college thing. Wait, don't you know where she's living?"

You stand there, trying to make sense of what she's telling you. A dance program? You glance at the rainbow cookies, the pink, green, and yellow layers inside. Layers on top of layers. Lies on top of lies. You're starting to lose track.

"Um, yeah, I just forgot," you say as you add another layer.

"Well, I hope she's doing great. Tell her I say hi the next time you talk to her."

"Oh, sure," you say, your head spinning. Then you remember what you wanted to do. Another layer. "I have to go to Jane's apartment. She's helping me with my math homework. Will you tell my dad? I'll be home for dinner."

Two customers have just walked in. A man is starting to squeeze the bread, a pet peeve of Gabby's.

"It's fresh, all baked today," she calls to him in her polite but sharp way. He stops. "Okay, Ari, I will," she says to you and heads over to the customers.

How to See a Ghost

You run all the way to your apartment. Luckily, Jane lives on the fourth floor and you live on the fifth. You climb up the stairs instead of taking the elevator. Ma always takes the elevator in her heels. She usually changes to comfortable shoes at the bakery and then puts on her heels to walk home, something you've never understood.

You press your ear to Jane's door and listen for a minute until you hear voices inside. Then you knock.

Jane's mom, Peggy, answers. Being at Jane's is like being in another world sometimes, even though the layout of their apartment is exactly the same as yours. Peggy couldn't be more different than Ma. When she's home, she wears dungarees that are often dotted with clay and glazes. She's a teacher's assistant at a nursery school as well as a potter. She turned her bedroom into an art studio, with a mattress on the floor in the corner and the rest of the floor covered in painter's cloth so wet clay doesn't get everywhere. She takes her pieces to a friend's kiln when they're ready. Then she brings back her shiny bowls and vases, piles them up on shelves in her room, and tries to sell them at art studios and craft fairs. And she makes you call her Peggy instead of Mrs. Cooper.

"Oh, hi, Ariel, I didn't know you were coming over. Jane!" she yells before you can say anything. "Come on in. I'm in the middle of some work, but Jane's in her room," she says as she walks back to her bedroom.

You walk in. Their apartment smells a lot different than yours, mainly because Peggy cooks entirely different foods than Ma. She's always experimenting with new recipes. She made Chinese food for a while but then switched to Greek food and once made you something called moussaka, which is kind of like lasagna but with different stuff in it, like eggplant. Once when Jane had you over for dinner, she made cheese fondue. She also makes extra-healthy things, like brown rice and lentil casseroles, which Jane is always complaining about.

You go over to Jane's bedroom and peek in. Her walls are covered with magazine posters of all her favorite

Hollywood stars and bands. Jane is sitting on her bed, cutting out pictures from the newspaper.

"Hi," you say, still breathless from running up the stairs.

"Hi!" She jerks her head up. "What's going on? Are you okay?"

You pace a little. You go over to her dresser and look at her little collection of makeup and perfumes. She doesn't wear makeup to school; she says she's just practicing for when she's famous. You pick up a lipstick and open it. Bright red. You twist it and smooth it on without even asking. You press your lips together and turn to face her.

"Looks nice," she says, but she doesn't smile. "Ari, I just don't know what's gotten into you these days. One minute you're crying. Then you're mad at me. Then you want to be friends again. Now you're in my room, trying on my lipstick, not saying a word. And you don't even like lipstick."

"Sorry," you say and put the lipstick down. "I have to tell you something, but it's a secret."

Jane's eyes light up. There's nothing she likes more than a secret.

"I solemnly swear," she says and salutes.

You sit cross-legged on the end of her bed, and she backs up, making room for you. You face each other like you're about to play cards. Her bed feels softer than yours.

"On your life?" you say.

"I never swear on my life. What if I was kidnapped and had to tell the truth to save my own life? Then because I told the truth to save my life, I *died* because I swore on my life? Just tell me."

"That would never happen," you tell her, but she has a point. It's a lot to ask. You've never really asked Jane for anything. You've always been happy to have her around, but now you feel different. You need her.

"I almost swear on my life," she says. "Really."

"Okay, I guess that's good enough. Here's the short version. My sister eloped, moved to the city, and now she's going to have a baby." The words fall out of your mouth. Jane doesn't say anything at first. You see her turning over what you just said. Then her face changes.

"WHAT?" she yells and jumps up, standing on the bed.

"Shhhhhhhhh," you say, putting your finger up to your

lipsticked mouth. "Come on. I'm not going to tell you the whole thing if you holler like that."

She plops back down. "Okay, okay. Sorry. Go on."

"And my parents have decided to pretend she's dead or doesn't exist, sort of. Because they didn't want her to marry him," you continue.

"Why?" Jane asks. "Is he some sort of criminal?"

"Worse, according to them."

"Worse, what's worse?"

"He's not Jewish."

"Ha," she says and laughs, but then she sees you're serious. "Uh, so is that a really big deal for you guys?"

You stop. *You guys.* Suddenly you want to put back the words in your mouth. Maybe Jane isn't the person you should be telling about any of this. Maybe a Jewish friend would understand, but you don't have any. What you have is Jane.

"You mean Jewish people? Isn't it a big deal for everyone?"

"I guess. I don't know," Jane says.

"I mean, they just made a Supreme Court ruling to say that different races of people are allowed to get married. It was against the law in a lot of states still."

"They did? It was?" Jane says.

"Yeah, I did a school report on it. And what if someday you decided to run off and marry a Jewish guy? Wouldn't your parents care?" You stop. Jane never talks about her dad.

Jane looks down. She traces a pink flower on her bedspread with her finger.

"Sorry, I mean your mom," you say.

"It's all right," she says and is quiet for another few seconds. "He left my mom when he found out she was pregnant. They weren't even married. And he never came back. My mom always tells people he's dead."

Now it's your turn to be quiet.

"I was always afraid to ask. I didn't mean to make you sad," you say after a moment.

Jane shakes her head. "It's okay. I don't think about it that much. I never knew him, but I also don't think my mom would care if I married someone Jewish. I guess most people aren't like Peggy, though."

Suddenly you feel the shape of your friendship with Jane changing, in a good way, like chocolate chips melting into a cookie as it bakes.

You would agree with that. "But it's not just about him not being Jewish," you say, bringing her back to what you're trying to tell her.

"What else is it?" Jane asks.

"He's Indian. Hindu."

"Hindu?"

"It's a religion from India."

Jane leans back and nods. "Oh, wow, that's pretty far-out."

You both get quiet again. You lie on your side and prop up your head with your elbow, scanning her shelf of Nancy Drews. You wonder if she's read them all.

"Where did Leah meet an Indian?" Jane says after a moment.

An Indian. It sounds funny when she says it like that, like he's another kind of person. You think of Raj that night at your house. You remember that he moved his hands a lot when he talked. You remember how he looked at Leah. How he ate all the cucumbers off his plate but left the lettuce. How he kept smoothing his hair back nervously when Ma asked him questions. At one point when Daddy was going on and on and on about the proper way to make a sourdough starter, Raj winked at you. You tried not to blush, but you did.

"He's from India. But he lives here now. He's just a fellow, Jane, a man who Leah's in love with. But if they would've gotten married in another state like Virginia only a few months ago, I think it would have been illegal."

"Illegal? Like the-police-can-arrest-you kind of illegal?"

You tell her about the Loving case.

"Holy smokes."

You nod. "There's more."

"How can there be?" she says, holding her hands to her cheeks.

You tell her about the bakery, about having to move. You tell her everything you've been wanting to tell someone.

"And I need your help," you say.

She looks like you just slapped her. "My help? What could I possibly do?" Jane gets up, starts walking around her room, crosses her arms over her chest. "This is crazy."

"I need to find Leah," you say, running a hand through your curls. Your scalp is warm, and your hair feels slightly damp at the roots. "You read Nancy Drews." You point to her bookshelf across the room. There they all are, neatly lined up, the yellow spines staring back at you. "You must have learned something about finding people."

Jane laughs. "That stuff is mostly about missing treasure and haunted houses."

Your body feels limp after explaining everything. You think of your grandparents who died, what they taught your parents, and how their ghosts float around in your parents' eyes. Leah's not dead, but you feel her ghost every time you walk into your room, every time you look at her bed, her posters, her clothes.

"My house feels like it's haunted right now," you say. "I have to find her. She needs to know about everything. I know my parents aren't bad people, but what they're doing doesn't seem right. I never thought we were that religious, but Leah marrying Raj changed something in them, especially in Ma. And Daddy seems to go along."

Jane walks over to her dresser and stands in front of a glossy picture of Elizabeth Taylor. She pats her nose with a powder puff. You wonder if she's even listening to you. Then she takes a small red notebook out of her desk.

"What's that?" you ask.

"This is where I write down my clues."

"Clues?"

"Yeah. How else do you think mysteries are solved, silly?"

You jump up and hug her.

"Oh gosh, Ari, it's not that big a deal," she says, but then she hugs you back. She smells like Johnson's baby shampoo and peanut butter, and you know that from this point on, those two things will always remind you of her.

When you get home that night, you don't say much to Ma and Daddy. They try to talk to you about school and about Jane, about anything else, but you just murmur your way through the evening and close yourself in your room again as soon as you can.

The desk is piled with books and paper. You sit down and try to face the homework you've been ignoring. Leah would have helped you get organized. She would have sat with you until you felt less overwhelmed. You remember her saying that you should do the harder things first, then the easier things. But you preferred to get the easier things over with first. It was like putting your feet into a cold pool to get used to the water.

You do a division page in your workbook. Then you read a chapter of *Heidi*, which, so far, you like. Then you look at your heavy history textbook. You're studying ancient civilizations, and there's a chart of world religions—Christianity, Islam, Hinduism, Judaism, and Buddhism.

It's hard to keep the details straight, but they all have gods, and they all have places to pray, and they all have a better place to go if you follow the rules. It seems like the same ideas, just different styles. It's like coats, you think. All coats do basically the same thing: protect you from the weather, keep you warm. They just look different around the world. You want to tell Ma and Daddy this, but they probably wouldn't listen.

The murmur of the TV in the living room stops. You hear the shuffling of Daddy's slippers, a glass being placed in the sink, more footsteps down the hall toward their bedroom, the door opening and closing, then nothing. Your conversation with Jane and what you said to her about ghosts comes back to you. You open your notebook and write.

Ghosts

I was never afraid of ghosts,

until one night

I heard the creak

of a door opening.

When I found the open door

I couldn't shut it,

as hard as I tried.

Something was there,

something that needed me.

Like I was the only person

in the world

who could see it.

After closing your notebook, you lie awake for a while, listening past the silence. You hear some sounds: the radiator in your room making a whispery noise, the small whistle of wind outside your window. You keep listening, waiting for a certain sound as your lids grow heavy, but it doesn't come. You don't know exactly what you're listening for, but you know you haven't heard it yet.

How to Have a Friend

Today Miss Field sets up an electric typewriter on a desk in the back of the classroom during your vocabulary quiz. She tries to do it quietly, but kids are craning their necks to see what's going on. You watch her out of the corner of your eye. She takes the smooth blue-gray machine out of the box. She sets the typewriter on the desk, looks for an outlet, and plugs it in.

You go back to your quiz. You like learning new words and memorize the meanings easily as long as you match them with a picture. If each word becomes a little picture in your mind, it stays there forever. The quizzes are multiple choice, so all you have to do is fill in a little circle to prove what you know.

Accelerate, homage, peevish, mirth. You know them all, but you stop on *mirth.* Usually words sound like what they are. *Accelerate* moves faster as you say the word in your head, like a little car. *Homage* sounds like you're handing something to someone else, a gift. Just hearing the word *peevish* makes you feel irritable, and you think of the way your face looks when Ma tells you to clean your room even though you already have. These words all make perfect sense.

But not *mirth*. *Mirth* sounds like *earth*, which reminds you of dirt, which makes you think of mud and mess and deep, dark holes. You picture someone falling in mirth, stuck in the mirth, sitting alone at night filled with mirth. But the dictionary says *mirth* means "gladness or gaiety as shown by or accompanied with laughter." *Mirth* makes you believe that something can truly look and sound like one thing and mean something exactly the opposite.

After the quiz, Miss Field makes an announcement.

"Please put your quizzes in the basket. I'm happy to say we have a new addition to our classroom. An electric typewriter," she says and walks over to it in the back of the classroom, where it sits on its own desk.

All eyes follow her.

"I'd like you to come around for a demonstration, but please try to make room for everyone."

The scrape of metal chairs becomes irritating. Then there's talking, sneakers squeaking, everyone trying to get close. It makes you want to put your hands over your ears. Miss Field waits for everyone to settle down.

"Let's try to figure out a way for all of you to see."

Miss Field does this often, lets you order yourselves. She says she'll wait and watches silently as the class figures out how to calm its own chaos. Most of the time it works, and it's very different from the usual harsh directing and scolding from your past teachers. Last year, Mrs. McKenna used to make people stand in the corner, facing the wall for ten minutes, if they didn't listen. She also pulled on people's ears sometimes. Never yours, thank goodness.

You stand back, waiting for the cheerful chaos to die down. Finally, people have arranged themselves around the typewriter in a large half circle, so everyone can see.

"Okay," she says. "I'm going to choose a student who can help me demonstrate." She looks around. Hands shoot into the air. She keeps looking and locks her eyes on you. "Ariel, why don't you come up here."

Normally, demonstrating anything for the class would be the last thing a teacher would ask you to do and the last thing you'd ever want to do. But since the presentation, you don't feel like hiding anymore. You walk over slowly, and people move aside to let you get by.

"Have a seat," she says, and you slide into the chair.

You place your hands on the keys, and the typewriter buzzes comfortably against the pads of your fingers. It says *IBM* on the front in big capital letters. Miss Field shows you a chart of where your fingers are supposed to go.

Your left-hand pinkie is supposed to go on *A*, then the other three fingers on *S*, *D*, and *F*. Then your right-hand pointer goes on *J*; the other fingers on *K*, *L*, and the semicolon. You use your thumbs for the space bar. It's like you're playing the piano. She shows you how to reach with each finger to the keys above and below. You can hear everyone breathing around you.

"Okay, try typing *The sad dog sat on a log*," she says.

The *T* is a little hard, then the *H*, then the *E*. Your fingers press down each key so easily, and there they are, the black letters on the white paper, as neat as a printed book. You think of how you would have handwritten the word, big and wavy, the *E* not really looking like an *E*.

You think of how much faster you could write once you learn how to type. You would never have to think about why your fingers can't make the words look the way you want them to.

"Great," she says. "Keep going."

You manage to type the whole sentence. Each letter makes a popping sound as you type it onto the paper. *Pop, pop, pop.*

"Can I try?" asks Lisa. This unleashes a wave of requests. Hands shoot into the air. Everyone is begging Miss Field to try. She says everyone will have a turn and picks five more people to type the same sentence. Then she passes around a sign-up sheet for five people every day. You're glad you got to go first, but you wonder when you'll get another chance.

The day goes by quickly. After the final bell rings, Miss Field calls you over. You stand before her desk. She rubs her hands together, like she's warming them over a fire.

"Ariel," she says. "How would you like to do a lot of your writing on this typewriter? You'll still work on your handwriting, but if you learn how to type, I think it will help you get your ideas out more easily."

You nod. You think she's right. A letter, a sentence, a paragraph like magic on the paper with just a little press. *Pop. Pop. Pop.*

"I've done some reading on this, and my understanding is that dysgraphia doesn't just cause messy handwriting, it makes it hard to think about what you're writing while you're trying to write each letter. Does that ring true to you?"

You think of how it feels when you pick up a pencil. First you have to think about holding it correctly. Then you have to think about forming each letter. Then there's spelling. It hardly ever comes out the way you want it to, and by that time, you've forgotten what you wanted to say. That's how one sentence is. A whole paragraph feels like climbing a mountain.

"It sure does," you say.

"Great, let's just get you typing and see how it goes. Our experiment."

"Okay," you say. "But how will I practice?" You think of all the kids clamoring for a chance at the machine.

"How would you feel about coming in at lunch twice a week? That might be easier than staying after school."

You nod; that way you don't have to tell your parents. And the kids won't know you're spending more time at the typewriter than they are. That also means less time in the cafeteria. She said it was a gift for everyone, but now you wonder if it was mostly for you and Miss Field, your secret experiment.

"I would like that," you say. Miss Field smiles, and you both stand there for a few seconds.

"Miss Field?" you say.

"Yes."

"Thank you."

"I just want to help get those amazing ideas out on paper." As she says this, she taps her own head with her finger. It's one of the nicest things anyone has ever done for you.

That night, you think about the typewriter, the way it buzzed under your fingers while all the kids watched. You wish you had one at home, but at least in your poetry notebook you don't have to worry about what your handwriting looks like. You scribble down another poem.

Mirth

Mirth is such a
sad and grumpy word.
I'm not sure if
I believe that "mirth"
actually means
a happy feeling.
Maybe
I'm just used
to people
lying to me.
Or perhaps
the real truth is
that lots of things
are not what they seem.

On Friday night after dinner, you go over to Jane's apartment again to plan. Ma and Daddy don't seem to mind. Ma hasn't been making her usual Shabbat dinner. Tonight, it was chicken salad sandwiches and leftover split pea soup. She always lights the candles and says the blessings but hardly ever goes to services these days. It's like that with Ma. Sometimes she goes a lot and makes you come with her, and she used to take Leah as well. But sometimes she goes months without attending; Daddy hardly ever goes.

Still, for Shabbat dinner, Ma used to make matzo ball soup, kugel, and a roast. Often, she would also make cholent for the next day. It was your grandmother's recipe, and Ma said she made it just to smell it—the meat, beans, and barley cooking all day. Daddy would save the biggest and best challah to bring home.

You didn't like being dragged to synagogue, but you miss the routine, the dinner cooking when you got home from school, the glow of Temple Beth Torah's sanctuary at night, the hushed rhythmic sound of the rabbi's prayers. It was something you could always count on—even if you didn't like taking the bus there, even if Rabbi Ackerman's low, gravelly voice could put you to sleep, even if you wondered whether you actually believed in God the whole time.

When you're inside Jane's apartment, you feel a

weight lift. There's no missing sister here, no sad, angry parents—just you and Jane sitting on her bed with a big bag of potato chips that you've brought from your place. Peggy isn't home yet, so you have the apartment to yourselves. Jane gets out her red notebook.

"This is what we know already," she says, nibbling on the end of her pencil. "Leah's in New York City."

"With Raj," you say.

She writes it down. "With Raj."

Then she looks up at you, and you both blink at each other.

"That's it," you say. "I can't find the envelopes her letters were in or the second letter she sent, telling us about the baby."

Jane taps the notebook with her pencil.

"So what do you think Leah does all day?" she asks. "Where does she go, or where would she go?"

You think about the city. You've only been there a few times. Twice for Broadway shows, once to see Leah in a special performance with her dance company at Lincoln Center, and once to meet your aunt Sheila to shop for your cousin's wedding at Macy's. You've been to your aunts' and uncles' apartments in Brooklyn lots of times, but when you go there, you never go anywhere else. You have no idea where Leah would actually live.

"Do you know Raj's last name?"

"Oh, yes! Jagwani."

"Did you try calling information or looking them up in the phone book?"

You shake your head. You wonder why you never have.

"Come," she says, and you follow her into the kitchen. The phone book is in a shelf beneath the kitchen counter, the same place your family keeps it. There's only one phone book, and it's just for Fairfield County, Connecticut.

"No problem. Just call information," Jane says.

"Will you call?" Calling people on the phone, especially strangers, always makes you nervous.

"Okay," Jane says and dials 411.

As you watch the dial spin back after each number, your heart starts beating faster and faster.

"Um, hello," Jane says into the receiver. "Do you have a listing for either Leah or Raj Jagwani in New York?" Her cheeks turn pink. She seems nervous, too.

"Manhattan," you whisper and poke her gently on the shoulder. "Tell her to look in Manhattan."

"In Manhattan, I mean?" she says. You put your head close to hers so you can hear the operator's response.

"What did you say the last name was?" the operator asks. Jane looks at you and raises her eyebrows. She pushes the receiver toward you. You shake your head no. She nods and pushes it back to you.

"Jagwani," you say again, louder. The operator asks you to spell it. You remember again how it looked when Leah wrote it, and you spell it slowly for her.

"What an unusual name," she says. You're not sure what to say and bite your lip. She puts you on hold and you hear a bit of static. The seconds go by slowly, then there's a click. She's back.

"Can you spell it again for me, hon?" You roll your eyes at Jane and spell it again, letter by letter. You wonder if people always react to Raj's name—which is now Leah's name, too—like this.

More waiting, then she returns. "I'm sorry. I don't have a listing for either."

"Okay, thank you," you say in a small voice and place

the phone back in its cradle. Maybe this was why you never tried; you didn't want to feel the way you do now. You hunch over and hang your head as you both walk back into Jane's room.

"Hey, come on," Jane says. "That's just one step. No good mystery is easy. We have to figure out what her daily life is like. Is she an uptown girl? Or maybe a hippie type? Where do hippies live in New York City? Greenwich Village? I think I read that somewhere."

Has your sister become a hippie? Maybe she has. You picture her in bell-bottoms, a headband around her forehead, flowers in her hair.

"In Nancy Drew, Nancy's always spying on people to see what they're really up to. We should probably spy on your parents."

"I guess." You wonder what you would find out if you did. You kind of do all the time just living with them, but it hasn't led you to Leah.

"Is there any place either Leah or Raj have to be? Does Raj have a job?"

"I think Raj is going to business school."

"Good," Jane says and gets ready to write. "Where?"

"Oh, of course!" you say, smacking your forehead. "New York University. Leah said he was going there for business school, but I'm not sure where it is."

Jane tosses the book on the floor and hugs you. The bag falls over, spilling potato chips on the bed.

"What?" you say, surprised, but you hug her back.

"That's where they must be, at New York University. Now we just need to go there and find them. We'll call information again. Or the library must have something about it."

"Oh, I don't know," you say.

"You said you wanted my help," Jane says as she quickly puts loose chips back in the bag, eating a few as she goes.

"True, I did," you say in a tiny voice. Jane could be like a little tornado when she got an idea in her head, swirling everyone up around her. Last year she read in some tabloid that Elizabeth Taylor was spotted at 21 Club, a restaurant in New York where all the stars went, according to Jane. She wanted to go there just to see a place that Elizabeth Taylor had been in. She had this idea that you both would take the train to the city and then a cab to the restaurant and try to have dinner there. "Bring all the money you have. Maybe we can get a hamburger," she had said to you.

The plan was that you were supposed to tell your parents you were going to be at her apartment, and she would say she was going to be at yours. But you didn't have the guts. Ma could smell a lie from miles away.

"So we can take the train there. We'll try that old—"

"There's got to be another way," you say, starting to feel nervous again. You picture your parents catching you in a lie or worrying them for some reason. You're finally the good child in Ma's eyes. You don't want to ruin that.

Jane puts her hands on your shoulders. "Ariel, you want to find your sister, right?" she says.

You nod. "More than anything."

"Then this is what we have to do."

You picture seeing Leah and Raj from far away on a college campus. They're holding hands. You call out Leah's name. She turns. She runs and hugs you and tells you she's so sorry for leaving, so sorry for not writing, that she misses you more than anything. Raj holds out his hand for you to shake, but you hug him, too. Then you tell them everything, and it's all okay. They come back with you on the train, right then and there.

"You're right. It's the only way," you say and take a huge handful of potato chips, some greasy pieces falling onto the bedspread. Jane smiles and wipes some crumbs off her face with the back of her hand. It's almost like you didn't really know each other before even though you've been friends for years. If you never asked her for help, you might have missed this: the chance to have a real friend.

How to Have a Nightmare

After an early dinner a few days later, you sit on the couch with your parents, and everything seems fine, almost cozy. Daddy's doing the crossword in his chair, and Ma is in her rocking chair with her stockinged feet in slippers, crocheting something in fuzzy yellow and white yarn. She hasn't crocheted in a long time.

You wonder if you need to let Leah go. Maybe you need to have faith that she'll come back when she's ready. Because if you actually find her, what do you expect will happen? She might be mad at you. Your parents will also be angry, and it won't bring Leah home. Even worse, what if you don't find her? Won't that be harder?

Walter Cronkite is on the TV, telling you how many more soldiers died in Vietnam last week—hundreds more, he says—and that fighting is hard during the rainy season. You think of all those families the soldiers belong to, hundreds and hundreds more people who will never be the same. You know girls can't be drafted, but would Raj ever be drafted? You remember Leah said he was in school so he wouldn't be. But will it change when he graduates? You don't want to ask Ma and Daddy what the rules are.

"We saw a Realtor again today," Ma says during a commercial. "We might have found a place."

"Already?" you ask. "You didn't tell me it would be that soon."

"They're raising the rent here next month," Daddy says.

"Can't we just wait until after the bakery is sold?" you ask. "Just a few more months?"

"Every month counts," he says. "But we're still not sure. This place isn't available for a few months anyway."

"How far is it from here?" you ask.

"It's closer to the train station, but on the other side of town," Ma says, her voice suddenly too cheerful. "Just a couple of miles from here on Cedar. It's a little smaller, but the kitchen has more space. There's good light. It only has one bathroom, though."

"A few miles?" You're about to ask how you'll walk back

and forth to Gertie's, but then you remember that eventually you won't need to. Only one bathroom. Leah took forever in the bathroom. You were always banging on the door, trying to get her to come out. But this new apartment will probably never be a place Leah lives in. And then there's Jane. You wouldn't be in the same building anymore. Would you stay friends?

"It just seems so unfair," you say. "How can Peggy and Jane afford to live here? Are they richer than us?"

"Darling, the earlier you understand that life is unfair, the better," Ma says. "And Peggy and Jane's financial situation is none of our business."

You roll your eyes. *Life is unfair. Don't talk about money.* You've heard Ma say that a million times. You wait for her to comment on your eye roll, but instead she puts her hand on her head. "Oooh," she says and leans over a little bit. Daddy asks her if she's okay. She waves him off, says she hasn't been sleeping well and needs to rest. She leaves, and you go to your bedroom, too. You've had enough of everything, even Ma's migraines. A part of you feels angry that she gets them.

The light in your room is off, but you don't even bother

turning it on. You lie on Leah's bed in the dark, thinking about the plan, because you're not going to be able to let Leah go. You and Jane will go to New York University and look for your sister. You're not sure when. You and Jane still have to figure that part out.

NYU, that's what it was called when you looked it up in the phone book. You and Jane looked up both Leah and Raj in the phone book, too, just in case, but they aren't listed. You hope you won't need to go to NYU, though, that somehow you'll hear a knock on the door just in time, and Leah will be standing behind it, holding her dance bag on her shoulder, like the day she left. You fall asleep with that image in your mind.

In what feels like a minute, Daddy is standing over you, shaking your shoulder. "Ariel," he says, and you think you're dreaming. You can't remember the last time Daddy was in your room. But then you realize you're not dreaming and sit up quickly. "What time is it?"

"It's okay. It's very late," he says, whispering. "Ma needs to go to the hospital."

You want him to explain, but then you look at him. He has a sweater on, and you see his pajama shirt sticking out of it on top of an old pair of dungarees. He looks shaken. Not much makes Daddy look that way.

"Why? Is it her headaches?" you ask him, though you don't know why a headache would send her to the hospital.

"We're not sure. She's very dizzy, and she fell."

"She fell?"

"She can't stand up right now. I've called an ambulance. You'll go to Jane's."

"An ambulance?" You keep repeating what Daddy says.

"I'm going to call Peggy now," he says. You wait for him to say that everything will be okay, but he doesn't.

You get up and follow him into the dark kitchen, and you flip on the light. The sink is full of dishes. Crumbs litter the counter. Nobody cleaned up. You hear Ma moan a little in the bedroom.

"Can I see her?" you say as he walks you to the door.

"No, Ari. She's very uncomfortable. You'll see her when she's better. I promise."

He sends you downstairs in your pj's holding your pillow and a key to the apartment so you can come up and get changed for school in the morning. He rushes you out before the ambulance gets there.

You and Jane watch outside her window when the ambulance comes. You see Ma being taken away on a stretcher. Daddy gets in after her, and off they go, sirens screaming into the night while Jane holds your hand. But even with Jane's fingers grasping yours, you feel alone. Her room smells a little musty from the rain outside. Another wave of anger makes the back of your neck feel hot and prickly. It should be Leah taking care of you while Ma is in the hospital.

"I'm mad at her," you say to Jane.

"Your mother?"

"No, Leah," you say. "It seems like everything is falling apart without her."

"But this isn't her fault," Jane says.

You walk away from the window. "Maybe it is, though," you say and get in the sleeping bag Peggy put down for you on the carpet, curling up on your side.

Jane gets in her bed. "The doctors will fix your mom," she says. "It'll all go back to normal soon."

You nod and press your face into the pillow so Jane can't see you cry because you don't think there will ever be a normal to go back to.

The next morning, Peggy wakes you up by gently rubbing your back. You jump, not knowing where you are for a second. Then you remember: Ma, the ambulance. Peggy kneels by your spot on the floor. "Ariel, sweetheart," she whispers. "Your mom's still in the hospital. They want to do a few more tests. I left some cereal on the counter, but I have to run to work."

Then she gives you a big, long hug. "Don't worry, she'll be okay," she whispers in your ear. She probably doesn't know for sure, but it still feels good to hear it. She smells like coffee and some flowery soap. You don't want to let go. For a moment, you wish Peggy was your mom and Jane was your sister. Then you'd be exactly where you belong, and everything would be fine.

She releases you slowly. "Gertie's will be closed tomorrow, and Gabby is coming to stay with you when you get back from school."

"Oh?" you say. "But why can't I stay here?"

She shrugs. "Your father thought it would be best for you to be in your own place. Probably didn't want to impose, I guess."

You want to stay with Jane. You think of Ma and

how she's always saying Peggy is a little "wild," which is probably why Gabby is coming. Peggy doesn't seem wild to you, just different from a lot of moms you know. She cares a lot about her pottery. She's younger than Ma, not too much older than Gabby. But mainly she seems to do the things she wants to do, things that are for her. She takes good care of Jane, but if she gets into her work, Jane makes her own dinner. She plays the music she likes and dresses how she wants, not how moms usually dress in this town. You wonder if that's what Ma calls wild, just being the person you want to be.

Ma always seems to be doing things for other people. She works hard at the bakery for Daddy's dream. She left her family and came to Connecticut so you and Leah would go to better schools. She always wears nice dresses and does her hair and puts on makeup the moment she gets up in the morning. Who would Ma be if she didn't care what anyone thought? Who did Ma want to be before Daddy, before the bakery, before you and Leah?

Peggy also tells you that Daddy said to put fresh sheets on Leah's bed for Gabby.

You eat some Lucky Charms with Jane and go upstairs

to get changed afterward. You stand in your room, about to make Leah's empty bed, and imagine Gabby sleeping in it, but you don't want her to. It will remind you of Leah, seeing someone else in her bed. You try to remember what it was really like when Leah was home. You're starting to forget a little, which makes you wonder what else you'll forget about her.

Leah was a restless sleeper. She tossed and turned and made little whimpering noises in her sleep. Sometimes she even snored. Once last summer, while she sat at the vanity getting ready for dance, she said she had just read an article in a magazine about how newlywed women could stay pretty in the morning for their new husbands. It said that one should always wake up before their husbands to brush their teeth, take out their curlers, and put on makeup. That way, the article said, you always stayed the girl he married.

Leah laughed as she told you this. She stuck bobby pin after bobby pin into her bun and said, "Who would be ridiculous enough to marry someone who didn't love them without their makeup on! Raj isn't like that at all."

Now you realize Leah was already thinking of married

life then, planning and imagining what it would be like to live as husband and wife. Did she still sleep the same way, tossing and turning and snoring, or was she different now that she was married? Was it better? Did Leah even want to be found?

You pick up a pen at your desk and open your notebook.

Nightmare

Sometimes she would have
nightmares—
cry and yell
in her sleep.
I would gently wake her
and ask her if she
was okay.
She always said yes.
And I was glad for her.
I was glad she never remembered
what was causing
all that pain.

How to Have Fun Anyway

When Gabby comes over after school, she brings a bag of fun stuff for you, like she used to do when she babysat, and dumps it out on the dining room table. She pulls out a deck of cards, nail polish, a new pack of jacks, and a bag filled with red shoestring licorice, Now and Laters, and Hershey's Kisses. It makes you feel ridiculous. You aren't a little kid anymore.

You stand, watching with your arms crossed.

"Listen, Ari. I know there's a lot going on for you. I can't make any of it go away. But I can still be your friend," she says, wiggling a banana Now and Later at you.

You take it and start unwrapping the sticky little square. Was Gabby your friend? She used to be your babysitter. Now she works at the bakery, but when the bakery is gone, what will she be to you? Will you even see her anymore?

"Thanks," you say and go off to your room, hoping that Gabby will just leave you alone.

You lie on the rug while Elvis sings about jailhouses and hound dogs. Then, after you switch to the Beatles and then to the Doors, and nothing seems to be the right music for how you feel, you picture Gabby sitting out in the living room all by herself.

Shoestring licorice would taste pretty good right now. You like to eat one string at a time, taking little nibbles until the whole string is gone. You and Jane have contests to see who can eat a string the fastest without using your hands. Jane always wins.

That's what your apartment needs—Jane.

When you come out of your room, Gabby is sitting with her feet up on the coffee table, reading a magazine and chewing on a piece of licorice, her favorite as well. You like that about Gabby. Even though she's a grown-up, she still likes things like magazines and licorice.

"Can I have my friend Jane over?" you ask.

"Of course," Gabby says, her eyes lighting up. "The more the merrier. We'll get pizza and have a proper slumber party."

You run downstairs and knock on Jane's door. She and Peggy are all set to watch a movie. You see a big bowl of popcorn sitting on the coffee table.

"Oooh, can we have a dance party?" she says after you ask her to come over. You agree, and Peggy lets her go, and then you and Jane run upstairs as fast as you can, Jane taking the bowl of popcorn and her copies of *Help* and *Sgt. Pepper's Lonely Hearts Club Band* with her. The two of you and Gabby pile on the couch with blankets and turn on the TV, first loading up on some candy and popcorn for energy.

Then you bring out your record player. Jane puts on *Help* and turns the volume all the way up. As the three of you dance, Jane holds out the album cover and pretends to kiss Paul, which sends you and Gabby into fits of laughter. You never thought you could have fun like this with Leah gone and Ma in the hospital, and you expect to feel guilty, but you don't, because for a few hours no one is going to get mad, or have a headache, or seem sad or tired. There are no secrets or missing sisters, only popcorn, candy, the Beatles, Jane, and Gabby.

The next day, Daddy calls early in the morning. He

tells Gabby that Ma is getting released from the hospital. He says that she has something called vertigo, which was caused by her migraines, which made her very dizzy. All she really needs is some rest. When Gabby explains this, you feel relieved, but you're also sorry to see Gabby go, because when she leaves, she'll take the fun with her. You both pick up the popcorn and candy wrappers, do all the dishes, and wipe down every surface. Gabby strips Leah's bed and decides to strip yours as well and wash the sheets. When she's downstairs starting the laundry, you look at both beds with no sheets or bedspreads on them, and you like the way it looks. It feels less like the room you're supposed to be sharing with Leah. Maybe you'll keep Leah's bed like that.

You head over to the bus, and Gabby rushes off to open up the bakery. Later, when you get home, Daddy's making coffee in the kitchen. It's so strange to see him there instead of Ma during a school day.

"Hi, Daddy," you say as he pours water into the percolator. He stops and gives you a quick kiss on the forehead.

"Hi, Muffin. Are you all right?" he asks.

"I'm fine. How's Ma?" you say.

"She's okay, just resting in the bedroom."

"But if Ma's okay, why did she need all those tests?"

He finishes pouring coffee grounds in the filter and plugs it in. He turns, and you see the dark circles under his eyes. He's never looked so tired.

"They wanted to make sure she didn't have something more serious," he says, leaning against the counter.

"Like what?" you ask.

"Like a brain tumor," he says flatly, but then he notices the shocked look on your face. "But she doesn't have one, Muffin," he says, pinching your chin gently. "That's why she stayed in the hospital, so we could be sure. She's going to be fine."

Even though it's scary, you feel like he's telling you the truth for once, and you're glad. Suddenly all your angry thoughts at Ma vanish. You just want to sit next to her and hold her hand.

"Can I go in the bedroom?" you ask in a small voice.

Daddy nods. "Just knock first."

You go over to the bedroom and knock gently. "Hi, Ma, it's me," you call through the closed door. "Can I come in?"

"Okay," you hear Ma say after a moment.

You open the door and look at her. She's sitting up against the pillows, but her eyes are closed. She's in her fuzzy pink robe, her hair is down, and she doesn't have any makeup on. You can't remember the last time you've seen her like this. She normally locks the door and doesn't come out of her bedroom until she's dressed and made-up, even on a Sunday.

She opens her eyes and smiles. "And I thought my migraines were the worst thing I could feel. You just don't know what's going to take you down. But I think the worst is over," she says and pats the bed for you to sit down. "For now."

"Are you feeling better?" you ask.

"Yes, less dizzy," she says. "But the medicine makes me tired, so I can either be dizzy or tired, isn't that a nice choice? The doctor says I should feel fine in a day or two. I'm glad to see that you and Gabby didn't wreck the house."

"Nope. We even did the laundry." But you think of last night with pizza boxes, popcorn, blankets, and candy everywhere. It would have sent Ma right back into the hospital.

She smiles and pats your hand. "Good girl."

Your heart leaps a little as you hear those words again.

Ma's eyes are getting heavier and heavier. She closes them and murmurs, "Leah, don't worry. I'm fine."

You freeze. Did she just mix up your names, or did she actually think she was talking to Leah? You watch her for a few minutes as her breathing becomes deeper. Her chest goes up and down.

"Ma?" you say, but she doesn't answer. She's already asleep.

You go back into the living room. Daddy sits at the table with his coffee and the newspaper spread in front of him. You sit across from him quietly and listen to him turn the pages. You can't think of the last time you were alone with him, really alone. Ma is usually around. She doesn't go many places. She's either here or at Gertie's, the grocery store, or sometimes at Temple Beth Torah. That's it, her whole life. Daddy, too. You glance over to the dark TV, where Jane was kissing the screen the night before, making you laugh. Everything felt like it was in color. Now it's back to black and white.

"Do you guys have friends?" you ask.

Daddy looks puzzled as he puts down the newspaper.

He takes a long sip from his mug. "Of course. We have lots of friends. We just haven't had much time to see them lately."

Lots of friends. You wonder if this is true. Your parents used to have two couples over from the synagogue for card nights, but they haven't been over since Leah left. "Who is Ma's best friend?" you ask.

Daddy thinks for a second. "Maybe Becky or Barbara." He murmurs the names of the women who came over to play bridge. "But I think when people get older, they don't have best friends like they do when they're younger."

"Oh," you say and put that on the growing list of why being a grown-up doesn't sound very good at all. "So did Ma have a best friend when she was younger?"

"Why are you asking?" he asks, looking down at you over the black rims of his thick glasses. "I'm not really sure."

You shrug and think of how you and Jane can sit on her bed with a bag of chips and for a little while nothing else matters. When it's like that between the two of you, you feel inside your life instead of outside of it, and you realize you've never thought of Jane as your best friend until now.

How to Make Soup

When you come home from school the next afternoon, you hope to see Ma up and about, but the kitchen is dark and gloomy. You can hear the low murmur of the public radio news station trickling out from under your parents' door.

You click on the kitchen light and see the bank calendar hanging on the wall. The pictures are of the shops around town or a pretty garden outside someone's house. You don't even know what date it is. You lean closer. Ma has written something in the little square, and it makes your heart stop. You cover your mouth with your hand. Tonight's the eve of Rosh Hashanah.

Daddy and Ma must have forgotten with everything going on. Normally you'd stay home from school and go to services in the morning. Ma would make her Coca-Cola brisket and apple-noodle kugel. You and Leah would make the honey cake. Daddy would bring home his round raisin challah. Sometimes you would bring food to Brooklyn, or your aunts, uncles, and cousins would come over. You think of Ma rushing around with a bunch of pots going on the stove, the apartment alive with relatives, talking, laughing, eating. Will it ever be like that again? Or is that part over, too, and you just don't know it yet?

You run to your parents' bedroom and open the door without knocking. The radio is on, but Ma is asleep. She looks so peaceful, almost like a young girl. You back out of the room, closing the door slowly. If she forgot about Rosh Hashanah, you don't want to be the one to tell her.

You go back in the kitchen and look in the refrigerator. You and Daddy had TV dinners last night, but the thought of having them again tonight feels wrong. There are some onions, celery, and carrots in the crisper. You take them out. They look a little wilted, but not rotten. In the freezer are some chicken parts. You've seen Ma cook soup a million times, so you try to remember what she does. You put the vegetables and chicken in Ma's big soup pot, fill it with water, and plop in a bouillon cube. Then you turn up the heat.

Ma always puts in fresh dill, which looks like big hairy pieces of grass, but you don't see any. She usually puts other vegetables in it, too, but the carrots, celery, and onion will have to do. You find some dry dill in the spice drawer. You sprinkle that in with some salt and pepper. You don't know how to make matzo balls, but there's a bag of egg noodles in the pantry, so you take those out. Ma always cooks them separately and then puts them in the soup, so you boil another pot of water for those.

When Daddy comes home, the soup pot has been simmering for a while and the noodles are done, drained, and waiting. You don't know how long you're supposed to cook the soup, but the apartment has started to smell the way it's supposed to, the steamy scent of boiled vegetables, chicken, and dill taking over.

"What are you making?" Daddy says to you, surprised. He doesn't seem mad that you were cooking by yourself.

"Soup. I think."

Daddy comes over next to you and looks in the pot.

"I'm impressed," he says and starts making his coffee in the percolator. You both stand there quietly, watching things boil. Daddy puts his hand on your shoulder and squeezes before getting a mug.

"Why is Ma sleeping so much?" you ask, stirring and stirring the soup.

He sighs. "Why don't you put the cover on so the water doesn't boil off?"

"Okay," you say and do as you're told. "I thought she was almost better."

"It's her medication," he says. "But she'll stop taking it when she's not dizzy anymore. Don't worry, your mother will bounce back. She's a fighter."

A fighter. You never thought about Ma that way. Maybe the way she puts on her heels and marches off to the bakery every morning—always ready to roll out dough, always ready to argue with the delivery people—then comes home and puts dinner on the table, no matter what, all the while keeping her lipstick fresh, is kind of a fight.

You find an apple. It's a little bruised, but it will do. You cut it up and put some honey in a little glass bowl. You set that on the table before serving the soup. Daddy looks at it, confused, and then his face fills with recognition.

"I didn't think you'd remember."

"Daddy, did you not want me to remember?"

He looks at you carefully. "Oh no, that's not why."

"It makes me sad to miss Rosh Hashanah." As you say it, you're surprised how sad it does make you.

"It was just too much right now, the trip to Brooklyn or having family here. We thought it would be easier if we didn't talk about it or make a big deal."

You swallow. "I think most things are easier if you do talk about them. I feel like everyone is lying to me all the time."

Daddy takes off his glasses and faces you. "Oh, Ari. I don't mean for you to feel that way."

A few seconds go by as you stare at the honey glistening in its little glass bowl. "Ma must be sad, too."

"She is," he says. "She loves this time of year."

"Are you sad?" you ask him.

"Yes, I am," he says.

You hand him an apple slice. "Baruch atah Adonai," he says in Hebrew as he begins the blessing over the apples and the prayer for a sweet new year. You say it along with him, and then you both dip the slices in honey, clink them together, and eat them.

Then Daddy says, "I'm kind of glad that you're sad."

"Why?" You wipe some honey off your lip, but now your hands are sticky.

"Because the holiday means something to you. When we decided to move to a place with such a small Jewish community, we didn't know how it would be for you and Leah. And lately I wonder if we made the wrong decision." He sits back in his chair and rubs his chin. Then he takes another apple slice and eats it slowly, bite by bite. "You make choices in life," he says while he chews. "But sometimes you want one thing so much, you don't see what you might lose if you get it."

You think about what your father is saying and drag an apple slice through the thick honey before putting it in your mouth. Maybe it also means that Leah wanted Raj so much that she didn't see what she'd lose, either.

"Let's have the soup before it gets cold," Daddy says.

The bowl of steaming broth heaped with noodles makes you feel a little better, and it tastes pretty good with lots of salt and pepper. After dinner, Daddy checks on Ma and then gets in his easy chair with the paper. You go to your room. You sit down and write:

Sticky Fingers

Tonight I said the blessing
for the sweet new year,
my fingers sticky
with honey
and the apples I spread it on.
It feels good
to at least be able
to make this wish.
I like how the sweetness
stays on my tongue,
even if all I can see
right in front of me
are hard days ahead.

You read the poem over a few times, even once out loud. You never do that. Usually just getting something out on paper feels like plenty, so you only read them once.

But this time, you see a few words that could be taken out and think of a few words you want to add. It's almost like remembering a dream: The more you think about it, the clearer it becomes. Then you do something you've never done before. You rewrite it.

A Blessing

Tonight I said the blessing
for a sweet new year,
my fingers sticky
with apples and honey.
And it feels good
to make this wish
and taste the sweet honey
on my tongue,
even if all I can see
in front of me
are bitter days ahead.

The next morning, Jane is at the bus stop, holding her gray wool coat together by the front, her schoolbag hanging off her shoulder. She's wearing a headband that pulls her bangs back. You don't think you've ever seen so much of her face.

"Your eyes look pretty," you say.

"Why, thank you," Jane says in a southern accent and bats her eyelashes. She shivers. "It's really cold. When is the stupid bus coming?"

You both look down. The air is brisk, and you can smell the drying leaves all around you. But your body feels warm.

"Time is running out," you say.

Jane looks alarmed. "What do you mean? Is your mother okay?" she asks.

"I think so," you say. "But I wonder if her migraine problem would have gotten this bad if she had just talked to Leah. It's gotten so much worse since Leah left. My parents didn't even want to celebrate Rosh Hashanah yesterday. I don't know what's going to happen next."

"What's Rosh Hashanah again?" Jane asks.

"It's the Jewish New Year," you say. You explain it to Jane every year, because normally you get to miss school for the holiday. It's weird that a holiday you've celebrated your whole life is a mystery to so many people around you.

"Oh, that's right." Jane kicks a pebble on the sidewalk. "Are you really going to move?" she asks, looking toward the pebble.

"I think so," you say and look at Jane.

"That would really be rotten."

"I know. We've lived in the same building forever. But we'll still be friends, right?"

"Of course," Jane says.

Then you both walk in silence for a bit.

"I also don't want to move without Leah knowing where we are," you say. "It's too much. I have to find her no matter what happens." Any doubts you had evaporated when Ma went to the hospital. You've never been more sure that this is what you have to do.

"Then we'll find her," Jane says. "Next Tuesday."

"Next Tuesday?"

"Yes, we'll find her next Tuesday. Because I have play rehearsal then. But I'm barely in the show. They're working on the opening number. They won't even notice I'm gone."

"But my parents will notice," you say.

"Not if you say you're in the play."

"Jane, they'll never believe me."

The bus comes. You both hurry to your usual seat toward the back and sit for a moment, thinking as the bus lurches forward.

"I could say I'm doing tech for the play. That sounds more believable."

"Great idea," Jane says. Then she taps you on the knee. "I think you'd be a good actress, you know. You have a presence."

"A presence. Like how?"

Jane turns her face up toward the bus window and then back at you. "It's kind of hard to explain. Sort of like you're more *there* than some people."

"Oh," you say. "Thanks."

All day you think about what Jane said. Miss Field once told you an old saying—that a razor blade is sharp but can't cut down a tree and that an ax is strong but can't cut hair. When you asked her what it meant, she said, "It means you have everything you need. You just have to find the right purpose to suit the tools you have."

To you, acting in a play feels like trying to cut down a

tree with a razor blade. Your presentation, though—the way people listened to you, wanted to know what you thought—felt like you were cutting hair with the razor. Or something like that.

How to Make Stuff Up

Missing

I am searching for her
because I need her
even if she doesn't need me.
And I promise
I will not be mad
when I find her.

You type this at lunch when Miss Field sits at her desk, going through papers, eating what smells like a tuna-fish sandwich. When you come up with a poem, you want to write it down as soon as possible because you forget it if you don't, and that feels like dropping an ice-cream cone.

As soon as you finish, you pull out the paper, fold it up, and stuff it in your pocket. Then you take a bite of your peanut-butter-and-jelly sandwich and chew for a moment.

"Ariel," Miss Field says. "I don't mean to pry, but I think I saw you put a poem in your pocket."

You spin around before you can even think about it and the color rises in your cheeks. Miss Field gets up, walks toward you, and pulls up a chair.

She leans forward. You lean back.

"I really would love to see more of your poems," she says. "I won't correct them if that's what you're worried about."

She holds her chin with two fingers and then lets it go. You study her face. Her blinking blue eyes, her long features, her pale skin. You wonder what she was like as a girl in school. Was she like Jane? Like Leah? Was she like you?

"I want you to read them," you say. "But I also don't."

"Okay. Why?"

You're not quite sure of the answer. You take the poem out of your pocket and grip it tightly. You think and think. "Because," you say after a moment. "Once you read it, the poem will change."

"Interesting," she says. "Tell me more."

"The words I wrote might mean something different to you."

Miss Field sits back in her chair and crosses her arms.

"They might," she says.

"I don't want them to. I want them to mean to you exactly what they mean to me."

"That makes sense," she says and pauses for a moment. "But that's art, Ariel. It's your gift to the world. People will see what they need to see. Sometimes it will mean to them exactly what it meant to you. Those people are your soul mates."

Your soul mates? You're not sure about that. Sometimes Miss Field talks like she has an *idea* of how she wants things to be, but it isn't how they really are.

"I just write the poems for myself," you say.

Miss Field nods. "That's good. That's why you should write them. I didn't show my poems to anyone for a while, either, but it got too hard for me to carry all alone. Writing is communication."

"What was too hard for you?" you ask. You've never spoken like this to a teacher, as if they were just another person, a friend.

"Hard?" she asks.

"Yes, you said it got too hard for you to carry all alone."

"Oh," she says. "Just some difficult things that happened in my family. So I wrote about what I was feeling. After a while, I started showing them to people. I started reading them out loud. I still do."

You want to ask her what exactly those difficult things were, but you don't, and you push the poem back into your pocket. The paper is a little damp now from the grip of your sweaty hand. Would it make you feel a little lighter to let Miss Field read it? Would it make you feel like you had less to carry?

She watches you, and you give the poem to her, slowly, carefully, like you're handing her a newly hatched chick. Miss Field seems to understand this, because she takes it from you just as delicately.

"Thank you," she says in a low tone. "It'll be just between you and me."

"It's just made-up stuff."

She reads it quickly with her eyebrows knitted together. Then she folds it gently and gives it back to you. "All poems are real and not real at the same time," she says. "But what's true and not true is your business."

"Okay," you say, but you know your poems are not made-up. They are all real.

"You manage to put a lot in just a few words. I like the way you connect the idea of needing and searching."

"Really?" you say.

"Really. Don't stop. You inspire me."

"Thank you," you say, but you wonder if she's lying to you just so you'll keep writing. But maybe a lie like that isn't so bad.

Back on the bus, you think about Miss Field. You still don't understand why she wants to help you.

"So, Tuesday," Jane says when she sits down next to you.

You remember and smile as you sink back into your seat.

"I drew up a plan," Jane says. She opens one of her school folders and takes out an intricate map drawn on white paper. Everything on it is outlined in black ink and then filled in with colored pencils.

It shows your town, the school, your apartment building, the train station, and even Gertie's. There are little drawings of you and Jane and descriptions and dotted lines marking the places you'll go. There are times and dates listed, even the train schedule.

You especially love the way she drew Gertie's. There are tiny pastries and cookies in the cases that sit near the window of the shop. You have never been more grateful for Jane. She's helping you carry some of this.

"This is really swell! I didn't you know you could draw."

"I'm a multitalented gal," she says, trying to brush off the compliment, but you see her grow pink underneath her freckles.

"How come you've never showed me anything before?"

Jane shrugs. "There was no reason to," she says.

You nod because you know exactly what she means. Maybe someday you'll show Jane some of your poems. You think of what Miss Field said about art again: *It's your gift to the world.* This map feels like that: like a gift to you from Jane.

You go over your plan. The first part takes place today. You'll tell Daddy that you've joined the theater tech club. Then you'll tell him that your first meeting is on Tuesday and you won't be home until eight. It's perfect.

How to Lie and Tell the Truth at the Same Time

At Gertie's, you burst through the door, wave to Gabby, take off your coat, and ask Daddy what you can help with. It feels like months since you've been here. You stretch out your fingers. You don't even want a snack. You just want to pull and push and pound and mix. The less you are at Gertie's, the less you feel like yourself.

"We need some more black and whites," Daddy says. "Can you make a batch for me?"

"Uh-huh," you say. You haven't made them in a while, but *step by step*, you remind yourself. Everything is easy like that.

You head to the file drawers to check the recipe. Usually Daddy and Ma don't need them anymore, but sometimes they change things, and you like to study them. The recipes make so much sense to you. In a way, they're like poems. You read.

FOR THE BATTER:

2 1/2 cups unbleached all-purpose flour

1 tsp baking soda

A big pinch of baking powder

1 tsp salt

2/3 cup buttermilk

1 tsp vanilla

2/3 cup unsalted butter, softened

1 cup granulated sugar

2 large eggs

4 tsp grated lemon zest

FOR THE FROSTING:

2 cups confectioners' sugar

1 tbsp light corn syrup

1/4 tsp vanilla

2 to 3 tbsp milk

1/4 cup unsweetened Dutch-process cocoa powder

Daddy sometimes likes to make notes on the note cards. He always uses red pen over the black or blue ink when he changes a recipe. You think about all the years he's baked these cookies and how many people have eaten them and how he says every time he bakes something he tries to make it even better than the last time.

On this recipe he wrote: *"An extra pinch of lemon zest for a special zing. Tried regular milk instead of buttermilk with a little yogurt, and I'm not sorry about it. Mrs. Frankel prefers the smaller cookies. Why do people like big and small cookies but not medium-sized cookies? I like them, so let's keep. Sometimes people don't know what's good for them.*

It's Daddy's art, his gift to the world. And it is true. Sometimes people don't know what's good for them, even adults.

You mix the vanilla and then the chocolate icing in separate bowls. After the cookies bake, you take out the golden circles and let them cool on the trays. You look to see if Daddy's watching you, but he's going through bills on the other side of the kitchen.

"Daddy," you call to him. "I joined a new club at school," you blurt out.

"That's great," he calls back, still opening envelopes with a frown on his face. "Which one?"

You start icing the cookies. You do the vanilla first on one half and then the chocolate, staying focused on the cookies because you can't look Daddy in the eye and lie to him.

"It's the theater tech club—you know, helping with costumes and sets for the play. That way Jane and I can spend more time together."

"Sure," he says as he writes a new sign for the day-old bread. "It's good for you to keep busy." You watch how easily the black ink cursive flows out from under his fingers onto the paper sign. Another gift to the world, one you don't have.

"So I'm going to be at the play rehearsal late on Tuesday. I just wanted to tell you if I forget to tell Ma," you say, because you've already decided you aren't telling Ma a thing. If you told Ma, she'd ask you if you actually spoke to Peggy in person because Peggy could be a little forgetful and why did rehearsal go so late and why were you joining this club now instead of at the beginning of the year and since when did you become interested in theater?

Daddy seems like he's barely listening. You've always wondered if that means he trusts you more or cares less.

"Peggy can pick us up," you say and take a breath. All the words that Jane told you to say are out. Jane's going to tell Peggy that Daddy will get you both after he leaves the bakery. Then you'll walk home together from the train station when you get back from the city. That way Ma will think you're at the bakery with Daddy, and Daddy will think you're at the rehearsal with Jane. And Peggy will think Daddy is driving you home.

"Okeydokey," he says and decorates the sign with some swirls. You watch him finish it.

"I wish I could write like you," you say.

He stops and looks at you, *really* looks at you.

"You could if you wanted to," he says.

"No," you say.

"Keep trying, Muffin."

"No, Daddy, I can't!" you say much louder. He holds the marker in the air, frozen. "And it's not because I'm lazy. Do you know how much work it takes for me to write a few lines? It's just the way I am." Your lip feels a little shaky, but no tears come. You aren't sad. You're angry.

Daddy has a funny look on his face, and you wonder if you've gone too far, if he's going to tell you never to speak to him this way and send you home.

"I'm sorry," you whisper.

"No, I didn't mean to upset you," he says, his voice softening. "I don't think you're lazy."

A few seconds go by. He puts the cap on the marker.

"Miss Field is teaching me how to type," you say.

"Yeah?"

"It really helps. For the first time something actually does."

He pushes up his glasses and blinks a few times. "That's so good to hear. Really." He wiggles the marker between his pointer finger and middle finger. "You know, school was always boring to me. I did fine, but it just seemed pointless. Then when I graduated high school, I couldn't wait to get a job and earn money. That felt exciting.

Productive. I got a job in a bakery, and it was so easy for me, using my hands to make things, coming up with new recipes. I actually cared about something for the first time. So I just thought . . . " he says and stops and shakes his head.

"You thought what?" Daddy never talks to you this way with Ma around. Normally he acts like he was born a grown-up dad and baker.

"I just thought you were like me and that maybe Gertie's would be where you'd land, too. But now that's changing."

Every time you think about your parents selling the bakery, you get a heavy, sinking feeling. Daddy shouldn't have to bake for someone else, use someone else's recipes. He already did that. You look at the sign sitting on the counter, the words perfectly centered, smooth, the letters curving up at the ends, as graceful as swooping birds.

"I'll never be able to write like that," you tell Daddy. "I don't think I'll be able to decorate cakes like you, either. But if I can learn to type, then it won't feel so hard. School could be something I like, at least sometimes. I like coming up with ideas. I like learning about things that make me think new thoughts and ask new questions."

Daddy sits down. He takes off his glasses, spits on them a little, and starts to clean them with his apron.

"I'm the one who's sorry, Ariel."

"Why?" you say.

He puts on his glasses. The lenses shine. "Because it's been a lot to handle lately, but you'll be okay. You always land on your feet."

"Daddy, the thing is I just don't understand what's happening with you guys and Leah. I try and I try, but I can't. I don't think it's the right thing to do." Your heart is thumping. You watch his face and wait for it to turn angry, but it doesn't.

"You might be right," Daddy says, leaning back against the wall.

"Wait, what?" You plop down on a stool next to him.

Daddy is silent. His eyes move back and forth, thinking.

"If my father hadn't left Poland when he did, who knows what would have happened?"

You just stare at him. You're not sure what to say.

He explains, "If they had stayed in Poland, my family might have been killed in the Holocaust like so many others. That was less than thirty years ago, a blink of an eye as far as history is concerned. I'm not very religious, but there's a duty you might not understand. I think about what my parents would have thought about Leah marrying someone not Jewish. Well, I . . ." He stops, swallows. "Ma and I feel like we've truly failed at something."

"The baby could still be Jewish," you say, hoping to take a little of the pain away, but maybe you're wrong. When there are two religions in a family, do you have to choose one, or can a family be both?

"When Leah told us about the baby," Daddy continues, "Ma started writing letters to her. She told me, and we went to see Rabbi Ackerman, right before she went to the hospital."

"Ma has been writing to Leah? All this time? But I thought she—" you say and stop, realizing you might never come to the end of all these secrets. "What did the rabbi say?"

"He said he understood how we felt and that maybe if they hadn't married already, we could change her mind, but it was done. He said we should listen to our hearts."

You think of Rabbi Ackerman and his serious way, his low, pious voice. You've always been a little afraid of him;

it feels as though if he studied your face too closely or looked into your eyes for too long, he wouldn't like what he'd see. Now you wish you could hug him.

Then Daddy looks up at you, his eyes a little red.

"What's in my heart is that Leah is my daughter no matter who she marries," he says. He fiddles with the marker in his hand again. "But it might be too late. They were staying in NYU housing before, but Ma's letters have come back. There's no new number listed. We don't know where she's living. NYU can't tell us because she's not a student there, and they won't give me information"—he stops again and clears his throat—"about Raj, either. It's my fault. She's going to have a baby in a few months. I always thought my grandchild would come to this bakery." His voice breaks, and he rubs his forehead. Tears start to roll down his face.

You've never seen Daddy like this. You've seen him get sad over things that didn't really matter, like TV commercials, but you've never seen him cry over something this real, and it scares you. You put your hand on his back.

"Don't worry, Daddy. Leah wouldn't leave us forever. She'll come home eventually," you say.

What you don't say is that she will come home because you will find her.

He straightens up and wipes his hand quickly over his eyes. "I'm just tired. Let's get these cookies in the case. They look great." He's suddenly moving so fast, you can barely keep up.

When you get home, Ma is on the couch with her crocheting and has dinner waiting—meat loaf, mashed potatoes, and salad. She looks better, her eyes a little brighter. You and Daddy eat like you've never had a proper dinner in your lives, and Ma watches you both, satisfied.

On the way to your room, you see the thing Ma is making on the couch. More of it is done now. It looks like a small blanket. Ma wouldn't say the things she says about Leah and then knit the baby a blanket, would she? You think about your talk with Daddy today and how hard it is to really know anyone. You sit down at your desk and take out your notebook.

A Poem for My Dad

Sometimes I get mad
and think he doesn't know
how hard it is
to be me.
But then I wonder
if maybe it's harder
to be him.

You run your fingers over the paper, feeling the indents from the pencil. Four more days until Tuesday.

How to Not Wear Lipstick

"It might be better if we both wear some," Jane says to you on the bus in the morning. She coats her mouth with Revlon Cherries in the Snow and hands you the tube.

"I'll pass. But it looks good on you."

"But think of Wonder Woman. You like her. It will make you feel like a superhero. This shade is one of Elizabeth Taylor's favorites." She presses her lips together.

"Isn't your teacher going to make you wash it off?"

"Nah," she says. "Mr. Canfield would never notice. I promise it will make you feel different." She wiggles the tube at you.

"Oh, for crying out loud." You roll your eyes and take the tube. She also hands you her silver compact. You're slowly smoothing on the bright red shade when *boom*, the bus goes over a huge bump. The lipstick jumps upward and paints a line starting from your top lip up to your cheek.

"Now see what you made me do!" you say.

"I did not make you do that," Jane says and doubles over laughing.

"Do you have a tissue?"

Jane searches in her bag. "Gosh, I don't think so." She rips off a piece of notebook paper. "Try this," she says.

You wipe your face with the paper, but it just seems to spread it over a bigger area.

"What do I do?" you shriek. The big red smudge covers almost half of your face.

Jane licks her fingers and goes to wipe your face like your mother used to do.

"Ewww, gross!" you say and duck out of the way. "I'll do it myself."

"I was just trying to help," Jane says.

After several more tries and a little spit, you manage to get most of it off. But your face is still red from all the wiping. You both sit back and catch your breath. You wonder if Jane understands that this is not a game to you.

"I know you're trying to help, but this is beyond lipstick. I was angry at my sister for not writing me, but now I'm worried that if things stay like this for too long, they might get stuck that way."

Jane presses her small red lips together. The lipstick makes her look like a doll. "I'm sorry. I just thought it would get us ready, you know. Like when I put on a costume and makeup before a play."

"But we're not in a play," you say and feel an energy growing inside you, like the way you felt when you gave your presentation. "This isn't about being someone else. I think it's about all of us being more *us*."

"You sound like my mom," she says.

"Is that a good thing?" you ask.

"Yeah, I guess. But I still don't understand why your parents won't talk to Leah anymore. Is that what they're planning to do forever?"

You shake your head. "My parents told Leah they wouldn't talk to her anymore if she married Raj, because he isn't Jewish, and there's a part of me that understands why they've been so upset. But I don't think Raj not being Jewish is the only thing that bothers them."

"So what else is it?" asks Jane.

You remember when Raj came over for dinner and the way they looked at him when he walked in the door, the questions they asked him: they wanted to know where he was from and when he was going back. Did they ask him those questions because of how his name sounded to them, his accent, or the color of his skin? It seemed like all of those things.

"I think it's the Indian part, too, but my parents don't talk about that."

Jane blinks and listens. The bus stops too short at a stop sign, and you both get thrown forward a little bit, then pushed back in your seats.

"To make it more confusing, my dad told me they talked to our rabbi about it and are starting to feel like they've made a mistake. He also told me that my mom has been writing Leah all this time, but that the letters keep coming back. Now nobody knows where she is. They might not even be at NYU anymore."

"It really is like a Nancy Drew mystery," Jane says.

"It's a mystery, all right," you say and watch the houses go by, square green lawn after square green lawn. You wonder what Raj's house is like in Danbury. Does it have a square green lawn? Or did he live in an apartment like you do?

"Maybe if my parents met Raj's parents, they'd like each other, and then they could all be happy for Leah and Raj. The good feelings would drive the bad feelings away."

"'Hate cannot drive out hate; only love can do that,'" Jane says quietly.

"What did you say?"

"They aren't my words. I heard it from my mom. It's something Martin Luther King Jr. said."

"I like that," you say and think about love and the courage it gives people. "But I wonder if it's true."

"If what's true?" Jane says.

"That love can really drive out hate."

"Isn't that sort of why we're doing this?"

You shrug and rest your chin on top of your schoolbag. If love is what drives out hate, does it mean that you should try to love the people who hate you? It makes you think of Chris Heaton. He seems to hate you. Maybe hating him back isn't going to solve the problem, but you can't think of a universe where you could love someone like Chris. And even if you could, would it make a difference?

You don't think your parents hate Raj, but they seem to hate the choice Leah made. So what is the answer for that? You shake your head.

"I don't know. I just want my sister back," you say to Jane and turn toward the window again.

The morning goes by painfully slow. Miss Field checks the math homework, which you didn't do very well on, and then Chris Heaton cuts in front of you at the pencil sharpener. You glare at him, and he glares back at you. You want to break his pencil in half, but you think of Dr. King's words again.

After lunch, it's Chris's turn to do his current events presentation. It's about the war. He says his brother has been in Vietnam for six months and that thousands and thousands of people have died already in this war that has lasted many years. The war isn't being fought in this country, but it's affecting everyone around us.

"I'm worried that my brother will be one of those thousands. That he won't come home ever again," Chris continues. Then he stops, and his face gets red. The room is silent. He looks like he might cry.

"Thank you, Chris, for sharing something so personal,"

Miss Field says. "We can detach ourselves from these headlines, but they are affecting people in our community in very real ways. You've shown us that."

He quickly goes back to his seat, red-faced. You see other boys elbowing each other, smirking. Chris stares at his desk, his shoulders hunched over. For a moment, you feel bad for him. At least you know that your sister is not a soldier in Vietnam with guns and bombs everywhere.

Chris starts to doodle on a piece of paper. Then he raises his head and sees you. You give him a tiny smile.

"What are you staring at?" he growls and goes back to his scribbling. You quickly look away.

The bell rings, and you get swept up in the rush of kids pouring out the front doors. You wait for Jane by the big oak tree in front of the school. You smell a bit of something cold in the air, like mint. *Winter will be here soon,* you think and shiver.

A few minutes go by, and Jane still isn't there. You think about the plan. You're taking the train to Grand Central Station, and from there you'll take the number 6 subway to the NYU stop. Then you and Jane will find the business school building and give Raj's name. You'll tell them you're his sister-in-law and that there's a family emergency.

It's the truth. This whole thing has been one big family emergency.

You start to feel warm despite the chilly fall wind nipping at your face. A squirrel runs by with a nut. It looks at you and puts the nut down.

"Hi, little squirrel," you say. It blinks and twitches, then picks up the acorn in its mouth and runs toward the nearest tree. You think of how simple things are for the squirrel. An acorn—that's all the squirrel needs to be happy.

You finally see Jane in her gray coat, thick wool tights, and black loafers, bounding toward you in the determined way she walks.

"You scared me," you say. "I thought you weren't coming."

"I'm sorry. Mr. Canfield held me after class because I didn't do the math homework. I said my mother was picking me up for a doctor's appointment and that I had to go."

"What if he calls your mom to check?" you ask. If Mr.

Canfield calls Peggy to check on the doctor's appointment, Peggy might call the theater department to speak to Jane, and Jane wouldn't be there. Then Peggy would call Ma.

"That probably won't happen," Jane says, a sliver of doubt crossing her face.

"Oh boy, this is not good. I knew we shouldn't be doing this," you say and start walking backward, away from Jane. "I can't, I just can't. It's too risky."

Jane walks toward you, grabs your shoulders, and gives you a little shake. In a strange, grown-up lady voice, she says, "Ariel, pour yourself a drink, put on some lipstick, and pull yourself together."

"What?"

"It's something that Elizabeth Taylor said. The drinks can be colas. But this is our chance, and maybe our only chance for a while." She takes out her Revlon Cherries in the Snow and paints it on thick. Then she points the tube toward you.

You smile. You can't help it. "No thanks, you're wearing enough for both of us. But okay, let's go."

How to Be Forgettable

The station is right in the center of town. On the bus in the mornings, you see lots of men standing in their hats and dark suits with newspapers tucked under their arms, drinking coffee and waiting for the train to take them to their jobs in Manhattan.

You hardly ever see ladies waiting for the train in the mornings. Ma and Peggy are the only mothers you know who go off to work. Lots of other mothers, the moms who live in the big houses outside of town, don't go somewhere to work. Sometimes they come into the bakery wearing brightly colored cardigans and with expensive purses hanging from their arms. If Ma were one of those ladies instead of being behind the counter, would she act like a different person or would Ma just be Ma with a more expensive purse?

You step onto the platform. There are a few people waiting, but not many. It's not a commuting hour. Maybe you and Jane should have both dressed up older. The ticket seller looks at both of you a little funny but sells you the tickets.

The conductor, a short, grumpy-looking man, doesn't even give you a second glance as he clicks holes in your tickets and sticks a piece of paper on the top of the seat. Then suddenly there you both are, with your hands on your laps, feet flat on the floor, watching Connecticut fly by and turn into New York.

"When was the last time you were on a train?" Jane asks you.

"We went to see Leah. Her dance company got to perform at Lincoln Center."

"Wow, Lincoln Center," Jane says, all dreamy.

"It wasn't in the main part, just in a smaller studio."

"Still," Jane says.

After a while, the buildings grow taller and taller. You remember that day last spring. Daddy didn't want to drive, so you all took the train. Leah went earlier with her dance company for rehearsal, and you sat in a row of three with Ma and Daddy, you in between them, but you had wanted to sit by the window.

You usually went into the city once or twice a year. Ma liked for Daddy to drive, but Daddy loved the train. He said that trains were the most relaxing place he could think of. There was no car to drive, nothing to bake, nothing to clean, nothing to worry about. "All I have to do is sit back and enjoy the countryside," he said.

He took along one of his favorite snacks, a can of roasted peanuts, and Ma brought a thermos of hot coffee. You remember burning with jealousy that Leah was the reason your parents were on this train to Lincoln Center, sipping hot coffee, eating something that they didn't make with their own hands—that taking part in her life was special, a holiday.

You remember thinking that you could never create something like that for your parents. But now, as you and Jane ride on the train with only a tube of red lipstick between you, you think that maybe there are other things you can do. Daddy said you're the type to land on your feet. So maybe that's what you're helping your family do—land on their feet.

After an hour, the train lurches into 125th Street, and you watch some people get off.

"Ten minutes to Grand Central Station," announces the conductor.

You lean back, your stomach growling, wishing you had a can of peanuts.

When you arrive, you both follow the sea of people out of the train and toward the main station, your heart pounding as people zoom by. The sounds are so loud. It seems like a place where people could easily get lost. You'd always worried you'd get separated from your parents when you were in the city, and now here you are, separated. Jane grabs your hand, and you see the panic in her eyes. The large black clock in the center of the station stands ahead of you, calling you to it. You've seen this clock.

"Okay," you say. "I know where I am."

"There," Jane says, pointing. "The subway is that way." She pulls you toward the sign, and you follow, looking back at the clock for a second.

When you get down to the subway station, it feels even more crowded and chaotic than Grand Central. Jane leads you to the token booth as you clutch your twenty cents. Jane slides her coins and yours through the little slot at the ticket window.

"Two tokens, please. What stop is New York University?"

The man behind the window points straight behind you. "Number 6 downtown, Astor Place," he announces. You get your tokens and head to the turnstiles. Jane drops her token in the tiny slot, and you follow. Ma never wanted to take the subway. She said there was a lot of mishegas on the subway, that she heard about someone getting mugged, someone getting stabbed, but now you're on the other side, amid the mishegas.

After a few minutes, Jane and you find yourselves sitting on a crowded, bumpy subway car hurtling downtown. A man comes on the train at the next stop and tells everyone he has an announcement. He isn't a conductor. Jane glances at you, then back at the man. His clothes are frayed and worn. A dirty hat sits on his long, tangled hair. Your back stiffens. Jane moves closer to you.

"My life has been hard, and I need help," he says. "But I'm not begging for your money. I'm offering you the only thing I have. My voice." He clears his throat, then clears it again.

"I think he's going to sing," Jane whispers to you.

"Oh," you say, relief washing over you as you look back at the man. He takes in a deep breath and sings "You Are My Sunshine," smooth and slow. The sound of his voice blankets the car. Your mother used to sing the same lullaby to you when you were little. You think of coming out of a bubble bath, dressing in a soft yellow nightgown, holding tight to your old teddy bear you named "Doggie" because you thought all animals were called dogs. Ma would sing the song as she tucked you in, and you knew, even as a little girl, that this was love and you were lucky.

You gaze at all the different kinds of people on the train: a woman wearing white gloves holding her white purse, a few men in business suits, a construction worker, some teenagers dressed in bell-bottoms and T-shirts, a sleepy-looking old man, a lady in red pants, a man in a black leather jacket . . . it went on and on. People of all ages and skin colors. You aren't that far away from Connecticut, but it feels as if you've traveled to another universe.

The car screeches to a stop. The man ends his song and holds out his hat, asking for money.

"Come on," Jane says, grabbing your arm. "It's Astor

Place." As you get up, you dig into your pocket and find two nickels. You think about giving him the money, but then suddenly feel afraid. You hear your mother's voice telling you not to talk to strangers. Before you can make a decision, the doors snap shut and you're hit with a sting of shame. You don't even have the courage to give a down-and-out fellow two nickels on the subway; how are you going to make your way through the city to find your sister? Fear starts to spread as Jane pulls you toward the stairs and up into the street.

Outside, you both look for NYU campus signs. It's different than you imagined. Where was the grassy square, the old school buildings surrounding it, students in smart outfits clutching books to their chests? All you see is city and more city, people pushing past you, rushing, rushing, rushing. You see young women in short miniskirts and tall boots. You see men in dungarees, hanging in front of shop windows, smoking and staring. You hold Jane's arm tighter.

"There," she says and points. You look up and see a white-and-purple sign. It cuts through your fear and feels like a signal, a beacon. "We can go in that building and ask where the business school is. That's where Raj is, right? The business school?"

"I think so," you say.

You head over to the building and stand in front of the large wooden doors. You look in the window and see a woman at a desk in the lobby. Jane tries the doors. They're locked. She starts knocking. Then she sees a bell and rings it.

"No," you say. "Don't."

"We only have a few hours before we have to get back. We need to talk to as many people as we can."

"But—" you say.

"Listen," Jane interrupts. "You brought me into this. You said you wanted my Nancy Drew expertise. How do you think Nancy finds her clues? She's not afraid to ask questions."

But you and Jane are no Nancy Drew with her sophisticated outfits, far-out cars, and never-ending confidence. Jane is right, though. You are risking a lot to be here, and Jane isn't afraid to ask questions even if you are.

"Okay," you say and start knocking on the door, hard. The woman looks up and lowers her glasses.

Jane waves in the window. "Could you let us in for a moment?" she yells.

The woman frowns and gets up. You wait for a minute, and the door opens.

"Hello," Jane says, her cheeks flushed from the cold. "We need to find a student at the business school. Where is that building?"

"Who are you looking for?"

Jane looks at you.

"Um, my brother-in-law," you say and stand a little straighter. It feels strange to say it. "There's some important family news, and we haven't been able to reach him."

"Try the Welcome Center. It's a few blocks down the street," the woman says and explains how to get there. Then she turns to file a stack of papers in the drawers behind her.

You yell out a thank-you and run around the corner and down a few blocks.

"I think it's here," Jane says, pointing to a brick building. Your heart is pounding so hard, you can feel it in your throat. What would you say to Raj if you saw him? Would he recognize you?

Jane tries the door. This time it opens. There's another woman sitting at the desk in the lobby.

"Hi," Jane says as you hang back. The woman, who is typing on what you recognize as an IBM Selectric typewriter, the same one Miss Field has in the classroom, stops and looks up.

"Can I help you?" she says in a stiff voice.

"We're looking for a student at the business school. Her brother-in-law," Jane says, pointing at you. "We haven't been able to reach him, and we have important family news. Can you let us know what classes he's in or what his address or phone number is?"

"A student in the graduate school of business? I can leave a message for him, but I can't give out his personal information."

"But we're family," Jane says, and you look at her funny. "And it's an emergency!"

The woman frowns, clearly not impressed by the word *emergency*.

"I'm sorry, but that information is confidential. Do you want to leave a message here for him? That's all I can do."

Jane looks at you. What do you say in a message to Raj?

Hi, it's Ariel. Just lied to my parents and came to NYU to find you and my long-lost sister. Call me!

"Anyway, if you want to find him, the graduate school is farther downtown, in the Wall Street area. Here's a map. I would take a taxi."

This information hits you like a brick. There isn't enough time. You had no idea the buildings would be so far apart. Your stomach feels hollow. You're cold. Your bottom lip trembles, and Jane puts a hand on your shoulder. You don't even have enough money for a taxi.

"Are you sure there are no business classes around here?" Jane asks, looking around.

"Not for the graduate school," the woman says. Then she lowers her glasses and peers over them. "Aren't you girls a little young to be wandering around all by yourselves?"

"We're older than we look," Jane replies and stands tall, her hands on her hips.

You pull on Jane's arm. "Let's go," you say and feel the eyes of the woman with her glasses still lowered watching your backs as you leave.

The wind whips around, making you both squint and turn in the other direction. People start pushing past you as you both move over and stand against the wall of the building. You feel the tears coming.

"This was a big mistake," you cry out. "How were we supposed to know the business school wasn't around here? It said the campus was near the Astor Place subway stop." You and Jane had gone to the library and mapped it all out. A lot of good that did.

You start walking toward the direction you came. You walk as fast as you can, not even checking to see if Jane is following you. A few blocks go by. You see a big stone arch near a park and keep going. You just need to put one foot in front of the other.

"Ariel," Jane calls after you, but you keep walking, the cold air in your face, your feet hurting. You don't care about anything right now, not even how much trouble you're probably going to get in when you get home.

"Ariel!" Jane yells again. "Wait up!"

You want to walk all the way to Grand Central and go home. If Leah and Raj want to disappear, if you're that forgettable to Leah, then you might as well forget all about her. She can see how it feels to be forgettable, too.

How to Break the World Open

You know Jane is behind you, but you keep walking. Her loafers slap on the sidewalk, and you walk just fast enough to be ahead. You want to be alone, but you don't. Finally, she catches up to you and grabs your arm.

"Just stop for a second. Please." She's breathing hard. You're not angry at her, just angry that you thought you had the power to change things. You're just a silly little kid. It seems like everyone's fighting to change things all around you, trying to make the world better. Protests, riots, war. People are fighting for peace, equal rights, freedom. You remember something Mildred Loving said: "We may lose the small battles but win the big war." But what if you lose both? What if nothing actually changes, no matter how hard you fight?

You stop and face Jane.

"We can try again. Do more research," she says.

"I don't think we'll get a second chance. It's already late. We're going to be in heaps of trouble when we get home. I've just got to let it go. I've got to let her go," you say as the tears sting your cold cheeks.

"Aww, don't cry, Ari. Let's just get something to eat. I'm starving. I can't think when I'm starving. There's a pretzel cart."

You let her lead you to the cart, because you're out of ideas. Jane asks for a pretzel and a soda. She gives the man a quarter, and he hands her back a huge pretzel wrapped in wax paper and a glass bottle of cola. Jane breaks off a large piece of pretzel and hands it to you. It's warm and soft with bits of salt on the top. You've seen pretzel carts in Manhattan before, but Daddy never wants to buy them, no matter how much you beg. He says he can bake better pretzels at home and passes around his peanuts.

You both stand on the street, passing the pretzel and the soda back and forth. For a moment, the wind dies down, and the food and drink soothe you. After you finish, you throw away the paper. Jane tosses the bottle.

"We have to go, Jane."

"I know, I know," she says, wiping her mouth. "We have

just enough for two more tokens. Let's take the subway back. It's freezing."

You nod and brace yourself against the wind that has started up again. One foot in front of the other, that's all you can do as you head back to Astor Place.

You still walk a little ahead of Jane, not completely sure of where you are. You want to ask someone where the subway stop is, but no one looks too friendly. You get the map out of your pocket, and as you're unfolding it, you hear your name. You think it's Jane, and you ignore it. Then you hear it again. This time you realize it's not Jane.

"Ariel?" you hear again and look up. Some lady is standing right in front of you, a lady who looks a lot like your sister.

You stare hard.

"Ariel, is that really you?" she says in a high-pitched voice.

You blink. You don't believe it. You never actually thought you'd find her, but you wanted to be able to tell her someday that you'd tried. It is your sister, but she looks different, older. She's wearing a brown coat over a dark green dress, and black low-heeled shoes. The coat is open, and her large belly is visible, but if she had closed her coat, you might not have noticed. Her face is full and rosy. She drops the two grocery bags she's holding. Then she grabs your shoulders and bends down a little. She's still taller than you, but not as much as she used to be. You've grown in only a few months.

"I feel like I'm imagining things. How are you here? Why are you here? Are Ma and Daddy with you?"

You're still not ready to speak. Jane cautiously steps forward and stands next to you.

"Jane!" Leah says. "You're here, too? Did you come in for a show? A school trip? I'm so confused."

No, you shake your head and keep shaking it. But the tears that were already in your eyes fall and fall.

"Oh, Ari," Leah says and hugs you hard. It's strange hugging her with her different body. Her baby will be your niece or nephew. You'll be an aunt. You can't believe it, any of it.

After Leah releases you, you see she's crying, too. With Jane's help, you sputter out the whole story. You tell her about the contract for the bakery, about Ma's migraines and vertigo, about having to move, about why that made you come here today to try to find her.

"I couldn't do it alone anymore," you say.

She hugs you again. You can feel her body shaking.

"I never meant for it to happen like this," she says in a thin voice. She pulls her body back, still holding on to your arms. "But why didn't you write me back?"

"Write you back?" you say, staring at her. "But you never wrote *me*."

"Ari, I wrote you so many letters, but then I stopped trying since I never heard back. I figured you were just too angry at me."

"You did? You wrote me letters?" The sidewalk feels a little tilted as you take in what she's saying to you. "I tried writing you. I didn't know your address."

"Ma finally wrote me back, but then we moved. I was angry, so I haven't written her since. We were in student housing farther downtown, but then we found this apartment that's cheaper. It's only a short commute for Raj. I was going to visit after the baby comes. I thought once Ma and Daddy saw their grandchild, they wouldn't be able to turn us away."

"You really wrote me?" you say again, wondering if you heard wrong. "Where did the letters go?"

"Something tells me you might have to ask Ma about that," Leah says, her face changing, becoming hard. Then she picks up her grocery bags and waves you toward her. "Come, it's chilly. Our apartment is a few blocks from here. You can call Ma and Daddy. Jane, you can call your mom, tell her you're safe," she says, ushering you down the block.

You and Jane follow your sister down the busy city blocks. You all walk silently, weaving through the people, still not believing how quickly everything changed a few months ago and was now changing again just as fast. While you walk, you think of part of a poem.

> The world breaks open
> and suddenly you see
> your sister as a mother
> and your mother
> as a person

You hope you'll remember it later.

How to Be In Between

"Here we are," Leah says, putting her key in a heavy metal door. To the left, in a dark hallway, is a row of metal mailboxes with numbers on them. Ahead is a black stairwell. You have to walk up four flights of stairs to get to Leah and Raj's apartment. By the time you reach the fourth floor, Leah is breathing hard.

"Why didn't you give me the bags?" You can't believe you let your pregnant sister walk up all those stairs with groceries.

"It's okay, I'm used to it, though Raj usually brings them up. His exams are soon, so I was trying to let him study."

You wonder if Leah wishes she were in school, too. What has she been doing all day? Probably not playing tennis and preparing for dinner parties like some of the moms who live in the big houses in Eastbrook.

There are only three doors in the hallway. Leah goes to

the one in the back. Before she walks in, she takes off her shoes and lines them up against the wall, next to a pair of men's loafers. You both follow her lead and take off your shoes. She opens the door and lets you and Jane in first. The apartment is small, but there's a big window ahead of you, letting in the light.

Raj is there, sitting at a little round table in a small kitchen area, with papers all around him. Against the wall to the right there's a couch with a coffee table. To the left is an alcove with a bed covered in a blue spread. A printed tapestry hangs on the wall over the couch. That's it. Raj looks up.

"Oh!" he says, startled. He stands and starts straightening the papers on the table. "Leah, you didn't tell me your sister was coming."

He smooths his hair to the side. He's wearing a white undershirt, pants, and brown sandals. You've never seen a man wear sandals.

"I didn't know myself," she says and drops the two bags of groceries on the counter by the stove and sink, and starts to put things away. Raj just stands there. You and Jane stand there. Jane's eyes are about to pop out of her head.

"Wow, Leah," she says. "Your own apartment in Greenwich Village. It's very bohemian. Or wait, are you guys hippies now?"

Leah laughs. "Is that what you think?"

"I have no idea what to think," Jane says and plops down on the couch. You feel a hum throughout your body, but you don't know whether it's from being upset or happy. You are so much of both things right now.

"You call Ma. I'm not ready to talk to her yet," Leah says and points to the big black phone hanging on the wall near the refrigerator. "We just got it connected. Before that, we had to use the pay phone down the street."

That's why they weren't listed. You glance at the phone. You aren't ready, either. You sit down next to Jane and look at her with pleading eyes.

"I'll call my mom first," she says and hops off the couch. Leah comes over and sits down next to you. Is this really Leah's new life you've suddenly walked into?

You cautiously turn to her. "Are you happy, Leah?" you ask her.

She smiles and looks at Raj. "We're happy together, but

we don't want to bring a baby into a family that's split apart."

"Can someone please tell me what's going on here?" Raj says, rubbing his hands through his hair again, worry in his eyes.

You want to answer Raj, but you don't know where to begin.

"I'm in the city," Jane says into the phone. "With Ariel. I know, Mom. I'm sorry. I know!" she says and rolls her eyes.

You put your cold hands on either side of your face and stare at Jane.

"Ari," Leah says and puts her hand on your back.

"Just tell Ari's parents we're with her sister," Jane practically yells to Peggy on the phone. "We're fine, I promise. They shouldn't worry." Then she pauses, listening for a moment. "Okay, but you don't under—" More listening.

"Let me," Leah says. She hoists herself up and takes the phone from Jane.

"Hi, Peggy, it's Leah. Yes, the girls are with me. I know. It's a really long story, but I think they were trying to help. Of course. We'll be calling my parents next, but if you talk to them, tell them everything's okay. We'll make sure the girls get home safe."

She tells Peggy her phone number before hanging up.

"Do Ma and Daddy have your phone number? Have you talked to them at all?" I ask after Leah hangs up.

Raj holds up a hand. "I'm sorry to interrupt again, but I'm really not clear on what exactly is happening here. How did they find us? Leah, did you give your parents the address? I thought you said you wanted to wait."

Leah takes a deep breath. You still don't understand why she didn't give Ma and Daddy their new address.

"You'd better sit down," she says to Raj. He sits back at the table, and she sits down in a chair opposite from him. You and Jane huddle together on the couch. Leah tells him about the bakery being sold, about Ma going to the hospital, about needing to move. She tells him about how you and Jane tried to track him down at NYU to find them and that she saw us a few blocks away while she was out for groceries.

"Wow," he says, leaning back in his chair, then picking up a pencil and pressing the eraser to his lips. "Wow," he says again.

"But, Leah," you say. "It's like you didn't want us to ever find you again."

"No," Leah says and leans forward. "That's not what I wanted at all. Do you know how many letters I sent? I asked to come and visit. They told me I couldn't bring Raj. That wasn't okay with me, and still I wrote. I called. They hung up on me. Both of them, two different times."

You swallow. "I don't want to believe they did that," you manage to squeak out. It makes you feel again like your parents aren't who you thought they were. But then you think of how hard this has been on Ma. You think of Daddy on Rosh Hashanah wondering if they made a mistake. You think of them talking to Rabbi Ackerman and trying to find Leah. Can people be good and bad at the same time?

"They did," Leah says. Your sister looks older to you, but still so young. "Ma wrote me one letter back, finally," she continues. "Her last letter to me before I moved. We've only been in this new place for a month. I told you I was planning to visit after the baby comes, Ari. I wasn't just going to disappear forever, but I needed them to know what they could lose. You didn't deserve any of this heartache, however. I can't tell you how sorry I am for that."

There's a part of you that feels a spark of anger at both Leah and Raj. You want to tell Leah that she's right, that you didn't deserve it, that she should have made sure somehow that you knew they hadn't disappeared. But you look at her face, and you see a pleading in her eyes. She's asking you to forgive her.

Leah gets up and goes over to a small white nightstand beside the bed. The bed makes you feel shy—the thought of Leah and Raj sharing it. She opens the drawer in front and takes out an envelope, carefully removes the letter, and hands it to you.

"Maybe it's better if you just read it," she says and goes back to the kitchen area. The folds in the letter are deep from being opened and closed many times.

"Should we start dinner?" Raj asks her.

"Make extra," she says, smiling and reaching for his hand. He takes it, and they look at each other in that way that makes you feel as if you shouldn't be watching.

You unfold the letter and start to read.

Dear Leah,

First I want to tell you that I love you. I will
always love you. Always know that in your heart,
wherever your life takes you.

You stop. This isn't what you expected to read. You take
a breath and keep going.

You may not understand why we have done
what we've done. We were trying to stop you
from making a mistake. Now you are married to
a foreigner, an Indian man, a non-Jew. This is not
what we hoped for.

I never told you this, but once when you
were young, maybe seven, and Ari was just a
baby, someone painted swastikas on the bakery
windows at night. It made the local news. I was
afraid to go to work the next day. My hands
shook for a week. But your father said we should
clean the windows and continue with business as

usual. He said we needed to show that we weren't afraid. So we did, but I was very afraid.

At the time, I regretted leaving Brooklyn for Eastbrook, but it was your father's dream to own a bakery, and we could afford the space and send our kids to good schools. We wanted a better life for you and Ariel. We also wanted you to go to college and marry educated Jewish men, raise Jewish children, and continue to thrive as Jews. To me, that is also showing those who hate us that we aren't afraid. Can you understand how important that is?

Eastbrook, by the way, rallied in support of us, and the bakery did better than ever for a while. But things like this, Leah, you never forget. I wish I had communicated that more to you. I wish you knew what you sacrificed when you didn't marry someone Jewish—and on top of that, a colored man from another country. I fear for the uphill battle I'm sure you both will face as a couple. Marriage is hard enough.

I'm sure he's a good man or you wouldn't love him, but how can your father and I support this decision?

My parents suffered so that I would suffer less. We did the same, but now you will suffer more. I can't bear it. It breaks my heart. I'm sorry. You can still divorce. We are in modern times. We will help you raise your child. You might have another chance at marriage. Please don't contact us unless this is your choice.

Your mother,

Sylvia

You finish the letter and lay it carefully in your lap. The smell of the onions Raj is chopping stings your nose. You're more confused than ever. You understand a part of what your mother wants—the part about wanting to show the people who hate you that you aren't afraid. But Leah and Raj are also showing people that they aren't afraid. Didn't the Lovings do that, too?

Raj has turned from the kitchen counter, where he was

chopping onions. "Ariel, what did you think of the letter?" he says, surprising you.

"Raj, don't," Leah says.

"What?" he says.

"It's not fair to put her on the spot. She's not my parents."

"I can't ask her a question?"

Their faces look tense, and you see something between them: anger. You remember hearing Leah on the phone before she left, the argument they had. You wonder how hard it has really been for them. Not even a year ago, Leah was living at home, going to high school, and now she's living with her husband in New York City, about to have a baby.

Raj looks away from Leah and back at you. "I don't mean to put you on the spot, Ariel. I'm just interested in knowing what you think," he says. "About us."

His voice is calm. His face doesn't seem upset. The anger between them passes.

"It's okay," you say. Leah is watching you carefully. "I want you to be together, but I miss my sister. I don't want it to be like this forever. Are your parents, um, against your marriage, too?"

"They aren't happy about it," he says, going back to chopping. "But they talk to me. We've visited them a few times. They've come here once. But they're disappointed and worried."

"So do you hate my parents for what they've done?" I ask.

"Ari," Leah says.

Raj heats some oil in a pan and throws the onions in. The sizzle reminds you of Ma cooking in your kitchen.

"She came all the way here, Leah, to find us, to talk to us. She should know our feelings," Raj says to Leah.

You watch Leah's shoulders drop, and she relaxes a little bit.

"To your parents I'm simply an Indian immigrant, a foreigner. Your parents' views don't surprise me, but I know this hasn't been easy for them. My parents' views don't surprise me, either. They wanted me to marry a Hindu girl. They had lots of choices lined up for me. But Leah and I love each other, and there's nothing we can do about that. It's sad that we can't come together, because we all know what prejudice feels like."

He stops talking for a few seconds. The onions make little popping sounds in the pan.

"And no," he continues. "Of course I don't hate your parents. I understand that their feelings are complicated, but so are ours. I hope they don't hate me, either. But Leah and I decided that we needed to be true to ourselves no matter what."

His words hang in the air. *We needed to be true to ourselves no matter what.* No matter if everything stayed broken forever? Was anything worth that? Maybe if you ever fall in love, you'll understand.

"It's just so much," Jane says. And then she puts her face in her hands and starts crying.

"Jane?" you ask gently. "Why in the world are you crying?"

"I don't even know. Sometimes it feels like I'm the only kid without a dad in Eastbrook, like my mom and I are outsiders. But this, what you guys are going through"—she circles her finger around in the air—"sure is tough." You put your arm around her shoulder. Raj brings her a tissue. She blows her nose in it, loudly.

You think about how many ways there are to feel outside of things, and settle back on the couch with Jane on one side of you and Leah on the other while Raj cooks dinner. There's too much to think about, and your brain feels like jelly. Raj stops stirring for a moment and goes over to the little black turntable in the corner. He puts down a 45 and goes back to his post by the stove as music fills the room.

You look around this little apartment in Greenwich Village. Different sounds drift in through the window: honking, sirens, things you never hear much of in East-brook. There is Raj, a man in sandals, cooking dinner. Leah, your sister, has a baby growing inside her. There's your best friend, Jane, with her red lipstick still on. A part of you doesn't even know where you are.

You've heard the song before, "Respect," by Aretha Franklin. It plays on the radio all the time. The music thumps, and her powerful voice hits your ears. Raj starts moving to the beat a little as he adds some spices to the pan with the onions, then chopped tomatoes, a can of chickpeas, and a bunch of shredded spinach. Rice boils in a pot. The warm scent is different than what your nose is used to. You've never smelled spices like these. Your mother mostly sticks to salt and pepper.

"You should call Ma," Leah says, and you nod. You

will in a minute, but suddenly all the confusing thoughts that have been swirling around for so long stop. Maybe it's the music. Maybe it's because you can feel the side of your sister's soft arm pressing against yours, or Jane's on the other side. Maybe it's the delicious smell of the food Raj is cooking for all of you, but for a moment, you feel something light and easy, something like joy.

How to Know When This Part's Over

Just before you all eat, you call Ma. The moment you say "Hi, Mom, it's Ariel," she starts yelling at you. She calls you untrustworthy. She grounds you for the rest of the year. She yells the whole story to you, and you hold the phone away from your ear. Jane and Leah both hover around you, listening, because they can hear her just fine as she hollers through the receiver.

She says that Peggy called and asked if Jane was there, because the director called Peggy when Jane didn't show up. Daddy told her you said you were doing tech for the play, but of course the director said you weren't there, either, and hadn't signed up for tech. Then all three parents drove around town, trying to find you and Jane. After that, they went back to their apartments and waited by the phone.

"My head is about to explode!" Ma says. "Are my daughters trying to kill me? Would it be easier for both of you if I just dropped dead?"

You start crying. "Ma, I'm so sorry I worried you. But I'm not sorry for finding Leah. I will never be sorry for that." Ma is suddenly quiet.

Leah takes the phone from you and only says one thing to Ma. "I'm bringing Ariel and Jane home tonight. With Raj. There is nothing you can do to stop me." Then she hangs up, and Ma doesn't call back.

After the phone call, you all try to calm down and eat the meal Raj has made. He calls it chana saag, which in Hindi means chickpeas with greens. He spoons it over a mound of soft, fluffy rice, and maybe it's because you're starving, but it's one of the best things you've ever tasted. Then you leave the apartment, and Raj gets a taxi to Grand Central.

You don't have time to get tickets at the booth, and you all run to make the train. It's crowded. You find a three-seater and a seat across the aisle for Raj. The conductor comes around and asks for money. Raj quickly takes out his wallet. "Four one-way tickets, please. I'm paying for them, too," he explains, pointing at Leah, you, and Jane.

The conductor looks at Raj and then at you, Jane, and Leah. "Miss, do you know this man? He says he wants to pay for all of you?" he says to Leah.

"Of course I know him," Leah says. "He's my husband." You notice several people on the train turn and look. The conductor gives you all the once-over again. You suck in your breath. It seems as if he doesn't believe her.

"If you say so," he says without a smile and walks off, shaking his head.

You watch Leah. She bites her lip. Raj reaches across and puts his hand on top of hers.

"Maybe he just said that because you look too young to be married," you offer.

"I don't think so," Leah says in a low voice.

"It's going to happen," he says. She leans her head back against the seat. You take her other hand, and she holds it for a long time.

When the train pulls up to the small platform in the center of Eastbrook, it's past ten. Leah gets up quickly, leading the way. She pauses on the platform for a moment, looking around.

"I'm home," she says quietly to herself. You and Jane follow Leah and Raj and walk the fifteen minutes to your apartment building. When you get to Jane's floor, she hugs Leah, Raj, and then you. "This was one of the best nights of my life," she whispers in your ear. "I know that sounds weird because our parents are mad at us and everything is kind of a mess, but it was just . . ." She stops, thinking. "So real, like we were all finally living our lives."

You know exactly what she means. Now you were people who did things, who *could* do things, real things, important things.

"Thanks, Jane. You're a good friend."

She pokes you gently on the shoulder. "A good friend or your best friend?" she asks.

Your heart lifts. "Best friend," you say. You already think of Jane that way, but it's the first time anyone has ever wanted to be yours. Jane smiles and nods.

She starts to open the heavy stairwell door that leads to her floor. "And remember, whenever you're not sure about things, just ask yourself: What would Elizabeth Taylor do?" she calls over her shoulder and then heads to her apartment.

Leah and Raj walk behind you for the next flight up. You turn when you get to your floor.

"Leah," you say.

"Yes?" she answers. Her face is pink, and a gleam of sweat shows on her forehead. You hope this isn't all too much for her and the baby.

"No matter what Ma and Daddy think, I support you and Raj. I don't want to ever be separated like that again, because I couldn't take it. Do you promise to never leave me?" You hold out your pinkie.

"I promise," she says and hooks her pinkie around yours.

"May I?" Raj says, holding out his pinkie.

You've never done a pinkie swear with a man before. You laugh nervously. "Okay. Sure." You hook your fingers together.

"There," Leah says. "The promise is fully sealed."

When you reach your apartment, Leah rings the bell. You hear footsteps coming toward the door, your parents' hushed voices saying something to each other, and then a pause. Leah makes a funny sound, sort of like a sigh, sort of like a little cry.

"It'll be okay," Raj says.

"How do you know?" Leah responds, but before Raj can reply, the door opens slowly. Daddy stands there with a strange look on his face, almost like he's embarrassed.

"Ari," he says, first looking at you. "You had us so worried."

You take a step inside. "I know, Daddy. I'm really sorry," you say, but he isn't listening anymore. Ma is standing by the kitchen, her hand on the counter as if it's holding her up. Ma and Daddy both look at Leah. Leah holds Raj's hand tight, and they stay in the hallway, waiting. Daddy is waiting. Ma is waiting, too. It starts to make you feel small and invisible. But that's not who you want to be anymore. That's not what you feel inside.

"Aren't you going to invite them in?" you say. All four of them look at you. "Because this is your chance," you continue, looking at your parents. "To change things."

Daddy looks surprised but walks toward Leah. She takes a step toward him. You watch Ma. She's still gripping the counter. Leah lets go of Raj's hand and walks a little closer. Then Daddy leans in and hugs her for a long time. You turn, and Ma has left the counter. She's left the room. You blink just to be sure you're not imagining the empty space she was just standing in.

"Ma?" Leah says, releasing Daddy.

"Maybe she needs more time," Daddy says.

Leah doesn't say anything. Raj takes her hand again and leads her to the couch so she can sit down. You sit down on the other side of her. All this time, you wanted to believe that if Ma could just see Leah again, it would fix everything. But sometimes things don't get fixed. They stay broken no matter what anyone does or how much love there is.

Then Ma comes out of her room. She's holding the finished yellow-and-white blanket she's been crocheting. She walks toward all of you on the couch. You and Raj stand up, leaving Leah sitting there, watching Ma. You both move away and let her sit down next to Leah.

"I made this for the baby," Ma says, handing her the blanket. Leah takes it, runs her hands over it. Ma is also holding a piece of paper. "I wrote that last letter before I was in the hospital. Did Ari tell you I went to the hospital?" she asks.

Leah nods. "She did."

"When I went to the hospital, I was so dizzy and in pain. I couldn't stand up. I couldn't speak. I thought I was having a stroke. Not knowing if I'd see the light of day or ever see your face again made me really think. I wrote this letter a few weeks ago. I just didn't know where to send it."

Leah hugs the blanket to her. Then she takes the letter from Ma. "I'll read it later," she says.

"I've certainly had too much tsuris for one day," she says and quickly looks at Raj. She nods, and it's hard to tell what she means by it. You wonder if it's simply a yes, that she's saying *yes* now to all of it. Then she turns her eyes to you. "We'll talk more tomorrow, Ariel," she says, her voice a little harder. Then she goes back to her bedroom. You reach out and touch the blanket sitting in Leah's lap. It's much softer than you thought it would be.

That night, you sleep on the couch. You haven't read the new letter Ma gave Leah, but the way Leah's face looked, the way she teared up on the couch after she read it, it seemed like a good thing. Raj and Leah are staying in your room and will head back to the city in the morning. A part of you is sad you don't get to sleep in the same room as Leah and finally see her actual self in the bed next to you. You've wished for it for so long.

But the apartment feels full, like the way it feels when you're having guests over and the refrigerator is stuffed with food. You lie in the dark, watching the unfamiliar shadows dance on the walls as the curtains move a little when the wind sneaks through the spaces in the window frames. A car drives by, casting new shadows. But you're not scared. You've never been less scared. Then you hear it, the low sounds of *Sgt. Pepper's Lonely Hearts Club Band* drifting from your room. Is Raj playing it for Leah? Are they remembering what last summer sounded like?

You get up and go over to the kitchen drawer and find a pencil and a small notepad. You start to write. It's hard with the dull pencil and a small piece of paper, but it doesn't matter.

The Yellow Baby Blanket

I knew what it was
and who it was for,
but I didn't let myself believe it.
Next time,
when I doubt myself,
I'll remember that blanket
and how soft
and real
it felt between my fingers.

You wake up to Leah's kiss on your forehead. The light is barely coming through the windows. It's early.

"We have to go. Raj has exams," she says. "But we'll be back soon, and I'll call you tonight."

"Wait," you say, blinking back sleep. "That's it? This part's over?"

Leah stands up. "This part?" she asks.

"You know, the you-being-gone part. And Ma-and-Daddy-pretending-you-aren't-with-Raj-and-that-you're-not-their-daughter-anymore part."

"Yes, I think it is," Leah says and gently touches your cheek before walking away.

Raj and Leah leave, and you get ready for school. Ma comes out of her room, her hair messy, her long silk robe on, no makeup. She's been doing that more lately, letting you see her undone. You used to think it meant she wasn't feeling well, but this morning you see it differently. Maybe it means she's caring more about her inside than her outside.

"Come," she says and pats the chair.

You go over. You don't know what to say to her. You want to shut your eyes tight and just get it over with, whatever punishment or words she's going to hurl your way.

"It's a lot, isn't it?" she says.

You nod cautiously.

"I made a mistake. Your father and I, we made a mistake with Leah."

You watch her hands. She plays with the thin gold wedding ring on her finger, turns it around and around.

"But, Ma, you fixed it, right?" The words come out of

your mouth rushed, worried that if you don't say them, they won't be true.

"No, Ariel. I think you did," she says.

You thought Ma was going to ground you until you turned eighteen. It makes you nervous, Ma saying nice things like this.

"I was livid yesterday," Ma continues. "But I can't stay mad, as much as you deserve it for scaring me like that. I don't know how you found her all by yourself. I took one look at Leah. Her baby," Ma says, her voice cracking. "And I thought about all the time I could have lost."

You don't believe it. Your mother is thanking *you* for something you did. Was it true? But then you remember the baby blanket, the poem you wrote last night.

"People think they have all the time in the world," she says and waves her hand outward.

"What do you mean?"

"I mean that everything counts, Ariel."

You want to ask Ma what happened to all the letters Leah sent you. You want to ask her where she hid them or whether she threw them away. But right now, in the quiet of the morning, you just want to sit with her and not fight. You study her face. Her blue-green eyes, her round cheeks, her small pink mouth, the loose curly hair she normally hides by hot-ironing and pressing into a bun. *A fighter*, Daddy called her. You never realized how much you look like her.

How to Take Responsibility

Months later, everything is different but also painfully the same. Raj and Leah are still in the city. Leah calls once a week, but it's mostly just you who talks to her. Things are still strained between her and Ma. Ma makes sure Leah's feeling okay, then she gives the phone to you.

Something also happened with the butchers who wanted to buy Gertie's. Daddy said the bank didn't approve their loan, but you don't really know what that means. It makes you hope that nothing is going to happen to Gertie's, but Ma and Daddy still say it is. It's just taking longer.

Today, there is another change. A substitute teacher sits at Miss Field's desk. He has on dark square glasses, brown pants, a white shirt, and a blue tie. He tells everyone to simmer down and writes his name on the board. *Mr. Carson,* it says.

"Miss Field is out. I'll be your substitute, and I expect you to be on your best behavior," he announces and then starts calling attendance. He sounds like a robot and messes up most people's names. After attendance, he writes *Multiplying Fractions* on the board. "Please open your math textbooks to page fifty-two."

Lisa Turner's hand shoots up.

"Mr. Carson?"

"Yes," Mr. Carson says.

"When will Miss Field be back?"

Lisa might be annoying, but she always asks the questions everyone wants to know.

"I'm not privy to that information," he says and starts writing on the chalkboard again.

"Mr. Carson," Lisa says again.

He turns around and sighs. "Yes," he says.

"Why is she out? Is she sick?"

"Again, I'm not privy to that information," he says and goes back to writing.

"Mr. Carson," Lisa says. "What does *privy* mean?" You suddenly admire her guts in a way you've never admired her before. Lisa's gift to the world.

"Young lady," he says. "*Privy* means having the knowledge of certain information, which I don't have. I will not be answering any more questions related to Miss Field. Now please turn your attention to your math textbooks."

Miss Field is probably just sick, but somehow you feel like this is your fault, Miss Field not being here. You spend the day trying to pay attention, but you can't. Every day, you've been eating lunch and typing out your poems with Miss Field in your classroom. Sometimes another teacher comes in and sees you and asks why you're in the classroom, typing. Miss Field just says, "Oh, Ariel's working on a special project."

You eye the lonely-looking Selectric sitting on its desk. There was a part of you that thought Leah being back would make all the other hard things fly away, but they're still here.

An aide stops into the classroom and gives Mr. Carson a note. He looks at it.

"Ariel Goldberg?" he asks.

You look up, surprised. "Yes," you say. Mr. Carson looks around, not knowing where the reply came from.

"Making trouble again, just like all you Jews do," Chris

Heaton whispers at his desk. You freeze. "And she's not here to protect you," he says.

You think about the fear that Ma and Daddy didn't want to show anyone after someone drew Nazi swastikas on the bakery windows. You will not show him your fear. "I can protect myself," you whisper back.

"Oooh, I'm scared," he says and wiggles his hands by the side of his face.

"Excuse me," Mr. Carson says, walking toward both of you. "Ariel?" he asks.

You nod.

"Here," he says and hands you a hall pass. "The principal wants to meet with you."

Your heart starts to beat faster. Chris has a smirk on his face.

"Go on," Mr. Carson says, and you clutch the pass as you walk toward the door.

"Yeah, go on," Chris says.

"One more word, young man, and you'll have a month's worth of detention," Mr. Carson says quickly, and Chris shrinks back. Maybe Mr. Carson isn't so bad.

You start to walk out, then turn. Mr. Carson is facing

the blackboard again, and Chris is watching you. You look at him and cross your wrists like Wonder Woman does when she blocks evildoers with her golden wristbands. *Take that,* you think. Chris looks at you, confused.

You walk down the quiet hallway, turn left, then right, and find yourself in front of the front-office lady, Mrs. Jones.

"Can I help you?" she says.

You hand her your hall pass. "I'm supposed to see Mr. Wilson?"

"Your name, dear," she says.

"Ariel Goldberg." There's a tremble to your voice. You've never actually spoken to Mr. Wilson. You've only seen him in the hallway, giving the thumbs-up to students, asking them for hall passes or telling them they have detention.

She picks up the phone and says your name.

"Go on in," she says and points to the door behind her. You walk around her desk and pull open the heavy door.

"Hello, Miss Goldberg, have a seat," Mr. Wilson says, leaning back in his chair and clasping his hands behind his head. You look at his desk, which has a bunch of

PEZ dispensers displayed on it. There's Popeye, Snoopy, a fireman, Mickey Mouse, Batman, Spider-Man, and Superman, but no Wonder Woman.

"So," Mr. Wilson says, breaking you out of your PEZ trance. "What can you tell me about Miss Field? I hear she's been helping you?"

You knew it. It is your fault. You wish your parents were here.

"Yes," you say slowly.

"With the typewriter?" he says, leaning closer.

You look down at your lap and notice a little stain on your navy pants, some dried milk from breakfast. You scratch at it and look back up. "Um, I guess so."

"Miss Field requested that you spend your lunches typing? Some of the other kids say you also do a lot of typing during class."

"Well, I," you say and swallow. "Maybe my parents should come in?"

"Ariel, you're not in trouble. We just want to know the facts. So is that true?"

"I did type during lunch. Typing is easier than handwriting for me. I was practicing. But I wanted to. She didn't make me."

"During lunch," he says. "The other kids type, too, during class?"

You nod.

"Thank you. I appreciate your help."

"Is Miss Field in trouble?" you ask. "Because she's helping me a lot."

"No one is in trouble. But teachers aren't supposed to request extra time with students without going through the proper procedures."

It sure sounds like she's in trouble. You both sit for a few seconds. Then Chris Heaton's words play in your ears.

"I also want to talk to you about something," you say, sitting up straighter.

"Okay," Mr. Wilson says, looking surprised.

"I'm being bullied by a classmate. He's always picking on me."

Mr. Wilson clasps his hands behind his head again. "Is there anything you've done to provoke him?"

"Something I've done?" you ask, pointing to yourself.

You wish you could be Wonder Woman right now and lasso Chris into this room, making him confess.

"Yes. I find that these conflicts are usually a two-way street."

"Oh," you say and think for a second. You should probably just leave. What made you think that telling the principal about Chris would do anything? But then you think about everything that's happened. You think about how brave Leah has been. And Raj.

You clear your throat. Then you look at Mr. Wilson. "There is something," you say.

He smiles. "I'm glad you're taking responsibility," he says. "So what do you think you're doing that's bothering him?"

"Being Jewish," you say with the straightest face you can. "That's what I'm doing to bother him."

How to Swallow a Bag of Rocks

That night, the phone rings after dinner as you help Ma clean up.

"No, that can't be true. Are you sure? How awful," Ma says and sits down, as pale as the white table. She puts her hand on her forehead.

"Sylvia," Daddy says. "Who is it?"

She puts her hand over the receiver. *Leah,* she mouths.

"Is it the baby?" he asks with a panic in his voice you've never heard.

Ma shakes her head. "Martin Luther King Jr. was shot," she says. "Leah just heard it on the radio."

After Ma hangs up, you all hurry over to the television and watch Walter Cronkite on the CBS evening news. He announces that Dr. Martin Luther King Jr. was assassinated that evening at his hotel in Tennessee and died in the hospital.

"This world is sick! Just sick!" Ma says, yelling at the television. She puts her hand over her mouth and shakes her head as she watches.

"What kind of person would want to kill him?" you say. It makes you feel as if you've swallowed a bag of rocks.

"First Kennedy, now Dr. King. Who's next? There are going to be more riots, I tell you. All over this whole farkakte country. And why shouldn't there be? This is pure evil. It's madness," Daddy says.

"Really, riots all over?" you say, your stomach twisting.

"Shush," Ma says to Daddy. "Don't frighten her."

You think of when Jane quoted Dr. King: *Hate cannot drive out hate; only love can do that.* Maybe there just isn't enough love. Maybe there never will be.

Daddy answers Ma in Yiddish, and then they go back and forth mostly in Yiddish, too. You can't tell if they're arguing with each other or the news, but there's no stopping them when they get like this. You don't know what to do, and you don't know how to feel, so you go into your room and take out a piece of paper. You grip the pen and stare at the paper, but no words come.

The next evening, Ma insists that you all go to Friday-night services, and before sundown, she lights the candles for Shabbos. She motions you over to stand with her and lets you light the first one. Then she lights two more and waves her hands over the light. You watch the way she waves the flames toward her, the way she puts her hands over her eyes and recites the blessing. You used to feel annoyed by how dramatic she looked when she did this, but it also made you ashamed because it didn't mean the same thing to you. Now you understand it doesn't matter anymore what it means to you, because you can see what it means to her.

At the service, Rabbi Ackerman talks about Dr. King and says he was a friend to the Jewish people and that we all must continue the fight for equality and justice together. He says Kaddish, the mourner's prayer, for Dr. King. People hang their heads. You've never seen so many grown-ups crying.

On the drive home, the news announcer on the car radio says riots are happening in many cities because of the assassination.

"What about New York City? Are Leah and Raj okay?" you ask. Daddy says there was some unrest in Harlem and Brooklyn last night and a big march today through Times Square, but things have quieted down.

"What are riots, exactly?" you ask your parents. That's the word you've been hearing on the news for a long time, that Black people are rioting.

Neither of your parents say anything at first. Then Daddy clears his throat.

"Well, people are very upset. They're angry."

"Who exactly is angry?" you ask.

"Well, Black people are angry."

"At white people, right?"

"Well, yes, but—" Daddy says.

"Because they aren't treated equally by white people?" you say.

"Yes," Daddy says. "And they're angry because Dr. King was trying to change things, and now he's been killed, and it's very tragic."

"So does that mean things won't change now?"

"Well, it's up to us to continue his message," Daddy says.

"His message of peacefully protesting. Nothing is solved by violence," Ma says.

"But what if we don't continue his message?" you ask.

"We will," Ma says. "Max, let's turn off the radio. I've had enough."

Daddy shuts off the radio, and you ride in quiet, but after a minute you have another question. "So is a riot when a protest gets violent? Like when people get so angry because nothing is changing and they don't know what else to do?"

"I suppose so," Daddy says.

"But why does the news always say riots? Why don't they say protests?"

"Please, Ariel! That's enough questions for one day," Ma says. "Things will be okay; let's just get home."

You bite your lip, feeling angry at Ma. Leah always said Ma liked things with clear answers, but nothing seems to have clear answers anymore. You think about the word *anger*. Then you think about the word *hate*. They seem like different things to you.

Back home in your apartment, the smell of stuffed cabbage and the sight of Daddy's challah and honey cake make you feel safe, but you know lots of people don't feel safe today.

The three of you sit down, and Daddy pours some wine for himself and Ma and gives you a little grape juice. He says kiddush and you all drink. Then he uncovers the challah and says another blessing. He passes the plate to you, and you twist off a golden-brown piece of challah and sink your teeth into the cakey bread.

With everything going on, you've put the sale of Gertie's in a faraway corner of your mind, but it comes rushing back as you taste the challah. "Daddy?" you ask, your mouth full.

"Finish first," he says.

You chew and swallow.

"Are you going to still make challah for us on Friday nights? After Gertie's closes?"

Ma looks at her lap. Daddy reaches out and tousles your hair.

"Sure, Ari," he says. "I'll try."

"When do the other people take over, again?"

"Hoping to close in three weeks, but they've moved the date twice already," Daddy says.

"Maybe it's a sign," you say.

"How do you mean?" Daddy asks.

"A sign telling you not to give up on your dream."

"Ari, darling," Ma says. "Let's try to have a nice dinner and not think about difficult things."

You cross your arms, feeling frustrated at Ma again, but before you can think of what else to say, the phone rings. Ma and Daddy stiffen. Normally Ma doesn't like to answer the phone during Shabbat dinner.

"It could be Leah," Daddy says. Ma nods. You hold your breath. *No more bad news*, you pray.

"Hello," Daddy answers. "No. No, thank you." He hangs up and sits down.

"Sales call," he says. Ma rolls her eyes.

You eat. You eat more challah. You eat the stuffed cabbage. You eat the mashed potatoes. Then the phone rings again.

"Leave it. They're just harassing us," Ma says. It rings ten times and stops. No one says a word. You take a sip of grape juice. Daddy has some more wine. Ma wipes her mouth and sighs. You look at her plate. She hasn't eaten much, only a few bites of potatoes.

"What if I worked more after school? What if you raised the prices or closed earlier? There must be more you can do," you say.

Daddy wipes his mouth and looks at you over his napkin. "I know the bakery has been a second home to you, but we don't want to be in debt forever. Maybe we'll own another bakery someday. A better one."

"A better one?" you ask. "There isn't a better Gertie's. Gertie's just is. Like me. Like Leah."

"Ariel, Gertie's isn't a person. It's just a shop," Daddy says.

"Not to me," you say and cross your arms.

Daddy starts to say something, but then the phone rings again, and rings and rings.

"Oh, I can't stand it," Ma says, but by the time she reaches the phone, it stops. "These salespeople, ruining our dinner like this. If they call again, I'm going to tell them a thing or two." She starts clearing the plates. The phone rings again, and Ma leaps on it in the middle of the first ring.

"You should be ashamed of yourselves, calling at this hour," she says. Then her face changes. She looks panicked.

"What? I'm sorry, I thought it was a sales call! Now?" she says. "Are you sure? Oy, let me get a pen. NYU Hospital."

You and Daddy stare at her. Ma mouths to you as she grabs a pen, *The baby's coming.*

After she gets off the phone, she moves so fast, you just stand there, holding your plate, frozen in place. She takes it from you and dumps the rest of the dishes in the sink. She wipes down the counter and the table. She covers the bowls of food with plastic wrap and sticks them in the fridge before you and Daddy even know what's going on.

Then she runs off to her bedroom and tells you and Daddy to be ready to leave for the hospital in five minutes. She comes back, hair in place, lipstick on, and grabs her purse.

"Let's go," she says.

"Maybe Ariel should stay with Jane," Daddy says. "The city could be dangerous."

You don't want to wait for them to come home, not knowing what's happening. You need to be there.

"I'm going with you."

They don't say anything at first.

"I don't know," Ma says.

"Leah needs me there. And you"—you point at your parents—"also need me there."

You don't wait for their response. You just get your coat, and they don't stop you.

In the car on the way to NYU Hospital, you stare out the window. As you're coming down the bridge onto the FDR Drive, there are police cars with lights flashing, stopping all the drivers. They ask Daddy to stop. He does, and a policeman comes to the window.

"What business do you have in the city, sir?"

Daddy tells him his daughter is in the hospital about to have a baby. The policeman hesitates. "There have been several disturbances. You're better off coming tomorrow."

Then Ma speaks. "Are there any disturbances by NYU Hospital?" she asks.

"I don't believe so, ma'am."

"Well, that settles it, then, because I'm not missing the birth of my first grandchild," she says. Daddy looks at her. "Sylvia," he says.

"Don't 'Sylvia' me," she says to Daddy.

"Ma'am," the cop starts to stay.

But Ma doesn't let him finish. "It's my daughter. We

have to be there. Please," she says and looks at him steadily in the eye.

The cop opens his mouth to speak, but then he stands back and waves you on. You feel a wave of relief, seeing how much Ma wants to be there for Leah, how much she loves her. Even though you're scared, this calms you.

"Will the baby call me Aunt Ariel?" you ask after a few minutes as the police lights disappear from view.

Your mother turns around. "Aunt Ariel?" she says. Then her face softens, and she looks sad. "Right, I guess so." She turns back to Daddy. "Oh, Max, she could have been at the American Ballet Theatre. She could have gone to Juilliard."

"You don't know any of that," Daddy says, keeping his eyes on the road.

"Well, now *I know* she won't be doing any of that," Ma says.

"Leah still has her whole life in front of her," Daddy says and pats Ma's leg.

Ma doesn't say anything for the rest of the ride. None of you do.

How to Have No Choice

Daddy parks in the garage of the hospital, and Ma speaks to the woman at the front desk. Before you know it, you're stepping off the elevator and heading into a waiting room, where Raj is standing, looking tired and very nervous. He's pacing and wringing his hands. Two other people are sitting near him. A woman is wearing a sweater over a long blue dress with an orange-and-gold pattern sewn in. The fabric wraps all around her. A man is wearing a tan sweater and pants. He's older and has a mustache, but he still looks a lot like Raj.

"Mr. and Mrs. Goldberg," Raj says quickly. "These are my parents, Mr. and Mrs. Jagwani." He forgets to introduce you.

Mr. and Mrs. Jagwani stand up. You move closer, then Daddy, then Ma. You watch as the four adults awkwardly shake hands, all staring at one another. After the hand shaking, Mrs. Jagwani sits down. Mr. Jagwani and Daddy follow. You, Ma, and Raj keep standing.

"How is she?" asks Ma after a few seconds.

"The contractions are two minutes apart," Raj says and clears his throat.

"I'm going in, room 403, right?" Ma says without waiting for the answer, and you follow her whether she wants you to or not. She walks ahead and goes into a room a few doors down on the right. You watch her go in, but you stand outside the door. You hear Leah say, "Ma!" Then a doctor's voice, speaking low. He walks out right past you. Then you hear Leah start to cry.

You peer through the door opening and watch. You think back to that first day Leah told you about Raj—back when everything seemed like a romantic movie.

Ma stands over Leah and holds her hand. Leah sits up in the hospital bed, looking pale and sweaty.

"I can't do it," Leah says, tears streaming down her face. She looks really young, sitting in the bed with a hospital robe on. "I really can't. I can't be a mother. I can't be a wife. You were right, Ma. It's going to be too hard. I've made a huge mistake."

"Listen to me," Ma says, pulling up a chair right next to her.

"Why should I? You abandoned me. I wasn't going to even tell you about the baby until after."

Ma starts to say something, but Leah turns away. Then her face screws up in pain. She starts breathing fast and moaning. Ma puts a hand on her shoulder.

"Because I'm here now. Just breathe through it. The doctor will be back and give you something for the pain. Count while you breathe. Follow me. Don't think about anything else." They breathe, and Ma counts, and Leah starts moaning some more, but then after a minute, she stops.

Ma wipes Leah's tears and places her hand on her forehead. Leah looks at Ma with wide, frightened eyes. She's shaking her head no. You wonder if you should be watching, but you can't turn away. You're frozen.

"Leah," Ma says in a firm voice. "Right now, you have no choice but to go forward. I promise you can do this. I was nineteen when I had you, and I wasn't half as brave as you are."

Leah's shoulders fall. She nods slowly. Then she sees

you peeking in. "Ari," she cries out. But before you can say anything, a doctor and a nurse come rushing into the room.

"Sorry, but you both need to leave. We'll take good care of her," the doctor says. "We're going to give her something for the pain. She'll be fine."

"Before you know it, you'll be holding your baby," Ma says to Leah, giving her hand an extra squeeze. "And then you'll decide what you think about everything." With that, she gets up and ushers you with her down the hallway. You look back for a second, but your sister is surrounded by the doctor and the nurse. You can't even see her face anymore.

Back in the waiting room, Raj is still pacing. Mr. Jagwani is reading the paper. Mrs. Jagwani sits quietly, looking down at her lap. Daddy sits a little farther away, looking off to the side, rubbing his chin like he does when he's nervous. Without even thinking about what you're doing, you go up to Mrs. Jagwani and hold out your hand.

"I'm Ariel," you say. "Nice to meet you."

Mrs. Jagwani looks up, startled. "Oh, yes. Nice to meet you," she says and shakes your hand lightly. She smiles a little and looks past you at Ma, who is standing behind you.

"Sorry, Ari, I should have introduced you. Ariel is Leah's sister," Raj says.

"I think we've figured that out," Mr. Jagwani says.

"How is Leah?" Mrs. Jagwani asks.

"The contractions are picking up, and they're giving her something for the pain. But everything seems on course," Ma says, and Mrs. Jagwani nods.

There's more silence. Finally, Mr. Jagwani speaks. "We know this marriage came as a shock to all of us."

"Pop," Raj says.

"No, no," Mr. Jagwani replies, waving him off. "It needs to be said. We can't just sit here and stare at each other all day long."

"Well," Ma says. "I have to agree."

"Why don't we all at least sit," Raj says and motions to the chairs in the waiting room. There are three other people sitting quietly on the other side of the room. You wonder what they think is happening, but no one seems to care.

Ma sits next to Daddy, across from the Jagwanis. You

sit on the other side of Daddy. Raj sits next to his parents.

You wonder what Leah would think of this. You wish you could be with her. Is she scared? Does the medication make her go to sleep? Can you have a baby if you're asleep? These are the questions you wish you could ask.

Mr. Jagwani leans forward. "We want to be honest," he says. "We were disappointed that Raj chose to marry a foreigner."

"Pop, are you sure this is a good idea? Maybe we can talk after the baby is born," Raj tries again.

Mr. Jagwani puts up his hand. "After the baby, this conversation might not happen."

Raj sits back in his seat, looking defeated.

"A foreigner?" Ma says. "With all due respect, Leah is not the foreigner."

Daddy rests a hand on Ma's leg. "Sylvia," he says quietly. She pushes his hand away.

Raj looks back and forth, a panicked expression on his face.

"With all due respect"—Mrs. Jagwani sits taller in her chair—"you are foreigners to us. And we are foreigners to you."

"True," Daddy says. Mrs. Jagwani nods, and Daddy continues, "And you seem like very nice people, but we hoped that Leah would marry within her religion. It has been a very difficult time for us."

"Don't you think we hoped for the same?" Mrs. Jagwani says. "But there is a baby now."

Then silence falls over the waiting room again. Ma crosses her legs. Daddy and Mr. Jagwani have their arms crossed over their chests. Raj has his hands on his knees like he's ready to jump up any second. Mrs. Jagwani touches the gold bracelets on her wrist, turns them around.

They don't know any more about what comes next than you do.

"So you have that in common," you say, using a cheerful tone. "You both wanted your kids to marry people more like themselves."

"Ariel, this is an adult discussion," Daddy says.

"She's right, though," Raj says and gives you a grateful look. "It's a place to start. At least you know what you're both feeling." He knits his eyebrows together when he says this, something you've seen him do before. You think of how he's starting to seem familiar to you, like an older brother, like family.

"Ma," you say carefully. "I heard what you just said to Leah—that right now we have no choice but to go forward."

Ma's serious face breaks open into a sad smile.

"Yes," she says. "I did say that."

Mrs. Jagwani sits back in her chair, and her face relaxes. Mr. Jagwani uncrosses his arms. You catch Raj's eye, and he also smiles.

Your parents and the Jagwanis sit quietly for another minute. Suddenly, Ma says it's been so chilly for April and Mrs. Jagwani says she's worried about her tulips and Daddy says he hopes this summer is cooler than last year, and they go back and forth like this until the conversation loses air like a punctured helium balloon. Finally, it seems there is nothing more anyone can do but wait.

You watch Raj's knee bounce up and down, up and down. Mr. and Mrs. Jagwani go get tea from the cafeteria and come back. Daddy buys peanuts from the vending machine and brings you a packet of M&M's. Ma sits silently, occasionally looking through her purse for no apparent reason. Finally, the doctor comes out.

"Well?" Ma says, jumping up out of her seat.

"It's a girl. Mom and baby are doing fine. Congratulations!"

That means you have a niece.

"A girl!" Ma says and puts her hand over her mouth. Daddy starts to cry, and seeing Daddy cry makes you cry. Mr. Jagwani quickly finds a handkerchief in his pocket and gives it to Daddy. Daddy takes it, dabs his eyes, then hands it to you. Mr. Jagwani squeezes Raj's shoulders before Mrs. Jagwani moves in and puts her hands on either side of Raj's cheeks, kissing him on his forehead. After Daddy composes himself, he goes over and pats Raj on the back. Ma comes over and takes Raj's hand in both of hers.

"Mazel tov," she says to him.

He nods and smiles at her. "Mazel tov to you."

Raj is a dad now and Leah's a mom and your parents are grandparents. It's like you've all jumped off a cliff together but have miraculously landed okay. You approach Raj, feeling a little light-headed. He holds out his hand for you to shake, but you hug him instead.

"Congratulations, Auntie," Raj says in your ear as he hugs you back.

Later, you get to see Leah in her hospital bed, holding her baby close. The baby is wrapped up like a little hot dog, only her face peeking through. Raj stands over both of them, proud and smiling. The baby's name is Geeta. Her Hebrew name will be Gitel. She's named after both her great-grandmothers, Gertrude and Gitali.

Leah's face is flushed and puffy. Her hair is matted, but her eyes looking down at the baby are filled with so much love, you can feel it fill the room. If there was any kind of love that could win over hate, it would look like Leah's face.

How to Read a Poem

When you enter your classroom, you're relieved to see Miss Field writing spelling words on the board when you come in. She was out all last week. She doesn't mention any reason why she was out, but the day goes along pretty normally at first, which is good. You need a big helping of normal.

But then you notice two strange things. First, the typewriter is gone. Also, Chris Heaton doesn't give you his usual glare. At one point, you drop your pencil case near his desk. You go to grab it, but he picks it up and hands it to you.

"Thanks," you mumble, but he doesn't say anything back. He doesn't look at you. Then, as school is letting out, Miss Field calls you to her desk.

"Ariel, Mr. Wilson wants to meet with us today after school. He called your parents in as well."

Your heart speeds up. "My parents? Did something bad happen?" you ask. You can't take in any more changes.

"No, no. Everything's okay. Sorry to spring this on you. I just found out myself," she says and takes in a deep breath. She leans forward in her chair.

"Sit down. I should explain a little before we go over."

You sit at the desk nearest to hers. Miss Field looks worried.

"I made a mistake, and I got into a bit of trouble."

"You got in trouble? Is this about the typewriter?" you say. You knew it. Mr. Wilson lied to you.

"Well, it's more than just the typewriter. I tried to help you on my own. I thought it would be less complicated that way. I didn't think your parents . . . Well, I wasn't sure how they felt about my understanding of your writing abilities. I just wanted to see if I could help you. It seemed simple at the time, but I shouldn't have done it that way. We're going to talk about that today with Mr. Wilson."

"Are you going to lose your job?" you ask.

"Mr. Wilson and your parents seem to understand I was only trying to help you. So no, but I'm lucky."

"Because that would be terrible," you say. "You have

helped me. You're the best teacher I've ever had."

Miss Field looks taken aback. Then her eyes get a little watery. You go over and hand her a tissue.

"Oh goodness," she says and quickly wipes her eyes.

"Don't be embarrassed. I cry all the time."

Miss Field laughs and wipes her nose. Then she turns serious again. "I'm sorry, it's just so nice of you to say that. But I also made another mistake," she says. "A worse mistake."

You feel scared again. Now you want to stop her from talking, just take the needle off the record.

"I didn't take you seriously enough with Chris. He's angry about a lot of things, but that's no excuse for him to treat you the way he does. He and his parents have met with Mr. Wilson. He will have two weeks of detention for the past incidents, and he knows he will be immediately suspended if anything else happens."

Two weeks of detention. The threat of suspension. Maybe you shouldn't have told Mr. Wilson.

"Because of me?"

"It's not because of you, it's because of him. It can't go on. And I'm sure other things have happened that I don't even know about, right?"

"Yes," you say. "But he's probably not a bad person. He just made a mistake. You said he's angry." You think of the way he talked about his brother in Vietnam. You have your sister back, but he doesn't have his brother back. He may never see his brother again.

There seem to be different kinds of anger: anger that somehow turns into hate, like Chris to you, and anger because of being hated for no reason, like you to Chris. Anger is what helped you stand up to Chris. So maybe anger can be good or bad, depending on what you do with it. But hate—that's something else. That doesn't seem to lead anywhere good.

"It's okay, Ariel. I don't think Chris is a bad person, but he needs to learn how to be better."

He did need to learn, but you're not sure detention or suspension will make him learn. It might just make him more hateful. You wonder what makes someone like Chris learn how to be better than they are? Is it love? And from who?

At the meeting, Ma listens to Miss Field about your writing and the typewriter and your poetry and all the things Miss Field was doing to help. Mr. Wilson and

Daddy listen, too. You also talk about Chris. Mr. Wilson says that Chris will have to write you an apology letter.

You wish you could say that you only want him to have to write the letter, not get detention. You also wish you could know if he's truly sorry and knows why his words were so wrong. That's what you care about. But you'll just have to see the letter.

Mr. Wilson says you're going to have some educational testing, too, to learn more about your disability and if it's what Miss Field thinks it is.

"I don't know about that," Ma says. "I don't want her to be in the slow class. Because they put me in there one year, and it was awful."

You all stare at Ma.

"Slow class?" you ask quietly. "What do you mean?"

"She isn't stupid, and neither was I," Ma says, crossing her arms. "I will take her right out of this school."

You feel like the whole room is spinning. "Ma," you say. "What do you mean *neither were you*?"

"I didn't have as much trouble writing as you do, but school wasn't that easy for me. Actually, math was the hardest. But spelling, too. And I never could pay attention.

There wasn't any talk of learning disabilities, extra help, and electric typewriters. There was just the 'slow class.' It's the same here. Don't you have a slow class?"

Miss Field looks at Mr. Wilson. He clears his throat. "No, that's not what we call any of our classes. We have a classroom for students who need extra support, but that's more than Ariel seems to need at this point."

"Well, that's where they put me in fourth grade. Then after that, I had to repeat the year. I was always teased about it. I don't want you treated that way."

"I'm sorry," Miss Field says gently. "I can understand why you might feel that way. But I think we can all agree that Ariel is intelligent and creative and should get the help she needs to do her best, as any child should, no matter how much support they might need," she says, looking at Ma. "Ariel's been working on some poetry. She's quite talented, and I've been seeing improvements in her writing in general. Typing also frees her up to think about her ideas instead of letter formation. Ariel, how would you feel about showing one of your poems to your parents?"

"Um, okay," you say. "But can I read it aloud?"

"Oh, absolutely!" Miss Field says. "It's your poem."

Just a few months ago, you thought you were supposed to be afraid of things like this. The truth is, that's not how you really feel. You want to read the poem. You want your parents to see what you can do.

In your notebook, you turn to a new one that even Miss Field hasn't seen.

A Poem for Baby Geeta

Does she know
about all that came
before her?
How could she?
She's just a baby,
with dark hair on her small head
that is as soft and as new
as spring grass.
But I know what happened.
I also see the sparkle in her tiny eyes
and how it could power the whole world.
All we have to do is love her.

When you're finished, a hush hangs over the room. You like this kind of quiet, a listening quiet. Daddy tears up and takes out his handkerchief. Ma nods and bites her lip.

"I didn't know you could write something like that," Ma says.

"It's really lovely, Ariel," Miss Field says. "If you want to try to get that poem published, I could help you send it out."

"Published, like in a book?" You can't hold back the wide grin that spreads across your face.

"I was thinking in a magazine," she says.

You nod. You don't think anyone will want to publish your poem, but just the fact that Miss Field thinks you should try is good enough. For now.

How to Be a Mensch

"Geeta's getting fussy. Want to take her on a walk with me?"

"Okay," you say and put down the cookie boxes you were folding. Ma turns the OPEN sign to CLOSED. The bakery now closes at five most days. It's only open late on Thursdays. Ma pokes her head out the door.

"It's a little chilly. Run up and get her blanket, would you? I'll tell Daddy we'll be back in a bit."

You nod and go up the back stairs. It's different living above Gertie's, and the apartment is smaller, but it's just you, Ma, and Daddy now. You kind of like it, being right in town and waking up to the smell of Daddy baking. At least you and Jane still meet at the bus every day, and you're only a few minutes down the road. Whenever the apartment feels too small, you just head to Jane's. Peggy says you have a permanent invitation to come over anytime.

Daddy decided to cancel the contract with the butchers, and Raj and Leah moved from the city to a cheaper apartment near the Eastbrook train station. It turns out that Raj can bake bread like nobody's business. He's even figured out a way to make Indian naan in the bakery ovens instead of a tandoor oven. He says it's not exactly the same, but it tastes good to you, and the customers seem to like it.

Raj's parents are helping them with the rent while Raj is still in school, so Raj works at the bakery a few mornings a week and takes the train to the city for his courses in the afternoons. Leah works at the bakery when Raj's mother can watch Geeta, but she also takes courses at the community college. That's when Ma watches Geeta.

The less expensive apartment, Raj and Leah helping, and not having to pay Gabby anymore has allowed Gertie's to keep going. You miss Gabby, but she took the bread-baking job at Caruso's that Daddy was going to take. She still visits when she can.

Gertie's might not last forever, but at least for now, it's still here.

"Can I push her?" you ask Ma. She stops and lets go of

the carriage. You take it and go gently over any bumps. The baby looks up from her nest of blankets and watches your every move. She has dark eyes, long lashes, and looks more like Raj than Leah. She's wearing a little white hat with a pink ribbon woven through it that Ma started crocheting the day she was born. A raindrop hits her nose, and she opens her mouth in surprise.

"Aww, look at her," you exclaim and realize everything is so new to Geeta. Even rain.

Ma smiles and pulls the hood over the carriage.

"It's just a drizzle," she says. "We'll be fine for a few minutes."

There were two baby-naming ceremonies. Mr. and Mrs. Jagwani had one very soon after Leah and Raj came home from the hospital. Raj said normally the Hindu ceremony would be the first time anyone would hear Geeta's name. "But we don't do anything the typical way, I guess. We're making it up as we go along," Leah said.

Ma invited everyone to the baby naming at Temple Beth Torah, even your Grandpa Myron. He didn't come because he doesn't approve of Raj and Leah, but you wish you could tell him Geeta is his great-granddaughter whether he comes or not. While they were planning it, Ma said to Leah that because she is Jewish, Geeta is really Jewish, not Hindu. Leah got upset and told Ma again that she and Raj are raising her as both.

"Good luck with that," Ma said under her breath. Then Leah got really mad. She took Geeta and stormed out of the apartment, slamming the door behind her. You wondered if things could fall apart as quickly as they came back together, that maybe what was holding everything together wasn't that strong. You didn't sleep that whole night.

The next day, though, Ma apologized and said she'd try to respect the way Leah and Raj wanted to raise their child. Things aren't always perfect with Leah and Ma. But they're not bad, either. In some ways, they're back to normal.

Sometimes you wonder why Leah and Raj were in such a rush, but maybe it was because they felt like getting married was the only way to make people see their love as real.

You both walk faster, the soft drops dotting the sidewalk. Neither of you say anything for a few minutes, and all you hear is the whisper of rain in the trees and the click of Ma's shoes.

"Can I ask you something important?" you finally say, breaking the silence. You've been waiting for a quiet time to ask her this question. But after Geeta was born and you moved to your new apartment and Leah and Raj came back, things have only been busy and loud.

"Okay," Ma says. She pulls her sweater closer around her.

"Why didn't you ever show me the letters Leah wrote to me?"

Geeta makes some funny gurgling sounds. You stop the carriage and make sure her blankets are tucked in. "Because I thought she forgot all about me. I thought she didn't care anymore. I spent months thinking that."

"Oh, Ari," Ma says and stops walking. Raindrops land on the printed silk scarf covering her hair. "I didn't mean for you to think that."

You nod. You've been waiting for her to be the one to bring it up, but you didn't want to wait anymore. Ma's hard sometimes, but she's your mother and she's a fighter. Sometimes, though, she doesn't always fight about the things that need fighting about.

"At the time, I thought it was simpler that way. But I was wrong," she continues.

"Do you still have them?" you ask, worried she might have thrown them out.

"Yes, I'll give them back tonight. They're yours, and I'm sorry I took them from you."

"Thanks," you say. You finally feel satisfied and full of the one thing you had wanted for so long, for Ma to say she was sorry.

Later, you might write a poem about it.

The rain gets a little heavier, and you head toward the bakery, which is also now home, two homes blended into one.

Ma brings Geeta inside, but you hang back. You want to stand under the awning and watch the rain. School is going to end in a month, and it will be summer again. You look in the direction of Rocky's Records and the Sweet Scoop. So much has changed, but Gertie's hasn't. It's still here, still beating, like a warm heart in the center of your new family, a family you never imagined you'd have, a family you weren't even looking for.

The mailman, Joe, covered in a gray raincoat, walks by

and hands you the stack of mail. You thank him and start flipping through the letters and catalogs before you bring them inside. It's mostly bills and the *Pennysaver*, which Ma likes. Then you see a letter addressed to you. It's from *Grasshopper* magazine. You tear it open. It says:

Dear Miss Goldberg,

We're pleased to let you know that we would like to publish your poem, "A Poem for Baby Geeta," in our fall issue. If you agree to this, please sign the enclosed form and send us a short biography, no longer than one hundred words, to the address below.

You feel something you've never felt before, like you've never been so in your body, like you've never been so *Ariel*.

"Ma!" you yell and run up the stairs to your apartment, waving the envelope. "Ma!"

You show her the letter, and she claps when you read it. She takes it and reads it again to herself. Then she stares at you.

"What?" you ask.

"I got you an early birthday present," she says. "I was going to wait, but now seems like the right time."

"Really?" you ask.

"Come," she says. You follow her into her bedroom, where Geeta's asleep now in her carriage. Ma opens her closet, and on the bottom, next to her shoes, sits an IBM Selectric typewriter.

"How did you get it?" You speak low so you don't wake up Geeta, and kneel in front of the typewriter. "Is it from my classroom?"

"No, it's one from the high school. They just bought new ones for their typing classes. But it works just fine. Miss Field arranged the whole thing," she whispers back.

There's a little card on a string hanging from the side, attached to the roller. It says: "To Ariel, may you always write what's in your heart. Happy Birthday. —Ma, Daddy, and Miss Field."

You jump up and down as quietly as possible, and you hug Ma.

"It's the best present I ever got. Can I put it on my desk?" you ask.

"Of course," she says. "I wanted you to have it because I don't want you to be like me."

"What do you mean?"

"I just want you to be better, that's all." Then she looks at the Selectric. "My daughter, a published poet. Such a mensch you are." She pats the space over her heart.

Ma's never called you a mensch before. You hug her again and give her a big kiss on the cheek.

"You're a mensch, too, Ma," you say, and then you try to pick up the typewriter, but it's too heavy, so you and Ma carry it back to your room together and place it on the center of your desk. Ma plugs it in, pats your shoulder, and leaves you sitting at your desk, staring at it. You can't believe you have your own electric typewriter. Last month, when you first moved, your new bedroom seemed so dark and small, only enough room for one bed. Leah took the other one for when Geeta's older. But now, sitting in front of this typewriter, the room feels bigger, brighter, filled with possibilities.

You think about the poem idea you had before and put your hands on the keyboard. You feel its electric hum.

You begin.

Author's Note

Sometimes, readers ask me if the book I wrote is based on a true story. The answer is always complicated. I think the best art emerges from truthful and authentic spaces, but how this happens in fiction is a complex journey for each storyteller. I often turn to my own family history for inspiration, and in this story, I've blended fact with fiction in possibly the most complex way I ever have in my writing.

In 1968, my mother, a Jewish American woman from Brooklyn, married my father, a recent Indian immigrant from Bombay (now called Mumbai). My mother's parents—my grandparents—were upset about the marriage. For a time, my grandfather thought it was his duty to reject my mother and her choice. He was devastated by what he felt was a renunciation of her Jewish identity and his—an identity deeply important to him. My father had lost his parents by then, but his brothers and sisters had hoped he would marry an Indian Hindu woman and were also disappointed by the choice my parents made.

My parents, however, followed their hearts, eloped, and have been married for 53 years. It wasn't an easy journey. Ultimately, love motivated people on both sides of my family to stumble through some difficult periods. By the time I was born, they had all evolved enough for me to enjoy close relationships with everyone, but the complex issues they grappled with persisted in a variety of ways over the years. I grew up in a community where there were very few Jewish or Indian American families, let alone both, and I continue to process and embrace the layers of my biracial identity and interfaith family.

I have often thought about what this time was like for my parents and admired their courage to forge their own path. I've also considered the historical context during which they made their decision. They were married in 1968 in Connecticut. This was only a year after the Supreme Court ruled, in the famous *Loving v. Virginia* case, that any state laws banning interracial marriage were unconstitutional. Before the Supreme Court ruling, sixteen states still had laws against interracial marriage. Though Connecticut did not have anti-miscegenation laws at the time, I wonder what would have happened if my parents had wanted to get married before the ruling in a state that banned interracial marriage, since some of those states had laws specifying South Asians on their list of "non-whites" and some didn't.

In the mid to late 1960s, the United States was deep in the Vietnam War and the civil rights movement. Protests against racism and the war swept the country. Along with other important pieces of civil rights legislation, like the Civil Rights Act of 1964 and the Voting Rights Act of 1965, The Immigration and Naturalization Act of 1965, which abolished the immigration quotas and allowed more immigration opportunities for people from all over the world, was passed. This changed and further diversified the racial and ethnic makeup of the United States, and a large number of Asian immigrants, including my father, entered the country.

But along with the strides toward equality made during this time, President Kennedy, Malcom X, and Dr. Martin Luther King, Jr. were assassinated as part of a violent and devastating backlash to civil rights progress. I've wondered how much my parents were affected and motivated by the breathtaking amount of positive and negative events happening all at once.

This was among the many questions I pursued when writing a story about Ariel, a twelve-year-old Jewish girl living in Connecticut, whose older sister falls in love with an Indian American college student. What would her awareness be of the many changes going on around her—both in her country and in her family? How would they affect her identity as both a Jewish girl facing anti-semitism in a mostly non-Jewish community and as a white girl experiencing white privilege?

Another part of my personal truth is that I'm a parent of a child with dysgraphia. I'm grateful that in our current world there has been an increasing amount of support and awareness in this area of education, but I've thought about what it would have felt like in a time like 1967, when such knowledge and resources didn't exist. This also played a part in Ariel's character.

So how true is this story? Who is Ariel? Is she a version of my mother, my child, or perhaps myself? Well,

Ariel is Ariel. That's all she can be. She, and all the other characters in *How to Find What You're Not Looking For*, are inspired by many influences. The story is infused with the experiences that my family had, that I've had, the historical context I've researched, and the things I've chosen to imagine—after all, this is fiction. Every story carries its own fingerprint, the unique pattern created out of the writer's singular quest, background, and imagination. A story that moves you with the depth of its own truth is truer than anything I know, and I hope you discover some truths meaningful to you while reading this book.

Acknowledgments

Many people had an integral part in making this book, and I'm beyond grateful to all of them.

First, I must thank everyone at Pippin Properties and my super-agent, Sara Crowe. You're a true mensch, and I wouldn't be where I am in my writing career without your magic.

Thank you to Kokila publisher and editorial genius, Namrata Tripathi. Somehow you always know precisely the right question to help me get to the heart of what I'm trying to say. Because of you I'm a better writer and a better person.

Thank you to everyone at Kokila Books/Penguin Young Readers who read the manuscript and added their wise thoughts, including the editorial team: Zareen Jaffery, Joanna Cárdenas, and Sydnee Monday; designers Jasmin Rubero, Kelley Brady, and Kristin Boyle; the production and managing editorial teams: Caitlin Taylor, Natalie Vielkind, and Ariela Rudy Zaltzman; Jennifer Dee and the rest of the PYR publicity team; and Christine Colangelo and everyone part of the PYR marketing team. I also want to thank the PYR sales, subsidiary rights, inventory, and warehouse teams, and finally, a big thanks to Jen Loja and Jocelyn Schmidt for your leadership and support!

I'm so grateful to my family, including my husband and best friend, David Beinstein, and my incredible kids, Hannah and Eli, for reading my work, cheering me on, and listening to me agonize at the dinner table over plot lines about made-up people.

Thank you to my sister, Shana Hiranandani, my forever trusted confidant in writing and in life.

Thank you to my in-laws, Phyllis and Hank Beinstein, who were excellent resources in many areas of Jewish culture, Jewish bakeries, and 1960s education. I must also thank the website myjewishlearning.com for their delicious black and white cookie recipe!

I'm blessed with the loving memory of my grandparents, Maurice and Gertrude Goldman, and I thank them for having the courage to open their minds to new ways of thinking and passing down their Jewish traditions to me.

I'm grateful for my extremely talented author friends and early readers: Gwendolen Gross, Barbara Josselsohn, Sheela Chari, Sayantani DasGupta, and Heather Tomlinson, who were crucial in helping me get this book just right. And to my ever-supportive friend, Sarah Hinawi, who always helps me get out of my comfort zone.

Finally and most importantly, a huge thanks to my mother, Anita Hiranandani, and my father, Hiro Hiranandani. Mom and Dad, I'm so appreciative of your willingness to share your stories with me. I'm so lucky you had the courage to follow your hearts and to have you as parents. I owe you everything.